THAT MAN JESUS

Dear Stephen and Pippa
With much love thanks
for your fellowship in
the Gospel
Martin.

OTHER BOOKS BY MARTIN DOWN

Speak To These Bones
Streams Of Living Water
Building A New Church Alongside The Old
Deluded By Darwinism?
The New Jerusalem
Low Cost · High Price (with Theresa Cumbers)
Love Each Other
The Best Is Yet To Be
The Gospel Truth

THAT MAN JESUS

An Historical Novel

by

MARTIN DOWN

Rehoboth
Media

Copyright © Martin Down 2014
The right of Martin Down to be identified as the author of this work has been asserted by him in accordance with the Copyright, Designs and Patents Act 1988.

This first edition published in Great Britain 2014

All rights reserved. No part of this publication may be reproduced or transmitted in any form or by any means, electronic or mechanical, including photocopy, recording or any information storage and retrieval system, without permission in writing from either the publisher or the author.

ISBN 978-0-9574813-2-9

Cover design by MPH.

Published by Rehoboth Media

The Well Christian Centre
Swaffham Road, Ashill, IP25 7BT
www.fountainnetwork.org

CONTENTS

	Note on biblical quotations	7
1	Setting Out	9
2	Baptism	20
3	The Wilderness	28
4	First Friends	39
5	Fishermen	50
6	Capernaum	59
7	Healing	70
8	Preaching	80
9	Magdala	91
10	Nazareth	101
11	Jerusalem	113
12	Teaching	123
13	Samaria	132
14	Now and Not Yet	141
15	Calling	149
16	Sending	159
17	Ploughing On	169
18	Returning	178
19	Prodigals	188
20	Caesarea Philippi	195
21	The New Community	205
22	Jerusalem Again	214
23	Blindness	224

24	The Wilderness Again	234
25	Dedication	243
26	Jericho	252
27	Arrival	261
28	Sunday Evening	271
29	Monday	279
30	Tuesday	290
31	Wednesday	298
32	Passover	306
33	The Olive Grove	316
34	Before Caiaphas	324
35	Before Pilate	333
36	Crucifixion	343
37	Burial	352
38	The First Day of the Week	358
39	Galilee Again	368
40	Ascension	378
	Two Thousand Years On	381

NOTE ON BIBLICAL QUOTATIONS

When Jesus or others are quoting from the Jewish scriptures, I have deliberately used the King James Version of the Bible and the Coverdale version of the Psalms.

The Jews in the time of Jesus heard and knew the scriptures in Hebrew, a language related to but not identical with Aramaic, the language of everyday speech. Therefore, to use an archaic form of English for quotations from those scriptures may convey something of both the familiarity and the unfamiliarity of the language.

one

SETTING OUT

He closed the door of the carpenter's shop and set out for the River Jordan. He had told his mother that he was going, and she had asked when he would be back. "I don't know," he said. "A few weeks, perhaps."

John was a sort of cousin. Their mothers had been related in some way. John's family had lived down near Jerusalem, where his father was a priest, and Jesus' up in Galilee, but the two families had met up at festivals.

John and he were much the same age and had grown up together, but John had been the child of aged parents, and after they had both died John had left word that he was going to withdraw to a lonely place to be with God. He had taken to living in a cave, where the hills of Judea and Samaria fall steeply into the Jordan Valley, living on whatever the hills and the valley provided and, like Elijah, he drank from a brook.

At first he was regarded as some kind of wild man by the inhabitants of the settlements in the valley, but then later as a holy man. People started to turn off the road to ask him questions about God and seek guidance about what to do.

Then, crowds had begun to gather about him and he would preach to them.

The crowds had increased; people were going down to the River Jordan from all over the country to listen to this strange prophet, and to be baptised by him. He was becoming known as John the Baptizer.

It was a strange thing for a birthright Jew to be baptised. A Jew might have a ritual bath if he had been a leper or had contact with the dead, but baptism was for proselytes: Gentiles wishing to be numbered among the People of God. Baptism was a sign of the washing away of the uncleannesses of their Gentile past. But these were Jews, who had been neither lepers nor in contact with the dead, submitting to John's baptism.

"Repent," he would say, "and be baptised for the remission of your sins."

And many were doing it.

It was not exactly kosher. The hierarchy in Jerusalem were not sure what to make of this new movement, for that is what it was. Various delegations of priests and Levites, of scribes and Pharisees, were coming down to investigate and analyse the doctrine of this strange, even threatening, man. They often went away angry and insulted, but John did not seem to care.

For some time Jesus had felt a growing prompting to go down to the Jordan and be part of whatever it was that God was doing there through

SETTING OUT

his cousin John. So, he had closed the door of the carpenter's shop and set off for the River Jordan.

In his bones he knew that he would not come back, that he would never again pick up the saw and the plane and lay pieces of sweetly scented wood on the carpenter's bench. That part of his life was over.

He left the village and began to descend the winding road into the plain below. Nazareth nestled in a bowl high up in the hills of Galilee, where they rose suddenly out of the plain of Esdraelon. He passed underneath the rocky outcrop to which the rabbi had often brought the boys from the synagogue school.

Like most of the boys of his age, he had started to attend the synagogue school when he was about five years old. Devout parents, like Joseph and Mary, were aware of their duty to teach their children, especially their sons, the history of their people and the commandments that God had given them. How else would they know who they were and what God required of them? But the Scriptures were in Hebrew, the ancient language of the Jews, not the Aramaic that they spoke every day. So they must go to the rabbi, to learn the sacred language and to become familiar with the sacred writings.

The old man with his prayer shawl and his phylacteries had started by teaching them to read the Hebrew letters by writing them with his finger in the sand. Then they had joined the older boys in reading from the great scrolls that contained the Word of God.

Jesus could remember the sense of awe and excitement that he felt as the teacher went to the sacred cupboard in which the scrolls were kept. Reverently, the rabbi would bring out a scroll and unroll it on the reading desk, until he found the place to which they had read. A boy would be summoned to come up and read, the younger ones following the words with the rabbi's finger, the older, more fluent boys, rocking backwards and forwards as they read.

It was not easy to read the ancient and holy words. Only the consonants were written, the boys had to be taught how to pronounce the words one by one. Then the rabbi had to translate or explain them. When a passage had been correctly read and understood, it would be read again, then again, then chanted by the whole class, and then again, until the words and their meaning were engraved in their young memories.

Then on some particularly exciting days, the old man would take them out to the bluff on the edge of the town and point out the places about which they had been reading. There, towards the Great Sea, which they had never seen, but which the rabbi told them was over the other side of the hills, was Mount Carmel, the place where Elijah

SETTING OUT

had summoned the prophets of Baal and challenged them to a great contest.

The prophets of Baal had wailed and cut themselves in vain as they called upon their god to send the fire. Then Elijah had stepped forward and a great silence had fallen. Elijah had knelt and prayed to the God of Abraham, Isaac and Jacob, and fire had fallen from heaven and burnt up the offering. Then he had prayed again and God had sent rain, a mighty torrent to water the thirsty land.

The old teacher would enforce the lessons upon the boys: not to have any gods but the LORD, to pray to God to meet their needs, and to cleanse the land that God might bless them. But Jesus had not needed the lessons that the rabbi taught. They were plain to him from the Scriptures.

He could not remember a time when God was not real to him, and when the Scriptures had not spoken directly into his heart. Sometimes the other boys would mock the old rabbi and impersonate his sing-song voice, but Jesus kept quiet and stored up the sacred words in the treasury of his heart.

Now he walked down into the plain and headed across the fields on the long, straight road to Afula. Afula was the great crossroads where travellers from East and West and North and South would meet. There were khans or inns there to provide for the merchants and pilgrims.

It was there that, since Jesus was a boy, they had gathered to begin the journeys up to Jerusalem for the great feasts.

From Afula there were two routes to the great city, the longer took you east to the Jordan and then down the valley as far as Jericho and then up and up and up through the wilderness of Judea to Jerusalem. The other went due south, through the hills of Samaria. Sometimes they would go one way, sometimes the other.

Relations between Jews and Samaritans were always fickle. At one time the Samaritans would welcome them at the khans on the way, welcome their money and their custom, if not their persons. At other times the Jews would be turned away. Either way, the Jewish pilgrims always travelled together in bands, large or small. If it was not the Samaritans, it was robbers, hiding behind the rocks in the wilderness, that could threaten the lonely traveller.

Today, Jesus took the road east, heading for the River Jordan where John was baptizing, up the valley towards Beth-shan, under the mountains of Gilboa where Saul and Jonathan had died.

Saul and Jonathan, and the kingdom of David – the stories came back to him as he walked steadily eastwards. The tragedy of Saul, called and anointed by God, yet betrayed by his own weaknesses and imperfections; the tragedy of Jonathan, struggling to be faithful both to his

SETTING OUT

father and to his friend David; beautiful David, the shepherd boy taken from following the flocks to be the shepherd of God's people Israel, the greatest of the kings, a man after God's own heart. The composer of psalms, yet also imperfect, tempted by his neighbour's wife into the sin of adultery, bringing endless trouble upon his family and his kingdom.

All God's people, called and chosen, yet tainted and destroyed by sin, unable to live up to their calling, pathetically falling short generation after generation, so long now under the heel of foreign invaders, Assyrians, Babylonians, Persians, Greeks and now, Romans.

Not that the Romans ruled Galilee as they ruled Jerusalem and Judea. Down in the South the Roman governor Pontius Pilate was clearly in charge, personally present at all the feasts, escorted by his legionaries. Up here in Galilee the Roman governor of Syria was a distant figure. But everyone knew that their local ruler, Herod Antipas, son of the old Herod, was, like his father, no more than a Roman stooge.

Life in Herod's new palace in Tiberius, down on the Lake, was the subject of endless gossip in the market-places. The latest scandal was that Herod had had an affair with his brother Philip's wife, that Herod had divorced his own wife and that Herodias had repudiated Philip, in order to allow them to marry.

THAT MAN JESUS

Certainly this new woman was now to be seen ensconced at Herod's side, as bold as brass. But while the present regime collected the taxes and kept the country quiet, it was acceptable and useful to the Romans: letting the Herods do their dirty work for them saved the Romans from doing it themselves. But as soon as there was any trouble, the Romans would come in.

The old men of Nazareth often told the story of how the Romans had come and destroyed the town of Sepphoris, just an hour's walk away from Nazareth, when rebellion broke out in Galilee after the death of the old Herod. Afterwards, some of the men of Nazareth had found work up in Sepphoris while the town was being rebuilt. They also told how, in the aftermath of the revolt, the Romans had crucified two thousand Jews; the roads of Galilee were lined with their crosses and corpses. It was a warning: people should understand who was in charge.

But then Jesus remembered another day, relatively recently. He had been going up to Jerusalem with a band of pilgrims who had stopped to rest in the middle of the day. There was a spring from which they and their animals could drink, and shade from the trees that grew by the water-side.

As they settled down for their rest, a quaternion of four Roman soldiers mounted on horseback had

SETTING OUT

come jingling down the road, and they also had stopped to rest and water their horses.

The two groups sat apart, but after a while some of the bolder Jewish children crept over to pat the horses which were standing tethered, with their heads down, dozing in the heat. One of the Roman soldiers beckoned some of the children over and offered them some dates from his pouch. The children were shy, but stood by the soldier munching their dates.

At one moment the soldier stretched out his hand and stroked the hair of a little girl. She smiled coyly and ran back to her mother. And in that moment Jesus saw, not a Roman soldier, but a man, a long way from home, in a strange land and among an alien race, and Jesus knew in his spirit that at home, perhaps in some Italian village, this man had a wife and a little girl, whose hair he longed to stroke and whom he longed to lift up in his arms – and whom he might never see again. And Jesus' heart ached for that man.

There were no such things as enemies, just other men like himself, and other mothers like his own mother, and other children like these little ones resting here beside him.

The kingdom of David – now a distant dream. Perhaps it was always a dream, the dream of a people living in peace and prosperity under the law of their God. Was it ever to come again, or was it ever to come? Yet the promise of God was sure:

> I have made a covenant with my chosen,
> I have sworn unto David my servant:
> Thy seed will I stablish for ever,
> And set up thy throne from one generation to another.

His own father had originally come from Bethlehem and was descended from David, so he said, but was a son of David ever to sit on the throne again, ruling over the people of Israel? Even in Jesus' lifetime there had been a revolt in Judea, led by a compatriot of his, known as Judas the Galilean. This Judas had obviously fancied himself as another Judas Maccabaeus: he would rise up and break the yoke of the infidel and restore the kingdom to Israel. But the Romans had dealt with him and his followers as they had dealt with the people of Sepphoris. Clearly, that was not the way to realise the dream.

Even if such a revolt were successful, it would only re-establish the regime that Israel had already known under the succession of their own kings long before, a regime that had only led to ruin and disgrace, to the present.

You could yearn to see the kingdom of God on earth, God's will being done on earth as it was in heaven, but that was clearly not the way to bring

SETTING OUT

it about. In the end, no ruler or king could force anyone else to love God or to love his neighbour, and without love, obedience was at best an outward conformity. It was not new laws that the people needed, nor new rulers, not even their own, but new hearts and new spirits. That was what the prophets of old had foretold,

> Then will I sprinkle clean water upon you, and ye shall be clean: from all your filthiness, and from all your idols, will I cleanse you. A new heart also will I give you, and a new spirit will I put within you: and I will take away the stony heart out of your flesh, and I will give you an heart of flesh. And I will put my Spirit within you, and cause you to walk in my statutes, and ye shall keep my judgements, and do them.

Was that what this new movement under John the Baptizer was about: sprinkling the people with clean water as a preparation for a new heart and a new spirit?

two

BAPTISM

The crowds began to gather from early in the morning. They came and sat down on the bank that sloped up from the river, talking quietly in subdued little groups. There was a sense of anticipation and suspense, of uncertainty but excitement. Was this what they had all been waiting for so long?

Jesus came and sat down at the back of the crowd, to wait like the others. About mid-morning his cousin John appeared, alone, roughly dressed, his beard uncut, picking his way through the knots of seated people, down to the water's edge. He prayed, facing the river, his hands and his eyes lifted up to heaven.

"When Israel came out of Egypt, and the house of Jacob from among the strange people, Judah was his sanctuary, and Israel his dominion. The sea saw that, and fled, Jordan was driven back. The mountains skipped like rams, and the little hills like young sheep. What aileth thee, O thou sea, that thou fleddest, and thou Jordan, that thou wast driven back? Ye mountains, that ye skipped like rams, and ye little hills, like young sheep? Tremble, thou earth, at the presence of

BAPTISM

the Lord, at the presence of the God of Jacob; who turned the hard rock into a standing water, and the flint-stone into a springing well."

Then he turned and began to speak to the people.

"'Tremble, thou earth, at the presence of the Lord.' The kingdom of God is close at hand. We've waited, my friends, we've waited. Many years, many generations, we've waited for this time. I'm not the one who is to come, but I'm sent to prepare the way for him. Someone is coming who is infinitely greater than me, someone whose sandals I'm not worthy to stoop down and untie. I am the one foretold by the prophet Isaiah, the voice of one crying in the wilderness, 'Prepare ye the way of the LORD.'

"'Prepare ye the way of the LORD.' That means you, and it means repent of your sins. You know what your sins are; you've coveted your neighbour's house and your neighbour's wife; you've spoken ill of your neighbours; you've held back your hand when your neighbour was in need; you've neglected your prayers and treated the Lord's ways with contempt. But there is a day of judgement coming, and coming soon. We need to be ready to welcome the Lord in the day of his visitation. I baptize you with water, but when he comes he will baptize you with the Holy Spirit and with fire.

"So, stand and pray with me our father David's prayer of penitence:

'Have mercy upon me, O God, after thy great goodness; according to the multitude of thy mercies do away mine offenses. Wash me throughly from my wickedness, and cleanse me from my sin. For I acknowledge my faults, and my sin is ever before me. Against thee only have I sinned, and done this evil in thy sight, that thou mightest be justified in thy saying, and clear when thou art judged. Behold, I was shapen in wickedness, and in sin hath my mother conceived me. But lo, thou requirest truth in the inward parts, And shalt make me to understand wisdom secretly. Thou shalt purge me with hyssop, and I shall be clean; thou shalt wash me, and I shall be whiter than snow. Thou shalt make me hear of joy and gladness, that the bones which thou hast broken may rejoice. Turn thy face from my sins, and put out all my misdeeds. Make me a clean heart, O God, and renew a right spirit within me. Cast me not away from thy presence, and take not thy Holy Spirit from me. O give me the comfort of thy help again, and stablish me with thy free Spirit. Then shall I teach thy ways unto the wicked, and sinners shall be converted unto thee. Deliver me from blood-guiltiness, O God, thou that art the God of my health, and my tongue shall sing of thy righteousness. Thou shalt open my lips, O Lord, and my mouth shall shew they praise. For

BAPTISM

thou desirest no sacrifice, else would I give it thee; but thou delightest not in burnt-offerings. The sacrifice of God is a troubled spirit; a broken and contrite heart, O God, shalt thou not despise.'

"'Wash me and I shall be whiter than snow.' Come then and wash your sins away in the river. And as you do so, make this the prayer of your heart: Make me a clean heart, O God. The Lord never despises a broken and a contrite heart."

One by one the people began to go forward. They took off their outer garments, were led into the water, and were baptised by John. Dripping wet, they came back up the bank to sit, their clothes steaming in the hot sun, sober and silent.

Towards the end, Jesus also got up from where he was sitting and went down to the river. He joined the queue of people waiting to be baptised. As Jesus stepped down into the water, John looked up and their eyes met in recognition.

"What, you? Have you come too?"

There was a pause, and then, on his breath, John said, "Is it you?"

A long silence followed while they looked steadily into each other's eyes.

Then John spoke again, "Then I need to be baptised by you."

Jesus replied, "Let's do it like this now. This is what God wants." And John took him down into the water, just like the others, and baptized him in the river Jordan.

As Jesus came up out of the water he heard a voice, distinct and clear, yet intimate and close, "You are my son. I love you and I'm pleased with you." And what was that? A shadow had passed over his eyes. Was it a bird? A breath of wind over his head, a sense of being filled with life welling up inside him, and of being enveloped in love, the love of God.

Had anyone else heard that voice? Had John? Had that been a bird coming down, or something else? Almost in a trance, Jesus came up out of the water, walked slowly through the crowd and on up into the hills.

A picture from the past presented itself to his mind. One day, when he was very young - only a little boy - he had been asleep. When he woke his father was leaning over him, looking at him with such love in his eyes. His father had bent down and kissed him, and he was filled with such a sense of being loved by his father that he had squirmed with delight. His father had picked him up and held him close to his chest, whilst he had buried his face in his father's soft beard. Now, he was filled with the same sense of love and of being loved, but this was the love of his heavenly Father.

On up into the barren hills of the wilderness of Judea he walked. He wanted no company or

BAPTISM

communication. He only wanted to be alone with this Father, alone as Adam had been at the beginning before anything else began, just the two of them, he and his Father, one with the other.

It lasted for several days, this overwhelming sense of intimacy with God. God was his all in all. He found water in a spring but thought little of eating. The presence of God seemed to satisfy him entirely.

He remembered another time when he been so absorbed in God that he had forgotten the time, forgotten his surroundings. He had been about twelve years old. His family had gone up to Jerusalem as usual, in the spring to celebrate the feast of Passover. During the Days of Unleavened Bread that followed he had sat at the feet of the scribes who were teaching in the temple. They expounded the Scriptures and explained what other rabbis had taught about them.

He had listened, spell-bound, asking them questions. Sometimes they asked him questions in reply and he would answer in his twelve-year-old simplicity. On the last day of the Feast, he had not realised until the evening that his parents had set off for Galilee without him. He had stayed on in Jerusalem, assuming that they would come back for him, still absorbed by the teachers of the law. He had slept in the temple precincts.

Then, on the third day, his parents had come bustling through the temple courts, searching frantically for him and calling his name. They were cross with him and scolded him, but even then he had said to them, "But you should have known where I'd be: in my Father's house."

"Naughty boy," his mother had said, but in such a way that he knew she was more relieved to have found him than angry to have lost him, perhaps also a little in awe of this strange son of hers.

Now he slept in the open air, often waking to look up into the night sky, filled with the glory of the numberless stars. He imagined old father Abraham and his family in their wanderings, sitting together at the door of their tent under that same night sky and retelling the old, old story of the creation of the world:

"In the beginning God created the heaven and the earth. And the earth was without form, and void; and darkness was upon the face of the deep. And the Spirit of God moved upon the face of the waters. And God said, "Let there be light." And there was light ..."

But whenever his thoughts strayed to such thoughts as these, he came back to that place of being enveloped in his Father's love, there in the desert where the only relief from the sun by day lay in the shadow of an overhanging rock.

Would this state of joy, of bliss, last forever? Would this love never let him go? As the days passed by he knew that this was but a preparation for the thing that God had called him

BAPTISM

to do. But here was a place to which he could come back at any time, not in the wilderness maybe, but in any place where he could be alone with God and come back into those arms of love, holding him close, holding him near - the everlasting arms of his Father's love.

three

THE WILDERNESS

What was it that his Father was preparing him to do? Throughout his childhood, whenever the Scriptures were being read in the synagogue, he remembered how he would feel, as it were, a gentle touch as he heard certain verses being read. It was as if a finger were laid upon him somewhere inside, and something within him quickened. It was as if the Scriptures were speaking to him personally.

> "I will put enmity between thee and the woman, and between thy seed and her seed; it shall bruise thy head, and thou shalt bruise his heel."

He was of the seed of Adam and of the woman Eve. Was it he that was to bruise the ancient serpent's head, and would it be his heel that was bruised in the conflict?

> "In thy seed shall all the nations of the earth be blessed, because thou hast obeyed my voice."

THE WILDERNESS

He was of the seed of Abraham. Would it be in him that all the nations of the earth would be blessed? And again Moses had said,

> "The LORD thy God will raise up unto thee a prophet from the midst of thee, of thy brethren, like unto me."

Was he that prophet? And God saying to David,

> "Thine house and thy kingdom shall be established for ever before thee; thy throne shall be established for ever."

But how was that promise to be fulfilled in a world in which earthly kings and kingdoms were continually rising and falling?

> "And there shall come forth a rod out of the stem of Jesse, and a branch shall grow out of his roots: and the Spirit of the LORD shall rest upon him."

Since his baptism in the river Jordan, Jesus could sense the Spirit of the Lord resting upon him.

"Behold my servant, whom I uphold; mine elect, in whom my soul delighteth; I have put my Spirit upon him; he shall bring forth judgement to the Gentiles."

Since his baptism, Jesus knew himself to be that servant, the servant of whom the prophet Isaiah had spoken so much. There was no escaping the knowledge, fearful though it was. He was "the one who was to come." But what was it that he had been sent to do?

As Jesus roamed the barren hills, enveloped in the great silence of the wilderness, he pondered many things: the goodness of his Father's creation at the beginning when all was good. The evil and wickedness of so much of it now, the oppression, the sorrow, the disease, death, the greed, the indifference to suffering, the poverty, the broken hearts and broken lives.

God had begun a new thing when he called father Abraham to come to this land; God had then persevered with Abraham's descendants through many generations. They had often failed him, but he had never failed them. But now they seemed to have lost the vision, the vision of a new world, of the redemption of this sad, old world. They had given up all hope of that, and reduced their expectations to mere survival.

When they had come back from exile in Babylon they had tried to rebuild the old nation and the

THE WILDERNESS

old temple, but their hearts had not been in it. Taught by the prophets, they had learnt their lesson: disobedience leads to disaster. So they had set themselves to be obedient to God lest worse should befall them. But now the scribes of the law and the Pharisees were lost in a rigmarole of their own making, arguing over ever more minute details of how to fulfil the law. Should you eat an egg laid on the Sabbath?

They loaded people with burdens that no-one, not even themselves were able to bear. The men of the leading families in Jerusalem, to whom the people might have looked for wisdom and guidance, seemed to have settled for anything that meant a quiet life for themselves and the continuation of their own power and prosperity.

Underground, everyone knew, there were cells of zealots and hot-heads who would suddenly break out into random acts of rage and frustrated violence. But no-one seemed to have an answer to what had happened to God's covenant or even, yes, to God's creation, and how it might be restored.

Then John had come, baptizing in the desert and saying, "The kingdom of God is at hand." And a new hope had arisen in people's hearts. Was God at last going to visit his people? Was redemption truly at hand?

Hope, that was what was driving people down to the river Jordan, a mixture of wild hope and the fear of being disappointed once again. And he, Jesus, the son of Joseph, the carpenter of Nazareth, he was sent to fulfil those hopes. He was the servant of the Lord, God's precious Son, with whom he was well pleased, and that experience at his baptism was his anointing with the Spirit of God for the task that God had given him. But how was it to be carried out?

Choice was the key, he saw: people had to choose to enter the kingdom of God. During those days of his wandering in the wilderness, Jesus often reflected upon Israel's own wanderings in the desert when they had come out of Egypt many generations before. How many of those people really loved God, really believed in their destiny as the chosen race, or had really caught the vision of the Promised Land?

No doubt they were pleased to be delivered from slavery, but how many times had they grumbled and rebelled against Moses and against God. Sometimes it seemed that only Moses held on to the vision of the Promised Land, the rest being unwillingly dragged along, like children dragged along by their parents on the long journeys up to Jerusalem. "Are we nearly there? How much further is it?"

And when they had arrived in the Promised Land, how easily they had fallen into idolatry and sin! They had not driven out the nations that were there before them. They had been enticed by their

THE WILDERNESS

pagan deities and their heathen festivals, even offering their own sons and daughters to the idols of Canaan. They had enjoyed occupying the houses that they had not built, and eating the fruit of the trees that they had not planted, but they had not caught the vision of a new people, loving and worshipping God, blessing one another and the world with a vision of how God had intended his creation to be.

The problem was that most of them had never chosen God for themselves. He had chosen them, but they had not chosen him. They had been born as Jews, born into the People of God; they had not chosen it. Some had said yes to God for themselves. Abraham, Isaac and Jacob, Moses at the burning bush, Isaiah and Jeremiah, and, no doubt, many others who had left no memorial. But many in every generation had merely conformed, gone along with the crowd wherever the crowd was going, sometimes up to Jerusalem, sometimes up to the pagan shrines under every green tree and on every high hill.

The kingdom of God had to be a choice. Everyone had to hear the call of God and respond to it for themselves. The kingdom of God was not a territory or a race. Unlike the kingdoms of the world, it was not located within a land but within the human heart. The kingdom of God was present wherever a human life was lived in the love and obedience of God.

THAT MAN JESUS

The troubles of the world had begun with an act of disobedience, Adam and Eve's. The redemption of the world had begun with an act of obedience, Abraham's. Always the decision was that of an individual man or woman. Within the borders of every land there would be those who would say yes to God and those who would ignore or refuse his call.

It would be the same within families. One man would say yes, his brother would say no. A mother would say yes, her daughter would say no. God, the Father of all, longed to draw his children into one loving and beloved family. But this call would at first bring, not peace, but division. Within families, between friends, between neighbours, within nations.

For the call must come to all, first to the Jews, then to the Gentiles, to the whole world. People would come from east and west to feast in the kingdom of God. But the kingdom of God could not be extended by the sword, as the Romans and the others extended their empires. It could only be extended as people's hearts were turned back to God.

But what was the fate of such people as John who spoke in God's name? The persecution of the prophets and of the righteous had a long history, from the murder of righteous Abel by his brother Cain, down to the prophet Zechariah, murdered in the temple in the days of Joash. Could John, and

THE WILDERNESS

could he, Jesus, God's beloved Son, escape the same fate?

An image arose in his mind of the crosses of which the old men of Nazareth had spoken, two thousand crosses lining the roads of Galilee and Judea, the punishment for challenging the power and authority of Rome. The kingdom of God might not be a kingdom like the kingdoms of the world, but it was a challenge to every ruler and every principality and power in the world.

People who said yes to God would be putting God first, before their earthly masters and before any other god, and there would be times when those loyalties conflicted. It was inescapable, and somewhere or other the conflict would have to be faced in his own life, and in his own death.

That was what God was calling him to do. To proclaim the kingdom of God, and to be faithful and obedient to that calling - even unto death - even death on a cross.

As these thoughts crossed his mind, he suddenly felt distanced from where he was. He saw himself as it were from afar, an insignificant speck, like an ant, sheltering in the cleft of a rock in the middle of a barren wilderness. How hopelessly unrealistic it was to imagine any redemption of the world: the unknown regions of the earth as violent and disordered as he knew his own homeland and its history to be. No one could change it, least of all him, a carpenter from

Nazareth. The most powerful and the wisest of men had made no more than a fleeting difference to the course of the world. It was madness even to try. Go back to Nazareth, open the door of the carpenter's shop and forget such absurd ideas.

But then the Scriptures that he had heard and learnt as a child started to come back to him: was that all absurd? That the God who had created the world had chosen Abraham, Isaac and Jacob to be his People; that he had promised through the prophets to send them a Saviour; that that Saviour would be, not just the Saviour of the Jews but the Saviour of the world? And then, what had that all been about at his baptism: the voice, the sense of the indwelling presence of God, the unmistakeable sense of his Father's love and purpose for him? Wherever he might go and whatever he might do, these things would never go away. There was only one way forward. If he was wrong, or if he was mad, then that was what he would have to be.

As these thoughts finally crystallised in his mind, Jesus felt the peace and the love of God enfold him once again, and he slept that night in the wilderness for the last time.

When he awoke as the sun rose above the line of hills across the Jordan, with a sudden blast of light and heat, he noticed how thin his arms and legs had become. He had not noticed before how much flesh his body had lost during those weeks

THE WILDERNESS

in the wilderness. He had seen the moon wax and wane and now it had waxed again. The promptings of hunger in the first few days had long since worn off, but now there was a much more urgent pain in his belly and he realised that it was time to return to the rest of humanity, and to begin the work which God was calling him to do.

As he began to make his way back, down towards the Jordan valley, he felt weak and light-headed. He was hallucinating now ... or was he? There seemed to be a figure dancing along in front of him and turning round to talk to him.

"Hungry are we? If you are the Son of God, you could turn these stones into bread."

Jesus felt his flesh creep. He replied, "It is written, 'Man doth not live by bread only, but by every word that proceedeth out of the mouth of the LORD,' and God hasn't said to me, 'Make these stones bread.'"

A little further on, the figure said to him, "It would really make an impression on people if, for example, you jumped off the pinnacle of the temple. The people love sensations. You'd be alright, you know; because it is written, 'He shall give his angels charge over thee, to keep thee in all thy ways. They shall bear thee in their hands that thou hurt not thy foot against a stone.'"

Again Jesus replied, "It is also written, 'You shall not tempt the LORD your God.'"

THAT MAN JESUS

Still this creepy presence would not leave him. They came at last to the brow of the hill, looking down over the Jordan Valley and across to the mountains of Moab and away to the distant horizon.

"All this I will give you, even all the kingdoms of the earth, if you'll bow down and worship me."

"Go away, Satan. It is written, 'Thou shalt fear the LORD thy God, and serve him only.'"

Jesus went down the steep slope towards the River Jordan ready to begin his work, leaving the devil to watch - and to wait.

four

FIRST FRIENDS

There was an extraordinary sense of the presence of God around the pool where John was baptizing. Sometimes people coming down the road would begin to weep as they drew near, crushed by a sense of their sin and their need of the forgiveness of God. Even before a word was spoken, they knew themselves to be sinners in the hands of an angry God. Then they would find peace and joy as the water flowed over them, washing away their sin.

John was preaching and baptizing in the morning and evening. During the heat of the day he would sit in the shade and people would group themselves around him, as if he were a rabbi in the temple, asking him questions: what to do, how to live their lives in order to please God. But John answered, not as the scribes did, with a lecture on the opinions of various teachers and schools of thought, making ever finer distinctions between what was lawful and what was not. He answered them in short pithy sentences.

Tax collectors would ask, "Is it possible to be a tax collector and please God?" And John would answer, "Yes, if you deal honestly and collect only what's required of you."

Soldiers would ask, "How can I be a soldier for God?" And John would say, "Use your sword to do justice and defend the weak. Don't use it to rob, or extract bribes: be content with your pay."

Rich people would ask, "How should we use our wealth?" And John would reply, "If you've got two tunics, give one away to someone who has none, and if you've got food, share it with someone who has none."

One morning John was preaching.

"God is merciful; he is always willing to forgive those who truly repent. But he is also just. There must be punishment for sin. The prophet Isaiah expounds this mystery as much as we can understand it; he speaks of one who is to come:

"'Who hath believed our report? And to whom is the arm of the LORD revealed? For he shall grow up before him as a tender plant, and as a root out of dry ground: he hath no form or comeliness; and when we shall see him, there is no beauty that we should desire him. He is despised and rejected of men; a man of sorrows, and acquainted with grief; and we hid as it were our faces from him; he was despised and we esteemed him not.

"'Surely he hath born our griefs, and carried our sorrows, yet we did esteem him stricken, smitten of God and afflicted. But he was wounded for our transgressions, he was bruised for our iniquities: the chastisement of our peace was upon him; and with his stripes we are healed.

"'All we like sheep have gone astray; we have turned every one to his own way; and the LORD hath laid on him the iniquity of us all. He was oppressed and he was afflicted, yet he opened not his mouth: he is brought as a lamb to the slaughter, and as a sheep before her shearers is dumb, so he openeth not his mouth.'"

As he was speaking, John saw his cousin Jesus approaching once again, now gaunt and thin, from the direction of the barren hills. He paused a long time, pointed to him and said in a voice hushed with awe, "Look! There is the Lamb of God, who takes away the sin of the world." The circle of people who were gathered around him turned their heads to look, bemused by what he said, as Jesus stood once again on the edge of the crowd.

Jesus returned to the baptism-place the next day and John repeated the same strange words. As Jesus went away, two men who were sitting at John's feet rose and followed him.

Turning round, Jesus saw them and said, "What do you want then?"

"Master, where are you staying?" they asked.

Jesus smiled, "Wherever! Foxes have holes and birds have nests, but the Son of Man has nowhere to lay his head. But there was an old fellow from a village nearby who heard John speaking about me yesterday and he's invited me to stay with him. Come and see."

They walked along with him. "I'm Andrew son of Jonah, and this is John son of Zebedee. We're fishermen up on the lake, but we love it down here with John. We've been here for several days. It's like the presence of God is here. I can't explain it, but we can't tear ourselves away. I've got a brother here somewhere as well. I'll go and find him."

And with that Andrew disappeared to find his brother in the crowd. Jesus smiled again.

"And I'm Jesus, the son of Joseph, the carpenter of Nazareth," he said to John. "Do you have a brother too?"

"Aye, he's called James, but he's at home with our father. He would've liked to come too, but father needs his help. I'm not sure I oughtn't to be going home myself. I want to stay here with John. In the presence of God, like - but I ought to be at home with father too; we've got to earn a living."

"Don't worry about that," Jesus said. "Put the kingdom of God first, and God will provide for you, and your family as well." And he warmed to this quiet and artless young man.

Andrew came back, almost dragging behind him a thick-set, muscular fellow who bore a somewhat quizzical expression on his face.

"Here he is," Andrew cried, as if in triumph. "This is my big brother, Simon."

FIRST FRIENDS

Jesus looked at him steadily, but with some amusement. "Aye, I can see he is. You may be called Simon, but I'm going to call you Peter, the rock."

Simon looked even more quizzically at him, but nevertheless replied with a shrug, "Alright, if you want to."

So the three of them went off to the place where Jesus was staying and talked to him until the sun went down.

The next day, Jesus decided to return to Galilee. The three fishermen also agreed that it was time for them to be going back to their nets. Andrew, again, announced that he would have to find someone else before they left, an old friend from Bethsaida with whom he had met up here at the Jordan. When Andrew came back there were not one but two more friends in tow. Philip and another friend of his, Nathanael from Cana.

"These two both want to meet you too," said Andrew. "We're all going the same way, so we can walk together."

Jesus looked hard at Nathanael and said, "I've seen you before."

"Have you? Perhaps we've met somewhere at home. You come from Nazareth, I hear, and I come from Cana. So we're sort of neighbours."

"No, no," Jesus replied, "I saw you this morning. You were praying under a fig tree, before Andrew and Philip fetched you. You're a man who's seeking God. You were asking God for a sign, weren't you, whether I was really the one John said I was? Well, here's the sign you were seeking."

"Yes!" exclaimed Nathanael, wide-eyed with astonishment. "You're right, I was. That's exactly what I was asking. So you really are the one John said, the one who is to come, the man born to be king."

Jesus laughed, "You believe that already! Just because I said I saw you under the fig tree. Stick around and you'll see greater things than that."

"Right, let's go then," said Andrew finally, and they set off northwards up the lush and wooded valley of the river Jordan towards Galilee.

Peter and John were walking a few paces behind the others. "So what do you make of that, old son?" Peter asked the younger man John. 'The Lamb of God who takes away the sin of the world.' What's that supposed to mean? And he doesn't look much like a king to me. They say he comes from Nazareth. Have you ever been to Nazareth?"

"No. Why should I go to Nazareth?" replied John.

"Exactly."

"But there's something about him. Something ... different. Isn't there?"

"Maybe, maybe not," answered Peter sceptically.

Andrew always tended to act on impulse, whereas his older brother took time to consider

FIRST FRIENDS

things, as he was doing now. Fishermen like Peter knew how to be patient: answers, like fish, would come swimming up to the surface in their own time if you watched and waited.

There was some discussion on the journey about where they were all going. Nathanael announced that he was going back to Cana to attend a family wedding.

"Why don't you all come," he said. They looked at one another, and they all looked at Jesus.

"Alright, why not?" he agreed. No-one wanted to break the party up yet and, as Peter murmured to John, "It'll be a chance to see Nazareth too."

So they retraced the road that Jesus had taken, past the hill of Beth Shan and up the valley of Jezreel to the plain of Esdraelon, before heading into the hills around Nazareth and over to Cana.

When they arrived in Nathanael's village the wedding festivities had already been going on for several days. Jesus was surprised to find his mother there.

"Son, are you back?" she said.

"For a few days perhaps," he replied. "What are you doing here?"

"I said I'd come over and help with the food," Mary replied. "They're poor enough, bless them. The bride comes from Nazareth - you know, Rachel, old Ephraim's daughter. The groom comes from here of course. They're a sweet couple, and I said I'd like to help them. What about you? How thin you are!"

"I guess I've been fasting. I needed to spend time in the wilderness, alone."

"Tell me later, I'm busy now."

Jesus and his followers mingled with the family and friends from surrounding villages who came and went, wishing the bride and the bridegroom well.

Sometime during the afternoon, Mary came up to Jesus and whispered in his ear, "The wine's running out."

He got up and moved away from the others. "Why tell me, woman? What d'you expect me to do?"

She said, "I've no idea, but it'd bring such shame on them if they ran out of wine, and they're poor enough already."

Jesus pondered, searching within himself, listening for the prompting of the Spirit of God. His mother watched him, and then, without another word, she said to one of the servants, "Do whatever he tells you," and went away.

Jesus smiled.

"Fill the water jars up, then pour some out and take it to the master of the feast."

Mystified, the servants went away and did as Jesus had said. They filled the large stone jars that held the water for the ritual washings, and

FIRST FRIENDS

took some of it to the master of the feast. He looked in the cup, turned the wine round in it and tasted it.

"Mmm, this is good," he said. "Most people serve the best wine first, and when the guests have had plenty to drink, they serve the ordinary stuff. But this is good!"

Most people did not realise what had been going on. Only the servants who had drawn the water and Jesus' mother knew, but the word soon began to go round among the assembled company.

Most were incredulous and laughed it off as some sort of joke, but those who had come with Jesus looked at each other and shook their heads in awe and perplexity.

"I used to think nothing good could come out of Nazareth," remarked Nathanael, "but perhaps I was wrong."

They all laughed.

Jesus glanced up at the sun, now beginning to decline in the west, and decided that it was time for him to go. Nathanael offered the others a bed for the night before they returned to their homes at the lakeside, while Jesus returned to Nazareth with his mother.

The two of them walked back in the twilight, over the hill, in a companionable silence, until his mother said to him, "So you're not back for good, son?"

"No," he replied simply.

"Before you were born, God told me you were going to be a king, not a carpenter. I didn't understand it then and I don't understand it now, but I know that you must do whatever he tells you."

"Only ..." she added hesitantly, "I'm afraid for you, my son. You'd be so much safer here at home as the carpenter of Nazareth."

"Don't be afraid, mother," Jesus replied, "'underneath are the everlasting arms.'"

They continued on in silence, enjoying each other's company as if for the last time in the old familiar way. But Jesus was already beginning to think ahead, of those five followers who had attached themselves to him at the river Jordan and had seen the miracle that had occurred at the wedding in Cana.

The kingdom of God, he realised, did not just mean individuals coming into a new relationship with God, but people coming into new relationships with each other as well. He and they had tasted the first-fruits of the kingdom during the three days that they had spent together. The kingdom meant a new community, bound to God, bound to him, and bound to one another; loving God, but loving God together, and loving one another in a new way.

When he had honoured his mother and his brothers and sisters by spending a last couple of

FIRST FRIENDS

days with them, he must go down to the lake and gather up his new friends.

* * *

"What do you think now, then?" asked John of Peter as they settled down for the night in Nathanael's house.

"Mmm. Perhaps he is different after all."

five

FISHERMEN

A small crowd had gathered round Simon and Andrew as they sat in their boat, moored to the quay in Capernaum, cleaning their nets.

"What did you think of that John the Baptizer then?" asked one of the crowd.

"It was good, really good down there," replied Simon. "Big crowds every day, lots of people coming to be baptized, a great sense of the presence of God. If you haven't experienced it, it's difficult to describe. You realise down there that you've got to get serious with God. It isn't a game, all this, you know. Going through the motions Sabbath after Sabbath isn't enough. It's about your whole life. And it isn't about impressing the neighbours or the rabbi either. It's about getting right with God. John says the day of judgement's coming and we need to get ready for it."

"And we met this man while we were there," continued Andrew, "Jesus of Nazareth. John was saying that he was the one who is to come, the Lord's anointed - you know, the Messiah! We met him and talked to him. We actually walked home with him some of the way."

FISHERMEN

"Really? What's he like then?" asked one of the bystanders.

"Great," said Andrew, "I love him. I've never felt so at home with anyone in my life before. He's not frightening, as if he was someone great and powerful. He's natural, down-to-earth, just like you and me. Except that he isn't. He's lovely. I can't explain it."

"I have to admit there's something about his eyes," mused Simon. "He looks straight at you, or rather he seems to look straight into you. But it isn't frightening, like Andrew says. It's not as if he's peering into the dark secrets of your heart. There's love in his eyes – aye, that's it. There's love in his eyes."

Simon smiled.

In the household of Zebedee and Salome, a similar conversation had taken place the evening that John had arrived back from the river Jordan. All sorts of stories began to circulate along the shore of the lake and in the towns and villages up in the hills, as the testimony of the five friends began to spread. Others also were coming back from the Jordan retelling the words of John the Baptizer about the one who was to come, and about the gaunt figure that John had pointed out as, "The Lamb of God."

Soon after their return to the lake, news had spread along the shore that John the Baptizer had been arrested and was being held as a prisoner in Herod's fortress at Machaerus.

It seemed that, not long after Jesus and his friends had been there, Herod had decided to visit John the Baptizer and see for himself what all the fuss was about. He had gone down with a small retinue and asked for a private interview with John.

"No private interviews," John had replied. "You can sit down and listen like everyone else."

So Herod had humbled himself and had a chair brought by one of his retainers, and sat with the common people during the midday session under the trees.

At one point he had asked, perhaps sarcastically, "And what advice do you have for a ruler, a tetrarch like me?"

"Put away Herodias," John had replied immediately, in front of the whole crowd. "The law of Moses forbids you to have her as your wife."

There was a stunned silence. Then Herod had stood up, furious at having been rebuked in front of the people, but unable to do anything about it. He had stormed away, with his entourage scampering after him. But Herod had taken his revenge: John was now in prison.

As this news was spreading along the waterfront in Capernaum, Jesus appeared. He stood among the little crowd listening to Andrew and Simon as they sat in their boat. Suddenly Andrew saw him.

FISHERMEN

"Master, you're here," he cried in delight. "Look everybody, this is Jesus, the man we've been telling you about. We met him at the river Jordan."

Eagerly, Andrew climbed out of the boat. The people greeted Jesus with a certain amount of embarrassment or hesitation, while Andrew ran off along the shore to fetch James and John, who were in the boat with their father Zebedee.

The crowd grew as others sensed that something unusual might be happening and stopped on their way by. People were telling one another what Andrew and Simon had been saying about this stranger in their midst.

Soon Jesus was hemmed in on the shore, and he suggested to Simon that they should get into his boat and push off a little from the land. Simon and Andrew rowed the boat out a few yards onto the water and dropped the mud weight over the side so that the boat swung lazily on the anchor.

Jesus was sitting on one of the thwarts. An expectant hush spread over the crowd, which was ever increasing as more and more people came to see what was going on. Some sat down, others stood. Jesus began to speak.

"Some of you have been down to listen to John the Baptizer. So have I. In any case, you've all heard about him, and you've probably heard now that he's been thrown into prison. For a time John's been like a new light shining in Israel. It's been exciting, hasn't it? But now, another light is coming into the world. A greater light. I'm the one for whom John came to prepare the way.

"'The Spirit of the Lord God is upon me, because the LORD hath anointed me to preach good tidings unto the meek. He hath sent me to bind up the broken hearted, to proclaim liberty to the captives, and the opening of the prison to them that are bound; to proclaim the acceptable year of the LORD.'

"Those are the words of the prophet, long ago. Today, they're being fulfilled in your hearing. In the beginning, God created the heavens and the earth, and he saw that it was good. The garden of Eden was a place where God and man and all the creatures lived together in harmony, but our first parents rebelled against God. They disobeyed him, they thought they knew better than God. They were wrong. So wrong! And today, the whole world has fallen into the power of the evil one.

"Life in every generation is a struggle, isn't it? A struggle to survive, a struggle to provide for your children, a struggle with sickness and infirmity, a struggle with anxiety and fear. Every generation faces the threats of war, of famine, of plague, of death. It was never meant to be like this.

"God is love. He loved the world that he'd created. He loves it still. He loves you, each one of you. He wants to redeem the world, save the world. He's been redeeming it from the day when

FISHERMEN

he first called our father Abraham to leave his country and his people, and go to a land that he would show him.

"It's a country God's still calling us to enter, but it's a heavenly country, not an earthly one. It's the land where God reigns, the kingdom of heaven. God's calling the world back to himself. He's calling *you* back to himself. His kingdom is coming. One day, he will rule the world again. He will rule the hearts and minds of his people, and rule over the whole creation once again.

"'The wolf shall dwell with the lamb, and the leopard shall lie down with the kid; and the calf and the young lion and the fatling together; and a little child shall lead them. They shall not hurt nor destroy in all my holy mountain; for the earth shall be full of the knowledge of the LORD as the waters cover the sea.'

"But you have to enter this kingdom by your own choice. You don't enter it by being born in a certain place or born of a certain race. People will come from east and west and will take their place at the feast with Abraham, Isaac and Jacob in the kingdom of God. But you have to say yes, your own yes to God. Turn to him in penitence and faith, confessing your sins and seeking his mercy.

"'The Lord is full of compassion and mercy, long suffering and of great goodness. He will not alway be chiding, neither keepeth he his anger for ever. Yea, like as a father pitieth his own children even so is the LORD merciful unto them that fear him.'

"Repent then and believe the good news. The kingdom of heaven is at hand."

There was silence as Jesus finished speaking.

No one moved.

"Now, put out into the deep water and let down the nets," Jesus said quietly to Peter.

"What? What do we want to do that for? We were out all last night and we caught nothing. The fish just aren't over this side of the lake at the moment. And what about what you've just said? The people are waiting for more."

"Go on, do as I say," replied Jesus.

Peter stood in the boat and looked at Jesus. "Oh, alright," he said, with a bad grace. "If you say so, I'll let down the nets. But don't say I didn't tell you ..."

He and Andrew pulled up the mud weight and rowed out further from the shore, leaving the crowd, who started to move away, talking about what Jesus had said.

A little way out Peter and Andrew cast the net, let it settle down into the water and then began slowly to draw it in. To their astonishment they could see at once a mass of silver bodies and scales thrashing about in the net. They hauled the net in further and could see so many fish that they feared that the net would break.

FISHERMEN

Andrew turned towards the shore and shouted to James and John who had returned to their father's boat and were cleaning their nets. Andrew's voice carried over the water.

"Come out here, come and help us! We've got more fish than we can pull in!"

James and John launched their boat and came rowing out quickly to join them. When they arrived, the four fishermen hauled the net up, tipping the mass of fish into first one boat then the other, until everyone's feet were covered in fish, flipping and flopping about and gasping for air, until one by one they died and lay still.

All four men stood speechless, gazing at this extraordinary sight. Peter finally turned towards Jesus who was still sitting on the thwart where he had preached to the people.

Peter was overwhelmed by a mixture of emotions. Astonishment, exhilaration, and some sort of fear. He knelt down in front of Jesus in the boat amongst all the dying fish.

"Go away, master. I'm just an ordinary fisherman, and a sinful one at that."

"Don't be afraid, Peter," Jesus said, putting a friendly arm on his shoulder. "One day you'll be catching people instead of fish. Let's go back then."

They rowed the two boats back in silence, each of the fishermen trying to understand what had taken place. Where had those fish been all night?

Where had they suddenly come from? Why just then? Was it something to do with having Jesus in the boat? Was it connected with what Jesus had been saying about the kingdom of God? If so, what?

When they reached the shore, they pulled the boats up and started to sort and put the fish into baskets, still speechless.

Jesus watched with a quiet smile on his face. He loved these fishermen with their hard and calloused hands, their broad shoulders, their arms strong from rowing, and their openness.

Finally, John came up to Jesus and asked him, "So, where are you staying now?"

Jesus smiled again.

"Wherever! Foxes have holes ..."

"... and birds have nests!' the others joined in. "But the Son of Man has nowhere to lay his head."

They all laughed.

"Who is this Son of Man?" asked James.

"You'll find out," replied Jesus.

"Tell you what," said John, "there's a guest room on the roof of our house. It's not got much in it, just a bed, a table, a chair, and a lamp. But it's got a roof, and it's a place where you could stay whenever you're this way. I'm sure mother'd be pleased to have you – you'd be like the prophet Elisha passing by!"

"Aye, I like the sound of it," replied Jesus.

six

CAPERNAUM

It was the Sabbath. Jesus rose before daybreak and went out of the little room in which he had slept above the house of Zebedee and knelt on the flat roof.

"Father, I begin this new day with you.

"'Ponder my words, O Lord, consider my meditation. O hearken thou unto the voice of my calling, my King and my God, for unto thee will I make my prayer. My voice shalt thou hear betimes, O Lord, early in the morning will I direct my prayer unto thee, and will look up.'"

He sensed the presence of his Father and listened for his still small voice. He would be going to the synagogue with the people of the town and the ruler of the synagogue would invite him to speak. After what had happened yesterday there would be a crowd waiting to hear what he would have to say.

A text from the prophet Isaiah came into his mind and he knew that he must read this passage and preach from those words. They were another manifesto of the kingdom of God.

After a while he heard the family in the house below beginning to stir. Breakfast was ready. The bread baked the day before, the water fetched, to avoid working on the Sabbath day.

"Blessed art thou, our Lord and God, King of the universe, thou bringest forth food from the earth, to thee be all glory for evermore," intoned Zebedee, as they sat together on the floor to break their fast.

The town was quiet. On every other day of the week the narrow streets would be filling up, with women fetching water, men going to work, merchants emerging from the khans with their loaded beasts, shouting their orders, people coming in from the country with their produce for sale, eggs, fowl, milk, cheese, vegetables and fruit, the fishermen coming back from their fishing and landing their catches. But on the Sabbath, all was quiet. The calm of the Sabbath rest seemed to envelop even the hills and the Sea of Galilee itself. The oxen dozed in their stalls, the asses stood still, tethered to their rings, flicking their tails and twitching their ears as the flies awoke.

By the third hour men, women and children were making their way to the synagogue, voices were beginning to fill the air. Not the weekday shouting of the drovers or the cries of the traders, or even the shrill voices of the children playing in the market place, but adult voices, talking seriously to one another as they gathered in the courtyard outside the meeting place.

CAPERNAUM

Who was this new preacher who had suddenly appeared in their midst? Was he a proper scribe? Was he a Pharisee? He was not dressed like one. And what were they to think of his message? What was this kingdom of God of which he spoke? Was God really coming to redeem his people?

There had been people before who had called for the re-establishment of the kingdom of Israel. Did they really want that sort of upheaval? Who knows what dangers and trouble it might bring if it meant challenging the rule of Herod or Rome again. This could be serious stuff for everybody. Did they want to know about it? Would this new preacher be in the synagogue this morning? They had all heard that Zebedee the fisherman had invited this man Jesus to stay at his house, and so he would probably come. What then?

As Jesus walked to the synagogue with James and John, following in the footsteps of Zebedee and his wife, he knew that he was being watched. There was a sense of anticipation, but also suspicion. Zebedee himself was wondering just what it was that his sons had brought into his house.

Some of those standing outside the synagogue greeted Jesus politely.

"Peace be with you, rabbi."

"Peace be with you," Jesus replied with a smile.

Inside, the synagogue people were pushing each other up on the benches as more and more crowded in. They sat facing the elevated dais, the most important people, the elders of the town, sat at the front. The administator of the synagogue took his place at the reading desk and began the Shema.

"Hear, O Israel, the LORD our God is one lord, and thou shalt love the LORD thy God with all thy heart and with all thy soul and with all thy mind and with all thy strength."

The whole congregation stood and recited the verses with him until they finished with the words, "I am the Lord who brought thee up out of the land of Egypt. I am the LORD."

One by one, selected people were invited to come forward to read from the Law of Moses, the passages from the lectionary appointed for the day. Finally, the ruler looked round the assembly until his eyes rested on Jesus.

"Would the new preacher like to come and read the Word of God and expound it to us?"

Jesus rose and went to the reading desk. He asked for the scroll of the prophet Isaiah to be brought and the synagogue servant went to the cupboard in the apse and brought the sacred scroll. Jesus unrolled it until he came to the passage he wanted, and he read:

"'Strengthen ye the weak hands, and confirm the feeble knees. Say to them that are of a fearful heart, be strong, fear not: behold your God will come with vengeance, even God with a

CAPERNAUM

recompense; he will come and save you. Then the eyes of the blind shall be opened, and the ears of the deaf shall be unstopped. Then shall the lame man leap as an hart, and the tongue of the dumb shall sing: for in the wilderness shall waters break out, and streams in the desert. And the ransomed of the LORD shall return, and come to Zion with songs and everlasting joy upon their heads: they shall obtain joy and gladness, and sorrow and sighing shall flee away.'"

Jesus rolled up the scroll and sat down.

"Today, this Scripture is being fulfilled," he began. "The kingdom of God is at hand. The time has come for God to visit his people again. Not just as in the days of old when he rescued us from slavery in Egypt. Not just as in the days of old when he rescued us from the hand of the Philistines. Not just as in the days of old when he restored our fortunes in bringing our fathers back from Babylon. But now he's fulfilling the promises we've heard from our prophets but which have remained unfulfilled for so long.

"For too long you've said to one another as Ezekiel said, 'The days are prolonged and every vision faileth.' But now, this is what the Lord says: 'The days are at hand and the effect of every vision.'

"Remember what the prophet Jeremiah prophesied: 'Behold, the days come, saith the LORD, that I will make a new covenant with the house of Israel, and with the house of Judah. Not according to the covenant that I made with their fathers in the day that I took them by the hand to bring them out of the land of Egypt; which my covenant they brake, although I was an husband unto them, saith the LORD. But this shall be the covenant that I will make with the house of Israel: After those days, saith the LORD, I will put my law in their inward parts and write it on their hearts, and I will be their God and they shall be my people. And they shall teach no more every man his neighbour, and every man his brother, saying, Know the LORD: for they shall all know me, from the least of them unto the greatest of them, saith the LORD; for I will forgive their iniquity, and I will remember their sin no more.'

"These are the days to which Jeremiah looked forward. God is replacing the old covenant that he made with our fathers, the covenant that they constantly broke, and replacing it with a new covenant. You will no longer go to the scribe or the Pharisee to ask him what to do. God's law will be written on your hearts, on the hearts of priests in Jerusalem and on the hearts of fishermen and shepherds in Galilee. The law of God will no longer be a burden but a joy. Not a list of rules to be obeyed, but a new life of freedom, grace and peace.

"Come to me, listen to me, learn from me. You're weary, and worn down by years of disappointment and discouragement. I'm a carpenter by trade. I'll

CAPERNAUM

give you a new yoke, one that's easy to bear, and you'll find rest and hope for your souls."

Suddenly, there was commotion at the back of the synagogue.

"What do you want with us, Jesus of Nazareth? I know who you are – the Holy One of God!"

The voice was harsh and constricted. Everyone turned to see where it had come from. A man they knew well, who wandered the quayside, a tortured soul often heard muttering to himself as he walked along, was screaming at Jesus with a contorted face.

"Be quiet, you," Jesus commanded in a loud voice. Jesus stood up, "Come out of him."

The man shook violently. A shriek came out of his mouth and was lost in the air.

"Go in peace," Jesus said quietly. "The Lord has put away all your sin."

A profound silence filled the synagogue.

"Aye," said Jesus again, this time to all who were waiting for his next word, "Go in peace. The Lord has put away all your sin too."

Jesus made his way slowly through the people and out into the sunshine. Peter and Andrew, James and John followed him and they all walked slowly back to the house of Peter.

The rest of the people emerged from the synagogue and stood about in the courtyard and in the streets, saying to one another, "What's all this about then? We haven't heard a sermon like that before - and he has some sort of authority too! He gave orders to an unclean spirit and it obeyed him."

On some people, the impression that Jesus had made was favourable.

"I'll come again if this chap's going to be speaking again this evening. Perhaps he's really been able to help poor old Ben. None of us could."

But others seemed less well disposed.

"Who does he think he is? Someone said he was the carpenter up in Nazareth. Ben'll be just the same in the morning, mark my words, muttering away as usual, same as always."

When Jesus arrived at Peter's house they were greeted by Peter's wife and children. Peter had married young and his children were growing up. His eldest son was already going out in the boat with them at night, and his eldest daughter was betrothed to a shipwright in the town.

Andrew's family lived off the same courtyard. There was a strong smell of fish from the outbuildings, where on weekdays the women gutted, salted and pickled the fish to be sent off to the markets of Jerusalem and Damascus as well as to other towns around the lake.

"I'm sorry," Peter's wife began, "mother's in bed with a fever. Otherwise she'd be here to help."

"I'm sorry to hear that. Will you take me to see her?" Jesus asked.

Peter's wife led Jesus into a small room off the main house where an old woman was lying on a mattress on the floor.

"Mother, this is Simon's new friend, Jesus. He's come to see how you are, mother. You're not very well, are you?"

"No, dear, I'm very hot. I don't feel well at all. I ache all over. But I daresay I'll get over it. I'm a tough old bird, but I'm very pleased to meet you, Jesus. Simon's told us a lot about you."

She held up a gnarled old hand. Jesus took it.

"Get up," he said gently. "You're better now. The fever has left you."

The old woman slowly sat up.

"Do you know, I believe it has," she said, wiping her hand across her forehead. "Would you believe it! I think I do feel better. Well, would you believe it ..."

She lay back on the bed for a few moments.

"I think I'll lie still for a minute, just to make sure it's really gone, then I'll get up."

Jesus left her and rejoined the rest of the family in the living room. Andrew and his family had also arrived with their elderly father, Jonah, to share in the midday meal. The room was crowded. There was a certain reserve towards Jesus, especially amongst the children, in view of the things that their fathers had been saying about this man, but Jesus put them all at ease by telling them a story.

"There was once a man who found some treasure buried in a field. He covered up the treasure again and went and sold all that he had in order to buy the field. What do you think he sold?"

The children joined in, suggesting which possessions the man might have sold, while Jesus encouraged them to think of more and more valuable things. His cloak, his donkey, his wife's jewelry, his house!

"Because the treasure was worth more than all these things put together. When he had sold all he had, he had enough money to buy the field, and the treasure was his."

"Tell us another one," the children asked.

So Jesus told them another story, about a merchant who saw a pearl, more beautiful than any jewel he had ever seen, so he sold all the rest of his merchandise in order to buy it. As he was finishing the story, Peter's wife came back into the room.

"Mother says she'll be with us in a minute, when she's done her hair."

Everyone waited expectantly until the old woman appeared in the doorway.

"Come on then, mother. What kept you?" Peter joked.

CAPERNAUM

"Well, would you believe it," laughed the old woman as she put on her pinafore and began to busy herself in the kitchen. "Would you believe it!"

seven

HEALING

Between the sixth and the ninth hour, during the heat of the day, the streets of Capernaum were deserted as the inhabitants rested or slept, grateful for the weekly release from the daily grind. The fishermen had not fished the night before so there had been no catch to sort and sell or preserve. In the early hours of the morning they would have to launch their boats again but today, everyone could rest.

Jesus was drawn out of the house to spend time with his heavenly Father. He walked slowly along the shore, past the idle fishing boats drawn up on the shingle, past the last houses of the town, to a place where he sat down in the shade of a tall palm tree and leaned back against the trunk.

A bird squawked at him from the top of the tree and, as he looked up, the bird flew off dropping an offering onto Jesus' forehead. Amused, Jesus wiped his forehead with his hand and washed his face in the lake.

"Bless you, bird," he said. "May my Father provide for all your needs."

He sat down again and thought over the events of the last few days.

HEALING

Sometimes the Spirit had given him an idea of what would happen, of the situations he would face, and then he had been able to prepare for them. At other times, such as at the wedding at Cana or in the synagogue this morning, he had been caught unawares forced to react on the spur of the moment. He had not been prepared for the demonised man in the synagogue, but he had recognised the source of the disturbance when it had occurred. He had commanded the spirit to leave, and it had gone.

Jesus recognised that there was a sort of spiritual warfare interwoven in all human life, a warfare that was reflected and manifested in every aspect of human affairs. A conflict between good and evil, between light and darkness, between truth and lies, between kindness and indifference or cruelty. In the end, a conflict between God and the Devil.

God alone was almighty, but the devil's power was real enough. God alone knew what lay behind the demonisation of the man in the synagogue, but for now at least the demon had gone and the man was free to make his own decisions. Jesus asked his Father to bring the man to full salvation.

Then, there had been Peter's mother-in-law. Jesus had not been prepared for that one either. The old woman's fever was probably not a sickness unto death; she would probably have got better in any case. But every sickness was like a little attack of death, and he had come that people might have life and have it more abundantly. It was part of the prophetic mandate of the kingdom of God, which he had read out in the synagogue, to bring healing and wholeness to those whose lives were blighted by disease and infirmity:

'Then the eyes of the blind shall be opened,
and the ears of the deaf shall be unstopped.
Then shall the lame man leap as an hart,
and the tongue of the dumb shall sing.'

So he had rebuked the fever and it had left her.

"Blessed art thou, O LORD, the Shield of Abraham. Thou, O LORD, art mighty for ever, thou givest life to the dead, thou art mighty to save. Thou sustainest the living with loving-kindness, thou revivest the dead with great mercy, thou supportest the falling, healest the sick, freest the bound, and keepest faith with them that sleep in the dust. Who is like thee, LORD of the mighty acts, and who resembleth thee, O King, who ordereth death and restoreth life, and causeth salvation to spring forth?"

Slowly and thankfully, Jesus prayed the Jewish benediction and felt the blessing of his Father resting upon him. The words he had heard first at the river Jordan re-echoed in his ears: "You're my

HEALING

son, with you I'm well pleased." Once again he felt his Father's love and pleasure.

Was he surprised when the demon had left the man in the synagogue or when Peter's wife's mother had been healed? He supposed that he should have been, but in a curious way he was not. He had, after all, never done or said anything like that before, but he had always been distressed by the sight of the leper and the lame.

He remembered, as a child, the man who used to sit every day at the door of the synagogue in Nazareth, begging alms from the villagers who passed by. From the knees down the muscles and bones of his legs and feet were shriveled and deformed so that he could not walk. To move at all he had to shuffle along on his bottom.

"Why's he like that?" Jesus had asked his mother as they passed him one day.

"He was born like it," his mother had replied.

"What does he live on?" Jesus had enquired.

"Anything people give him. The almoners give him money from time to time. That's why we give our alms to the synagogue – to help people like him."

On another occasion during his childhood, Jesus and his father had been walking up to Sepphoris where his father was working. Out in the country they had passed a ramshackle hut a little way back from the road. In the doorway sat a man swathed in cloths from head to foot.

"Why does he live out here, all on his own?" Jesus had asked.

"Because he's a leper," his father had replied.

"What's that?"

"He has a skin disease. Underneath those cloths his skin's all blotchy and swollen. That's why he covers it up. It's also very contagious, that's why he has to live out here all alone."

"What's contagious?"

"It means you can catch it if he touches you or if you touch something that he's touched."

"Can't it be cured?"

"No, not by man anyway. There's a story in the scriptures in which a leper is cured by the power of God, but not by man. He was called Naaman the Syrian and he came to Elijah or Elisha – I can't remember which, I get those two confused – and Elijah or Elisha told him to go down to the river Jordan and wash seven times and he'd be healed."

"And did he?" Jesus had asked.

"Aye."

"And was he healed?"

"Aye."

"Then why doesn't that man go down to the river Jordan and wash seven times and he'd be healed too?"

HEALING

"It doesn't work like that," his father had replied. "It wasn't the waters of the Jordan that healed him but the power of God."

"Why did he have to wash in the river, then?"

"Obedience. The prophet told him to wash, and he had to obey the word of God in order to be healed. It's called faith. Faith and obedience go together. God says it, and you do it. Never mind whether you understand why. You do it in obedience to God – in faith."

For the rest of the walk Jesus had been silent, thinking it all over.

Now it was the power of God working through him and his word, not the word of Elisha (for Elisha it had been, not Elijah), but now through him. If he continued to listen to the Spirit of God within him, prompting him, the power of God would continue to work through him to bring healing and wholeness even to the lame and the leper.

He was not surprised then by the manifestations of the power of God that he had seen, invisible and mysterious though this power was. It was the Lord's mighty hand and outstretched arm that had delivered the demon-possessed man and healed the feverish old woman. Jesus knew that it was not him, but his Father's power, that was doing these mighty works. It was God's kingdom coming on earth.

THAT MAN JESUS

So what would happen next? Sabbath or no Sabbath, word would spread, about what had happened in the synagogue, perhaps about Peter's mother-in-law as well. There were plenty of laws about what could not be done on the Sabbath, but there was no law against talking.

Once the sun had set and the Sabbath was over, people would start to come, some out of curiosity, some out of desperation. No-one else had been able to help them; perhaps this new prophet could.

The sun was beginning to decline behind the hills of Galilee. Jesus stood up and walked back into the town for the evening service in the synagogue.

He was not asked to speak again.

Afterwards he went back to the house of James and John.

"Jesus, you're here," Salome greeted him. "Come in and eat with us now the Sabbath's over. I'm making something hot."

As they ate, a small crowd began to gather in the street outside in the dusk. A blind man with a stick supported by a friend beside him, a sickly child crying quietly in its mother's arms, a cripple on crutches, all patiently waiting in the street.

Jesus' heart melted within him. Tears came to his eyes. They were like sheep without a shepherd, harassed and helpless. He went out to

HEALING

meet them, and James and John followed to see what would happen.

Moving among them, Jesus laid his hands on them one by one and spoke healing to their diseases and infirmities. One by one, quietly, their tears turned to smiles, limbs straightened, the eyes of the blind were opened.

The blind man looked into the first face that he had ever seen, and it was the face of Jesus. Tears began to flow down his cheeks. He flung his arms around Jesus' neck, holding on to him, sobbing with gratitude and joy and saying, "Master, master."

Darkness drew on, and the crowd dispersed. Jesus and Zebedee's family went to bed. The house and the street under the night sky seemed to be enfolded in an aura of wonder and peace. Everyone slept. But long before dawn, as the fishermen were going out quietly to fish on the lake, Jesus woke and went up into the hills to pray.

What should he do? The town would be a hubbub with the news. More would come, some from the towns and villages round about, as the word spread. Should he stay in Capernaum where it had all started?

No. He must set out, to preach the good news of the kingdom of God to those other towns and villages as well. Not everyone would or could travel down to Capernaum to hear and be healed.

THAT MAN JESUS

He must go to them. All must hear and have the chance to believe, or at least as many as possible. He would come back to Capernaum no doubt, but today he must move on.

As Jesus returned towards the town the sun was rising over the hills across the lake, creating a shining path of light across the water. He went again to the quayside where the fishermen were at work. Simon and Andrew were in their boat mending their nets.

"Everyone's looking for you," Andrew exclaimed, as he jumped out of the boat.

"Let's go on somewhere else," Jesus replied. "To the nearby villages – so that I can preach there as well. That's why I've come out."

"Do you mean us too?" Simon asked.

"Aye, come, follow me." Jesus said.

So, not knowing quite what they were doing, or why they were doing it, the two brothers left their nets and their boat and followed Jesus.

A little further along the shore they saw James and John in the boat with Zebedee, their father. Jesus said the same thing to them, "Come, follow me."

James and John looked doubtfully at their father, but Zebedee could see in their eyes that they wanted to go.

HEALING

"Go on, lads," he said, "I can manage. I think this is more important than fishing. I'll tell your mother."

"Thanks, Dad."

And they all went off together.

eight

PREACHING

Between the market place and the quay stood the customs house, with the tax collectors running in and out with their wax tablets to record and assess the cargoes of the ships arriving and the merchants passing through.

Capernaum's quay and market were the largest on the lake. Merchants from every corner of the earth passed along its shores, their camel trains often jamming the narrow streets of the town. From Egypt and Syria, from the ports of Tyre and Sidon on the Great Sea, the caravans went to and fro. Silks from the East, spices from Arabia and India, goods in bronze and iron, cloth and perfumes and jewelry, as well as the produce of the towns on either side of the lake and of the fertile plain around it – everything passed through Capernaum. Goods coming from the north, from the tetrarchy of Philip, or from across the lake, from the region of the Ten Towns were subject to taxation as they entered the tetrarchy of their Herod, Antipas.

In spite of all these widespread comings and goings, Capernaum remained a staunchly Jewish town, in which the law of Moses was observed by

PREACHING

the residents as strictly as a life mixed up with so many unclean Gentiles and their commerce permitted.

With their bronze badges the tax collectors were conspicuous amongst the crowd. Like all tax collectors they were treated with a mixture of tolerance and resentment. Tolerance, because they were only men doing their job, making a living for themselves and their families like everyone else; resentment, because nobody liked paying taxes and the tax collectors were always suspected of adding another few denarii for themselves.

The taxes collected in Capernaum went to a regime, that of Herod, which was itself treated with a mixture of tolerance and resentment by the Jews. Tolerance, because it was useless to complain; resentment, because Herod was not a proper Jew, nor a proper Roman for that matter, merely a stooge.

As Jesus and his friends passed the customs house, a tax collector was sitting at the table receiving the taxes. He looked up as Jesus passed and their eyes met.

"Didn't I see you down by the Jordan?" Jesus asked him, standing in front of the table.

"You could've done," the tax collector replied. "I was there."

"You were asking John if it was possible to be a tax collector and to please God."

"Aye, I was. It bothers me. And I was in the synagogue yesterday and heard you speaking." The tax collector paused. "I want to know more about this kingdom you were talking about."

"Come on then, follow me," Jesus said. The tax collector hesitated a moment, then called over to a colleague, "Joseph, will you take over here for a while?"

With that, the tax collector took off his badge, stood up with a broad smile and said, "Alright, where are we going?" And he joined the little band of followers.

"What's your name?" Jesus enquired as they went along.

"Levi," the tax collector replied, "but there are three of us called Levi in the tax office, so they call me by my other name, Matthew."

"Right, Matthew it is. Men, this is Matthew," Jesus said, turning to the other disciples. "He's one of us."

They made their way out of Capernaum, down the main street full of donkeys, camels, carts, and people. Some recognized Jesus and his companions. Of these, some had listened to Jesus before, others had seen or heard of his miracles. As he passed by, some turned to follow him, to see where he was going, hoping to hear or see something more.

By the time they left the town and emerged into the fields in the open country there were perhaps

PREACHING

thirty or forty people following Jesus, most of them not sure where they were going or why, but with a curious longing that at that moment they could not name.

"Hello, James," said a man called Judas, "What are you doing here? Does anyone know where we're going?"

"Search me," replied James. "I heard this man speaking from Simon's boat the other day. Just as I was coming into town this morning I saw him heading out. I see my brother Levi, the tax collector, up there with him as well. I'm not sure where they're going. I just have the feeling that something's happening round here and I don't want to miss it."

"Aye, I know what you mean," said Judas. "I was in the workshop when I saw them go by and I had this sudden feeling that I had a choice. Either I could carry on sitting at the old bench, stitching leather for the rest of my life, or I could get up and go. So I got up and went, and here I am."

"You know me. I took over the farm when Dad died. There was not enough land to support all of us. That's why Levi took up the tax collecting," continued James. "But there's been many a time I've thought to myself, is this all there is to it? You get up in the morning, you go out to work, you come home in the evening, you go to bed, you get up ... da-di-da-di-da. You sow, you reap, you sow again. Then one day you die. Is that all there is to it?

"The Pharisees say we'll rise again and shine like the stars, if we keep the commandments of God. But which ones? I don't know. I don't work on the Sabbath, I don't keep pigs, but I can't spend my life worrying about whether I'm breaking the Sabbath by untying the donkey or fetching her a bucket of water. Come to think of it, I haven't always kept the Ten Commandments, far less all the others they make up. But is that what life's all about - trying to keep your nose clean with God?"

"But you have to admit the Pharisees love God, and they love our nation too," argued Judas. "We'd be in a fine old mess if we didn't have them to remind us of who we are and of what we ought to be doing."

"Maybe. I don't know. All I know is that I'm hungry for something. I don't know what it is, but I think maybe this man's got it, and I want it."

They were coming to a village where the hills of Galilee rose up from the plain of Gennesaret. They stopped at the well for water. The villagers who were about in the street were curious about this large group of people arriving all together.

"Who are you?" they asked. "Where are you all off to?"

"We're with Jesus of Nazareth," they replied. "He's over there. He's a teacher and a healer."

PREACHING

As Jesus' followers shared the water that was drawn for them, others came out to see what was going on. Jesus raised his voice.

"Fetch your friends and neighbours and come out onto the hillside. I've something to tell you."

He led the way out of the village, climbed a hill, and sat down on a rock overlooking the plain. The hills formed themselves into a sort of bowl here, a natural amphitheatre. Jesus waited as people appeared from their houses, some even started to leave the fields where they were working, drawn by what looked like an event that was out of the ordinary in the routine of their daily lives.

Eventually a hush fell on the crowd and Jesus began to speak.

"What do you want from life? Enough to eat and drink? Health? Happiness, for yourselves and your children? And what do you think is the way to get it? Who do you think is happy? The rich? The powerful? The important people? Those who live in big houses and recline beside groaning dinner tables?

"Listen, I'll tell you something. Happy are you poor, for yours is the kingdom of God. Happy are those of you who are hungry now, for you'll be satisfied. Happy are those of you who weep now - you'll be laughing in the end! Happy are you when everyone speaks ill of you and hates you for the sake of the kingdom of God, for that's how their fathers treated the prophets before you.

"But woe to those who are rich now. They've already had their good things. Woe to those who are well fed now, for they will be hungry. Woe to those who are laughing now, for they will mourn and weep. Woe to you when everyone speaks well of you, for that's how their fathers treated the false prophets.

"I don't expect you to understand that all at once, but it's simple. When you feel secure, you don't depend on God. When you feel insecure, you depend on God. God wants you to be happy and God is the only source of happiness and security. Learn these words then. Say them over to yourself. Depend on God, and you will find true happiness."

Jesus repeated his teaching phrase by phrase and made them repeat it after him, just as the rabbi had done when they were all back in the synagogue school.

"The rabbis teach you to keep the law of Moses. That's right. I haven't come to teach you *not* to keep the law of Moses, but to teach you *how* to keep it. You've heard it was said to the people long ago, 'Thou shalt not kill'. But that's not enough. I say to you, if you're angry with someone or if you insult someone, you're the same as the person who kills someone.

"Again, you've heard it was said to the people long ago, 'Thou shalt not commit adultery". But that's not enough. I say to you men, if you look at

PREACHING

a woman lustfully, you're the same as the person who commits adultery with her.

"You've heard it was said to the people long ago, 'An eye for an eye and a tooth for a tooth'. But that's not enough. I say to you, if someone hits you on the right cheek, let him hit you on the left one too.

"You've heard that it was said to the people long ago, 'Thou shalt love thy neighbour and hate thine enemy'. But I say to you, love your enemies, pray for those who persecute you. Your Father in heaven makes the sun rise on the just and on the unjust. He sends rain on the righteous and the unrighteous – all alike. So be like your Father in heaven. Pour your goodwill down on everyone you meet, like rain or sunshine. I tell you, unless your righteousness exceeds that of the scribes and Pharisees you will never enter the kingdom of God.

"Don't worry about things like what you're going to eat and drink, or what you're going to wear. There's more to life than food, and more to what you do with your body than the clothes you put on it. You need all these things, and so do I, but do you think God doesn't know that, or that he doesn't care about you? Consider the birds. There, that one over there, on that rock, for instance – he seems to be listening, doesn't he? - he doesn't sow or reap or store up food in barns like we do, but

God feeds him all the same. You're more precious in the sight of God than that bird.

"And look at the flowers around you. They don't spin and sew, like you do, but God clothes them in these wonderful colours. Not even Solomon, in all his glory, was dressed like one of these. You see, the problem is that you don't have enough faith. If God clothes the flowers of the field and feeds the birds of the air, can't you rely on him to look after you too?

"Don't store up for yourselves treasure on earth. Whatever you do with it, it's never safe. Rust and moth eat away at your possessions. You put your money in a box and thieves break in and steal it. Store up for yourselves treasure in heaven where there is no rust, no moths, no thieves. One day in any case, you'll have to leave it all behind and whose will it be then?

"There was once a man whose land produced a bumper crop. So he thought to himself, What shall I do? I haven't got enough room to store all this lot. I know what I'll do. I'll pull down my barns and build bigger ones, then I can stash it all away and put my feet up. I'll have enough to last me for years to come. I can say to myself, 'Have a good time, lad.'

"But God said to him, 'You're a fool! Tonight your life will end, and whose will all this be then? And more important still, where will you be then?' That's how it is with everyone who spends his life

PREACHING

storing up riches and possessions here on earth and is not rich towards God.

"You see, loving God and being loved by him is the most important thing in life. The things you can see are all going to pass away. The things that you can't see will last forever. If you don't know the love of God then you're missing out on the most important thing in the world. God has made us for himself, and our hearts are restless till they finds their rest in him. Come to me, listen to me, learn from me. I'm a carpenter by trade, I'll make you a yoke that's easy and light to bear. In me you'll find rest for your souls."

Jesus finished.

The people were still hanging on his words, reluctant to move, but Jesus got up and made his way through the crowd. Standing at a distance, he had seen a leper who was carefully keeping away from the others, but listening intently to what Jesus had been saying.

Jesus went over to him.

"What do you want God to do for you, my friend?" he asked.

The leper knelt down before Jesus.

"Master, if you will, you can make me clean."

Jesus stretched out his hand and touched him. There was a stifled gasp from the watching crowd.

"I will," said Jesus, touching the man's head, shoulders and hands and helping him to his feet. "Be clean."

Slowly the leper took off his bandages and the cloths covering his face. His skin was like the skin of a new-born babe.

The crowd slowly dispersed, back to their homes and their fields to get on with their daily work and to ponder the things they had heard and seen.

Was God really concerned with their happiness? Was it possible that he cared for each one of them? This seemed to be a different God from the one they had heard about before. That God was the God of the nations, the God, above all, of their own nation, the nation that he had chosen out of all the nations to be his own, the nation of Israel.

He was the God of their patriarchs and prophets, of their priests and kings, but not a God who cared about them – surely?

nine

MAGDALA

James the son of Alphaeus and Judas walked back to Capernaum together.

"Wasn't that extraordinary?" exclaimed James. "Not just the leper, but the teaching, the talk, the sermon, whatever you want to call it. He doesn't teach like the other rabbis. They're always telling you what Rabbi This or Rabbi That said, or at the most they're telling you what Moses or the prophets said. This man just gives it to you straight. 'I tell you this, I tell you that.'"

"Mmm," agreed Judas. "He seems to know what he's talking about himself. He hasn't got it from other people or from the teachers in Jerusalem. In fact, I doubt if he's ever been to Jerusalem. Folks like us don't go to Jerusalem, except for the feasts of course. We don't go there to study."

They walked on in silence for a while.

"Where do you think he get's it from then?" asked Judas.

"I've no idea," replied James, "but I've never heard anyone speak like that before."

"D'you think he'll be going out to preach somewhere tomorrow?"

"Maybe. If he does, I want to go again."

"Me too," agreed Judas.

As Jesus re-entered Capernaum that evening, the centurion from the local garrison met him. Capernaum was at the frontier between the tetrarchy of Herod and the tetrarchy of Philip at the head of the lake. The town had a garrison of auxiliary Roman troops permanently stationed there. The centurion stopped in front of Jesus, surrounded by some of the Jewish elders.

"Are you Jesus of Nazareth?" he enquired.

"I am," replied Jesus.

"I'm so glad to have found you," the centurion continued. "I've been looking for you all over town. My servant's been taken ill. He's paralysed all down one side. He does not look good to me. I heard that you'd healed some of the people here in the town."

"He deserves that you should help him," interrupted one of the Jewish elders. "He's not like most of them. He loves our nation and he helped us to build our synagogue."

"I'll come and heal your servant," replied Jesus.

"No, no. Whatever they say, I don't deserve anything," the centurion said, "and I'm not asking you to come to my house either. I know that that would make you unclean. I only ask that you say the word, and my servant will be healed. I'm a soldier, I understand authority. I say to this man,

'Come', and he comes, and to another, 'Go', and he goes. I believe that you only have to say the word and my servant will be healed."

Jesus was noticeably surprised. He had been reminded at once of the Roman soldier whom he had seen years before, sharing his dates with the Jewish children. He was now struck by the humanity of this centurion, by the concern he was showing for a man who was no more than his servant. Above all, Jesus was struck by his faith.

After a few moments, Jesus finally said, "I haven't met anyone with faith like this. You're a Gentile, but you put our people to shame. I tell you," he said, turning to the crowd around him, "many will come from east and west and sit at the table with Abraham, Isaac and Jacob, in the kingdom of God, but some of those who should be there..." he continued in a quieter voice, "... they will find themselves outside, in the dark, wishing they had come in while they had the chance."

"Go home," Jesus said to the centurion kindly, "your servant is well."

Day by day, Jesus went out to preach and teach in the towns and villages around the lake, sometimes returning for the night, at other times accepting hospitality from those he met. Always, as he set out, a crowd gathered about him and went with him.

Among them were usually Peter and Andrew, James and John. But then there were others who seemed to have become permanent members of the group and whom Jesus was beginning to know by name. Matthew and James, the sons of Alphaeus, and Judas. Then there were the two whom Jesus had met down by the river Jordan, Philip from Bethsaida at the top of the lake, and his friend Nathanael from Cana. These two had reappeared and were now always with him.

An assortment of other people accompanied him day by day, some of whom Jesus knew and some he did not. They often picked up others on the way. People would stop as they went past and ask his followers what was going on, and those who knew would tell them about Jesus.

Meanwhile, back at the quayside, Zebedee and his family carried on the family business, sometimes questioning what James and John were doing, going off everyday like this with Jesus, sometimes wishing that they might go too. Simon's wife and mother-in-law and Andrew's wife started gutting and cleaning fish for other fishermen and kept the family home going while Simon and Andrew were away. It seemed to work.

One day, on his travels, Jesus visited Magdala, a town about five miles down the lake. The road lay across the plain of Gennesaret. Along the north-west shore of the lake, the hills of Galilee drew back, leaving a fertile plain that produced an abundance of fruit and vegetables that supplied the whole region. Figs, dates, grapes, apples,

MAGDALA

pomegranates, leeks, onions and garlic. Magdala, like Capernaum, was another thriving lakeside town, famous and prosperous from the manufacture of its cloth.

Many of the inhabitants made their living in the spinning, dying and weaving of the wool that came down from the flocks on the hills of Galilee and from the lake shore opposite, in the territory of the Ten Towns.

As Jesus and his friends entered the streets of the town, a woman sitting on a stool in the doorway of her house, with her hair uncovered and her veil round her shoulders, stared at Jesus with a provocative smile, even pulling up her skirts to reveal her ankles. Jesus stopped and looked into her face.

As he looked steadily into the woman's eyes, they changed. The brazen, provocative stare faded, and pain and despair filled her eyes. She looked down.

"Woman, your sins are forgiven," Jesus said to her quietly.

Her eyes filled with tears and she began to cry, burying her face in her veil.

They walked on, the men following Jesus not knowing what to think or to say. Normally, they would have smirked or passed some remark, either disapproving or insulting, depending on their attitude to women such as her. Today, they passed on in silence, embarrassed perhaps by her tears or else by their own incomprehension.

THAT MAN JESUS

Amongst the crowd who gathered to hear Jesus teach that day was a certain Pharisee. You did not see as many Pharisees in Galilee as you did in Judea, but every town, and even some of the villages, had a small community of them.

They met together to debate the finer points of the law and to bewail the general laxity of the people around them. They would keep themselves as much as possible apart, especially from contact with Gentiles, whose food and clothing might make them unclean, but the Pharisees would also try to keep themselves apart from their fellow Jews - 'the people of the land,' who did not follow the traditions of the scribes as strictly as the Pharisees did.

When Jesus had finished speaking, this Pharisee came forward and invited Jesus to dine with him. That evening, Jesus' followers went home while Jesus went to dine at the Pharisee's house.

The Pharisee introduced himself as another Simon and invited Jesus to recline at his right, in the place of honour. Simon had invited a considerable number of other guests, including some of his fellow Pharisees. As the self-appointed religious leaders and experts in the town, they thought they ought to hear what this untaught preacher had to say.

Simon said the blessing.

MAGDALA

"Blessed art thou, Lord God of all creation, thou bringest forth food from the earth. To thee be all glory for evermore."

All the company responded, "Amen."

The servants brought in the dishes of hot food and placed them in the middle of the table where all the guests could reach. The lamps were burning on the table.

After they had been eating and drinking for a while, a woman slipped quietly in at the Pharisee's door. At first no one noticed her, but Jesus recognized her as the woman whom he had seen that morning.

She looked around surreptitiously, saw where Jesus was reclining and crept round in the shadows by the wall until she was opposite his feet. She knelt down, uncovered an alabaster jar of perfume that she had concealed under her cloak, and began to pour it over Jesus' bare feet, crying silently, wetting his feet with her tears. Embarrassed by her tears, she began to wipe his feet with her veil and her hair.

A stunned silence fell in the room. There was not another woman there. The men who reclined with Jesus around the table could not believe what they were seeing – and smelling. They pulled up their own legs and skirts lest they should be touched by her.

One whispered to another, "If this man were really a prophet he'd know what sort of a woman she is, and he certainly wouldn't let her touch him like that. What does she think she's doing anyway."

The silence continued while the woman went on wiping Jesus feet with her hair.

Jesus was conscious of the closeness of the woman, of her hands and her hair touching his feet. The man in him could not but be aware of the sexual frisson of the act. Many a time, as he had been growing up in Nazareth, the subject of his marriage had come up. His mother and father had often discussed the matter with him, assuming that like all the other young men of his age he would be wanting to find a bride.

Jesus had not been averse to the idea in principle. He felt the attraction of the opposite sex and the common desire for intimacy, for someone to love and to hold. But whenever the subject of marriage came up, he had known that it was not for him.

It was not a matter of suitability. There were a number of girls of his acquaintance, girls he had grown up with in the village, friends of his sisters whom he had known all his life, who would have made perfectly suitable wives for a carpenter. But always there was the sense that he had something else to do that would be incompatible with having a wife and a family. So he had kept himself from women. But it was not easy.

MAGDALA

Now, here was this woman, kneeling at his feet, touching him, indeed caressing his feet. He knew that she was not thinking of him in terms of the other men she had known, and that her touch was innocent of any sexual meaning, but it reminded Jesus at that moment of what he had renounced.

"Master," interrupted Simon, "I'll send her away. I had no idea anyone would intrude upon us in this way. I don't know who she is, except that we all know that she's a woman of the streets. I really do apologise for this. I'll have her put outside."

He was about to rise and instruct the servants to pick the woman up and throw her out, when Jesus said to him, "Simon, I've got something to say to you."

Simon paused, "Go on then."

"Once upon a time, there were two men who owed money to a certain money-lender. One owed him five hundred pounds, the other fifty. Neither could pay, so the money-lender cancelled both their debts. Which of them, do you think, will love him more?"

"Well, I suppose the one who owed him more."

"Good," Jesus said, "That's right. Now, you see this woman. I came into your house. You didn't bring water to wash my feet, but she's been washing my feet with her tears, and wiping them with her hair. You didn't give me the usual kiss of peace, but from the time she came into the room she has not stopped kissing my feet. You didn't give me oil to anoint my head, but she has poured perfume over my feet. Her many sins have been forgiven, so she loves me a lot. Those who have fewer sins to be forgiven love me less."

Jesus looked at the woman.

"What's your name, my dear?" he asked.

"Mary," she replied.

"Mary of Magdala, go in peace, the Lord has put away all your sin."

A smile spread across the woman's tear-stained face. Joy welled up inside her. She got up, somewhat clumsily, and still smiling broadly, slipped out of the room and out of the house.

More whispering started amongst Simon's friends.

"Who does he think he is, if he thinks he can forgive sins?

"We shall have to have a discussion about this some other time, but it sounds like blasphemy to me, and we'll have to stop it."

"Or stop him."

Meanwhile, Mary was dancing down the street, spinning and twirling with her arms outstretched.

ten

NAZARETH

He was becoming famous. Stories of the things he had said and done were spreading throughout the towns and villages of Galilee. People were beginning to come up from Judea and from the towns across the lake, wanting to see and hear this man Jesus for themselves. Wherever he went, crowds gathered.

It was, of course, the miracles that were attracting the most attention. If you became ill or had an accident there was not a lot that you could do. If you had a strong constitution you might recover. If not, you might become a permanent invalid or die. In the Greek-speaking towns, like Sepphoris or Tiberius, or in the Decapolis over the lake, there were doctors who had studied anatomy and the properties of plants and herbs, but they required payment for their skills and their medicines. And, it had to be said, their cures were often worse than the diseases.

Both amongst the Greeks and the Jews, there were also to be found those who practiced the dark arts. In Jewry at least, they were frowned upon, but nevertheless people sometimes resorted to them in their desperation. Perhaps they did have some sort of supernatural power, and some of them did acquire a considerable, if questionable, reputation. They also charged for their services.

But Jesus did not fit into any of these categories. He did not prescribe infusions of leaves, he did not manipulate bones. Here he was, operating in full view of everyone, and everyone could see that there was no hocus pocus. Just a touch and a word.

Above all, Jesus did not charge for his cures. No wonder people were saying, "We never saw anything like this before."

Some were even beginning to say, "When the Messiah comes will he do more miracles than this?"

Not everyone, however, was so easily persuaded. The Pharisees in particular were less than impressed, and let anyone who was prepared to listen know it.

In his teaching, Jesus never cited any authority for what he said. He quoted the scriptures freely enough, but often only to qualify them, as if he thought he knew better than God what God had meant. Similarly, they were not sure about the source of his authority over illnesses and unclean spirits. Was his power from God or from some darker spiritual source?

NAZARETH

One day the fishmonger from Nazareth, who had come down to the lake to buy his fish, saw Jesus as he was about to leave the town.

"Hello there," he called out. "We've been hearing all sorts of stories about you, my boy. Why don't you come back to your old home and do some of the things in Nazareth we hear you're doing down here?"

There was something that Jesus did not like about the tone of this man whom he had known all his life, but he agreed that he would come. After all, Nazareth had as much right to hear the good news as any of the other towns and villages of Galilee. Passover was only a few weeks away and Jesus had decided to go to Jerusalem and show himself to the people there. He could make a longer excursion and revisit his home town on the way.

Two days later, he rose before dawn and taking with him Peter, James and John, they set out to walk the twenty-five miles to Nazareth. Andrew had promised to come up to Jerusalem later with their families for the feast.

Mary was delighted to see her son when he knocked on the door in the evening and welcomed him and his companions into the old home.

"Come in, dear man. We've been hearing about some of the things you've been doing down by the lake. Come and tell us all about it."

The next day Jesus went out into the village. People were pleased to see him again and spoke politely to him, but he sensed a certain reserve, as if they were not sure what to make of him any more.

He was not any longer simply the village carpenter, one of their own. If the stories about him that were circulating were even half true there was something unsettling about seeing again this man they thought they knew so well.

There was the man with the withered legs, for example, still sitting by the synagogue door as he always did. He saluted Jesus, but eyed him with suspicion. What was he thinking? Certainly there was not even a glimmer of hope in his eyes that Jesus could heal him. Perhaps he was even afraid that Jesus might heal him. He had been sitting there outside the synagogue all his life, what would he do if he were healed?

So Jesus greeted him, "Peace be with you, old friend," and walked on by to spare the man any more uncertainty. One or two people came up and shyly asked him for his help, pleased that someone they knew was now renowned as a man of God, but for the most part, there was a reticence towards him.

Jesus sensed that people had conflicting feelings. Were they proud that this person who had grown up among them was now a famous preacher and healer, or were they jealous of him? He had never

NAZARETH

shown such gifts or tendencies in the years he had lived in the town, so what were they to make of his sudden celebrity? How had he apparently changed so dramatically? Was he really a man of God or an imposter or a charlatan?

On the evening of the Sabbath, the ruler of the synagogue called at Mary's house to enquire whether Jesus would be willing to speak in the synagogue the following morning.

"Gladly," Jesus replied, but knowing that many of their hearts would be closed to what he had to say ...

* * *

"'The Spirit of the Lord God is upon me, because the LORD hath anointed me to preach good tidings unto the meek. He hath sent me to bind up the broken-hearted, to proclaim liberty to the captives, and the opening of the prison to them that are bound; to proclaim the acceptable year of the LORD.'

"Those, as you know, are the words of the prophet Isaiah long ago. Today, they are fulfilled in your hearing."

It was the message that he had proclaimed before, down by the lake, and in the synagogues by the lakeside. There, he had been heard with a mixture of excitement and incomprehension, but here he could feel indignation rising in his audience.

"I know that you've been hearing stories about me. God is indeed doing a new thing down by the lake. It's the beginning of something new in the world, a new way of life, a new covenant between God and his people. You're witnessing a new visitation of God: the one the prophets foretold long ago. You can accept it or reject it. This is a day of judgement. By the way in which you judge me, you yourselves will be judged.

"But I tell you the truth," Jesus continued, "no prophet is ever accepted in his own town or country. There were many widows in Israel in the days of Elijah, when the sky was shut up for three years and there was a famine in the land. But Elijah wasn't sent to any of them, rather he was sent to a widow of Zarephath in the territory of Sidon, a Gentile. And there were many lepers in Israel in the days of Elisha, but none of them was healed, only Naaman the Syrian, a Gentile soldier who you would despise."

At this point a murmuring arose in the building, a muttering, "Who does he think he is? Talking to us like this. We've known him since he was a boy. We knew his father. We know his mother. How dare he talk to us like this?"

The murmuring grew to a hubbub of noise as people rose to their feet and began to surround the dais on which Jesus was seated. It was the

NAZARETH

elders who began to drag Jesus out of the chair and down onto the floor of the synagogue. In their eyes he was still the boy Jesus, and here he was with the cheek to think he could teach them.

Surrounding him in a group, they strong-armed him out into the street. The people poured out after them and, without knowing what they were doing, the crowd pressed forward.

Down the street they went, past the well, up the hill, to the sheer outcrop of rock from which the old rabbi had once shown the boys the land of their fathers. But as they reached the brow of the hill, their ardour seemed to cool. The elders realised the futility and wickedness of what they were doing and the spirit went out of them.

Ashamed, they let go of Jesus and drew back. Jesus turned and looked at them. It was a pathetic sight. These respectable old men, who used to pat him on the head as a boy in the synagogue, covered in confusion and shame. They parted to let him through, and the crowd did the same. Jesus walked quietly down the hill, back to his mother's house.

"Oh son," his mother cried, "don't be too hard on them. They were offended. They didn't think what they were doing. To them, you're still just Joseph's little boy. Come and sit down. Tomorrow you must go."

Jesus sat down with his friends and family.

"When you were a baby," his mother continued, "we took you up to the temple, as the law says, to present you to the Lord. In the temple courts we met an old man whose name was Simeon. He spoke strange words over you. I've never told you this before, but all these years I've kept them in my heart.

"He said, 'This child is destined to cause the falling and rising of many in Israel, and to be a sign that will be spoken against, so that the thoughts of many hearts will be revealed.' And then he went on and said to me, 'A sword will pierce your own soul also.' So you see, it's coming true. Some believe in you, and some stumble over you. I don't think I understand it all, son, but I do believe. Your mother believes in you."

"Thank you, Mum," Jesus said softly, and kissed her head.

The next day, they took their leave and went down the winding road into the plain, the road that Jesus had taken on the day that he had closed the door of the carpenter's shop for the last time.

The feast of the Passover was approaching and they had decided to visit some of the towns and villages on the plain on their way up to Jerusalem. So Jesus, now with his three friends, descended the same steep path into the plain. As they went along through the towns and villages of

NAZARETH

the plain they picked up a crowd of followers as usual.

They came to a town called Nain. As they approached the gate a procession was coming out. A dead body wrapped in a sheet was being carried out on a bier. Behind the bier came a solitary woman, weeping, and behind her other women keeping up the customary wailing, and a crowd of neighbours and other townsfolk.

Jesus stopped those who were carrying the bier. They set it down and stood still. Jesus addressed the woman.

"My dear, who is this?" he asked.

"My son," the woman replied. "He was my only son. I'm a poor widow. He was all I had. What's to become of me now?"

"Don't cry," he said to her kindly. He went up to the body on the bier and touched it. "Young man, sit up."

Everything went quiet.

The corpse sat up under the sheet with which it was covered, and slowly swung its legs over the side of the bier. There was gasp from his mother and a buzz went through the crowd.

The mother came hurrying up and began to untie the sheet and the bandages in which the body of her son had been wrapped. She pulled them down and there, sitting inside, with a bewildered smile on his face, sat her son.

"What happened?" he said. "Where've I been? What am I doing here, in this lot?"

It was a strange procession that made its way back into the town. The bearers raised the bier to their shoulders again and, with the young man sitting up on it cross-legged, and his mother clinging to his left hand, he waved and smiled to the passers-by as they made their way home through the streets, like some potentate being born in on a royal palanquin.

The townspeople escorted Jesus into the town telling each other excitedly, "A prophet has come to visit us," and "God is visiting his people once again."

Soon the whole town had heard what had happened to the widow's son, and people were coming from far and wide to see the person who had performed this miracle, and the person on whom the miracle had been performed.

"These are the days of Elijah, coming again," people were saying to each other. "Elijah raised a sick boy from the dead, and he was the son of a widow. Now it's happening again here, in little old Nain. Hallelujah!"

Jesus himself realised that in responding to the widow's distress he had been the agent of a further manifestation of his Father's power: the power to raise the dead. It was a power that had been manifested occasionally in the past, as the townspeople were saying, and now was being

NAZARETH

manifested in the present, a power that would one day be seen in all its fullness:

> 'He will destroy in this mountain the face of the covering cast over all people, and the veil that is spread over all nations. He will swallow up death in victory; and the Lord GOD will wipe away tears from all faces.'

The three disciples were becoming ever more impressed by the miracles that they were witnessing with their very eyes. Some of those whom Jesus touched and healed might have been responding because of their own desperate hopes or because of the hopes of others. In any case, the disciples were not often in a position to know whether the 'healings' had lasted beyond the moment, so some scepticism remained in them. Was all this real or just wishful thinking? But there was no doubting the reality of the blind receiving their sight, of withered limbs beings restored, or of this corpse coming back to life.

The excitement in the town was palpable and Jesus was able to heal many sick people there. He stayed and preached to them and taught them for several days. In Nazareth he had offended his fellow townsfolk, and had hardly been able to heal anyone. Here he was a hero, and people were hungry for more.

It was as his Father had shown him in the wilderness, and as agéd Simeon had prophesied to his mother years before. Some would see and believe, others could not see and would not believe. Somewhere in their own hearts, each one was making up his own mind.

Now he was on his way up to Jerusalem. How would he be received there?

eleven

JERUSALEM

Most of the Galileans who made the pilgrimage to Jerusalem for the great feasts had their own quarters in and around the city where they stayed. Some with family, some with friends, some in inns or houses where they were regular and familiar guests.

The great influx of pilgrims, not only from Judea and Galilee, but from all over the world, was an important source of income for many of the families in Jerusalem. The pilgrims swelled the population of the city three or four times a year, for a week or more at a time, swelled it to three or four times its normal size.

Many families from Nazareth used to lodge in Bethany, a village some two miles outside the city to the east. Joseph and Mary had always stayed there with a family of three siblings, none of whom, strangely, had ever married - Martha, Mary and Lazarus. They were hospitable people, always pleased to see their friends from Galilee. It was to this house that Jesus now took his disciples.

The Bethanyites, as Jesus' family had called them when he was younger, greeted him warmly when he and his companions arrived at their house.

"We wondered if you might be coming for Passover. How are you all? Your mother, and brothers and sisters?" And to Jesus' companions, "Pleased to meet you. You're very welcome. Any friends of Jesus' are welcome here."

Later, they gathered round the table for the evening meal and fell to exchanging news of their mutual friends and acquaintance.

"We've been hearing strange stories about you, Jesus, from friends and visitors from Galilee. What are you doing now? Are these stories true?"

"I don't know what you've heard," replied Jesus. "But it's possible they're true. I believe that God has sent me to proclaim the kingdom of heaven. He's certainly honoured my words, by bringing healing to those I've touched. Is that what you've heard?"

"Yes, and the rest," added Lazarus, "You seem to have upset some of the Pharisees in your part of the world. There are all sorts of rumours that they're jealous of you, of the crowds who come to hear you teach, of your influence among the common people. They don't seem to like you much."

"Well, I can't help that," Jesus continued. "I must do what I see my Father doing, and say what I hear my Father saying. I can't do more - or less."

JERUSALEM

"Take care," said Mary. "They may not be pleased to see you here."

The following day, Jesus and his companions went into the city to go up to the temple. As they came down the Mount of Olives, the new temple buildings gleamed white in the sun, except where the rays glanced in dazzling, blinding light off the golden ornamentation.

They climbed the great steps on the south side of the temple precincts, the same steps up which Jesus' mother and father had brought him at forty days old to present him to the Lord and to offer the sacrifice of two young pigeons. It was somewhere here, in one of these courts, that the old man Simeon had spoken those strange prophetic words to his mother.

Jesus looked around him. Here in the outer court, the Court of the Gentiles, were the usual stalls of the moneychangers and of the traders selling sheep and cattle and doves. The pilgrims who had travelled from afar, even from abroad, needed to be able to buy their sacrificial animals on the spot, and to change their currencies into the temple coinage. So, particularly at the major feasts, there were always these exchanges and transactions going on in the temple precincts.

But all of sudden the irreverence of it all struck Jesus like a thunderbolt. The disrespect for God's dwelling place and for the devout souls who visited it, particularly the Gentiles, many of whom had travelled great distances to worship the God of Israel, and who could penetrate no further into the holy place than this. The blasphemy towards God, and the insult towards them, suddenly appalled Jesus.

Without thinking twice, he overturned the table of the money changer nearest to him, sending the piles of coins rolling and tinkling across the stone pavement. Then the next and the next. Nobody moved. They all just sat there, overcome by astonishment.

Then he shouted at the men selling animals, "Get these animals out of here! How dare you turn my Father's house into a market-place."

He began to push the men towards the gate, letting the animals loose and herding them in the same direction with a stick. So fierce was his anger that the traders quailed before him.

"Alright, alright. We're going, we're going. Alright. We heard, we heard."

In about ten minutes the great court was clear, except for a mess of animal dung, spilled coins, overturned furniture, and bemused pilgrims and visitors standing in groups, watching and wondering what was happening.

"This is supposed to be a house of prayer for all nations," Jesus spoke to all who could hear him, "so pray here in peace. God welcomes all who come to him in penitence and faith."

JERUSALEM

Jesus went over to the colonnade beside the court and sat down as if he were one of the rabbis, and began to teach, as he always did, about the kingdom of God.

People began to gather, standing warily at a distance at first, then moving closer as they were attracted by his words. Slowly the life of the temple courts resumed, but now in almost complete silence, except for the sounds of praying voices.

The next day was the Sabbath. Jesus went up to the temple again to pray. The mess of the previous day had been cleared up and there was no sign of the money changers or the traders.

Peace and tranquillity continued to reign in the great outer court, but there were some priests and temple guards, who had witnessed Jesus' righteous anger of the previous day, who now saw him entering the Court of the Jews. A little group of them confronted him.

"Who are you? What do you think you were doing here yesterday? Who gave you authority to order people about in the temple of God?" they challenged him.

"I'm Jesus, from Nazareth. What authority do you have for allowing the temple of God to be used as a den of thieves?"

"God appointed the sons of Aaron to be priests of the altar. Those men you drove out supply the animals for the sacrifices appointed by Moses.

They have legitimate business in the temple. As for you, what credentials do you have?"

"'Will God indeed dwell on the earth? Behold heaven and the heaven of heavens cannot contain him; how much less this house?' God destroyed this temple once because what went on in here displeased him, and he will do the same again. Perhaps for ever. The Spirit of God is upon me. My body is a temple of the Holy Spirit. You can destroy this temple, but if you do God will raise it up again in three days. As the prophet Hosea has said, 'He hath torn and he will heal us; he hath smitten and he will bind up. After two days will he revive us; in the third day he will raise us up, and we shall live in his sight.'"

"What're you talking about? We've no idea what you're talking about. It has taken forty-six years to build this temple and it's not finished yet. You're a madman, and a cheeky devil at that. Be off with you. Go away, and don't you dare interfere again in what goes on here."

So Jesus and his companions left the temple.

As they were going out of the city by the Sheep Gate they passed the pool of Bethesda. There was the usual crowd of sick and infirm people, sitting and lying by the pool. The pool was thought to have magical properties, because from time to time the water was mysteriously troubled. Some said that it was an angel that came down from heaven and stirred up the waters. Folklore said

JERUSALEM

that whoever entered the pool first on the stirring of the waters would be healed of their sickness or infirmity.

So every morning, there was a competition amongst the early arrivals to secure a good place. Some of the sick even sent friends ahead of them to lay out a towel or a mattress to reserve them a good place beside the pool.

As Jesus passed through the porticoes around the pool he saw a man lying well away from the edge.

"Have you been coming here long?" he asked.

"Thirty-eight years this year," replied the man. "Most of my life, in fact. Never really known anything else. Come here in the mornings – my old mother helps me – stay for the day, then she comes back for me in the evening."

"Do you want to be healed?" Jesus inquired.

"Well, I've got no-one to help me into the pool when the waters are troubled, have I?" replied the man.

"No, but you don't look as if you're really trying, do you?"

"Probably not," confessed the man. He reflected for a moment. "But I would like to be healed, to know even for a day what it's like to be normal, to get up and walk about like everyone else."

"Go on then," Jesus said, "pick up your bed and walk about, like everyone else."

By now all those around were looking and listening. The lame man slowly raised himself to his feet and finding that they held him, he bent down and folded up his mat.

"Well, thanks," he said as he walked off, slowly shaking his head.

As he left the portico he turned again, and called out to Jesus, "I don't know what mother's going to say!" and smiled broadly.

That evening the Bethanyites were having dinner when they were surprised by a knock at the door.

"Who can it be at this hour?" Martha demanded.

Lazarus got up from the table to open the door. There, with a lantern in his hand, stood a Pharisee, alone.

"I'm sorry to disturb you," he said, "but I understand you have the teacher Jesus of Nazareth staying with you. My name is Nicodemus, and I'd really like to speak to him."

"Come in," said Lazarus hospitably. "Jesus is definitely here and I'm sure he'll be pleased to see you. Would you like to join us at the table?"

So Nicodemus came into the light of the room, and reclined with them beside the table. They all waited expectantly.

"Rabbi, some of us believe that you're a teacher sent from God," Nicodemus began. "We've heard of the miracles that have been taking place in

Galilee and even of the healing by the pool today. You couldn't do the miracles that you're doing unless God was with you. I want to know more about this kingdom of God you're talking about. How do I become part of it?"

Jesus loved the man. He was not the typical Pharisee with a dogma or an answer to fit every situation. The study of the Law obviously did not satisfy his spiritual hunger.

Jesus replied, "I tell you the truth, no-one can enter the kingdom of God unless he's born again."

"Born again?" Nicodemus queried. "What does that mean? How does that work? Must I get back into my mother's womb and be born again?"

"Not quite," Jesus smiled, "but it means starting all over again - leaving behind your old ideas, your old ways, the person you've been so far, and starting again, like a little child, with a new relationship to God, a new relationship to other people, a new hope and a new assurance."

"How do I do that then?"

"You can't do it by yourself. The Spirit of God will help you. It's the Spirit of God who's put this hunger into your heart. He's already convicted you of your need. You want to get right with God in a new way, don't you?"

"Yes, I do," affirmed Nicodemus. "That's why I sought you out. Many of the priests and the scribes are suspicious of you, but I want to know more. That's why I came."

THAT MAN JESUS

"It's a mystery, how the Spirit of God moves," said Jesus, addressing all of them at the table around him. "He's like the wind. You see trees moving in the wind, but you don't know where the wind comes from or where it goes to, or why it blows here and not there. Why you, Nicodemus, and not the others? I don't know, and neither do you. But you're not far from the kingdom of God. Come again. Listen to me in the temple among the teachers. God loves the world so much that he's sent his only Son into the world, so that all who believe in him won't perish but will have everlasting life."

Nicodemus went out into the night, his heart on fire.

twelve

TEACHING

After the Days of Unleavened Bread, the pilgrims began to leave Jerusalem and make their way home. Many had come long distances. For some of them Passover in Jerusalem might have been a dream realised once in a lifetime.

As well as the Jews who lived in their own land, there were others dispersed all over the world - Jews in Mesopotamia, Persia, and Egypt, Jews who had never returned after the great exile hundreds of years before. There were Jews who had more recently settled along the coasts of North Africa and Asia Minor; there were colonies of Jewish traders even in Greece and Rome. These would all be returning home.

Jesus, however, decided to stay on in Jerusalem and Judea, to preach and teach there.

In the towns and villages around Jerusalem, let alone in Jerusalem itself, there were more Pharisees than in Galilee, due to the proximity of the schools in Jerusalem, and more priests and Levites due to the proximity of the temple. These all tended to look down on Jews from the north - Galileans - as people ignorant of the Law, compromised by the proximity of the Gentiles in their midst, and not least as people who spoke with a strong regional accent.

But Jerusalem was the capital city and Judea was the heartland of Judaism, so here too they must hear the good news and be given the chance to respond to it. So Jesus, and the group of disciples who had come with him, began a tour of the hill country of Judea, preaching in the synagogues and in the streets, healing any sick people who came to them, and announcing the kingdom of God, just as they had done in Galilee.

From time to time they returned to Bethany to rest and Jesus would go up to the temple and take his place in Solomon's Colonnade, where the rabbis gathered their pupils, to teach. The custom was for the rabbis to teach, and then for their disciples to ask them questions. Jesus would do the same.

One day he said, "I'll teach you about the three great acts of devotion to God - almsgiving, prayer and fasting. Be careful not to do them so that people can see what you're doing. If you do, you've already received your reward here on earth, and you'll get no reward from your Father in heaven.

"So, for example, when you give to the poor, don't blow a trumpet, or wave your money about in the synagogue or in the streets. Only hypocrites do that sort of thing. If you do, you'll have received your reward already – the impression of your generosity that you'll have made on all those

TEACHING

people. But when you give to the poor, don't even let your right hand know what your left hand's doing, and your Father who sees what you do in secret will reward you.

"And when you're praying at the hours of prayers, don't be like the hypocrites. They like to do it standing in little groups in the synagogues or on the street corners for everyone to see them. I tell you, they've already received their reward. No, go into your own room, shut the door, and pray to your Father who sees in secret, and he will reward you.

"And when you're praying for something don't babble on like the pagans do. They think that God will hear them because they say it over and over again, but you don't need to go on repeating yourself over and over again. Your Father knows what you need, even before you ask him.

"When you pray, say 'Our Father in heaven, hallowed be your name. Your kingdom come, your will be done on earth as it is in heaven. Give us today our daily bread. Forgive us our sins as we forgive those who sin against us. Lead us not into temptation, but deliver us from evil.

"If you forgive other people when they sin against you, then your heavenly Father will forgive you. But if you don't forgive other people, then your heavenly Father won't forgive you either.

"And when you're fasting, don't look grim like the hypocrites do. They make themselves look haggard and miserable so that everyone can see that they're fasting. I tell you, they've received their reward. But when you fast, put oil on your hair and wash your face so that it isn't obvious that you're fasting. Then your Father who sees in secret will reward you."

Jesus paused.

Someone in the crowd asked, "Master, which is the most important commandment in the Law?"

Jesus replied, "Love the Lord your God with all your heart, and with all your soul, with all your mind and with all your strength. This is the first and greatest commandment and the second is like it, namely this: love your neighbour as yourself. There is no other commandment greater than these. On these two commandments hang all the Law and the prophets."

"And who is my neighbour?" the questioner pursued, for this was a thorny point amongst the Pharisees. Some of them would only recognise another Pharisee as their neighbour!

"Let me tell you a story," Jesus said. "A man was going down the road from Jerusalem to Jericho, a dangerous road as you know, and he was travelling alone. As he went down, a band of robbers leapt out on him from behind the rocks. They beat him up, stripped off his clothes, robbed him, and went off leaving him half dead.

TEACHING

"A little later a priest came up the road on his way to Jerusalem. He saw the man, but he passed by on the other side. He didn't want to make himself unclean by possible contact with the dead, did he? Again a little later, a Levite came up the road – he too passed by on the other side, for the same reason.

"Next, there came along a Samaritan. When he saw the man and the mess he was in, he stopped beside him, knelt down, put oil and wine on his wounds to clean and disinfect them, and bandaged him up. Then he lifted him onto his donkey, and brought him down to the inn.

"Next day, he took out two pence and gave them to the innkeeper and said to him, 'Take care of that man, and if it costs you more than that, I'll pay you back when I come again.'

"Now, which of these three, do you think, was neighbour to the man who fell among thieves?"

"The one who looked after him."

"Right then, go and do likewise," Jesus replied.

Later that day, as Jesus was in the house at Bethany, Mary and some of the others were sitting at his feet and listening to him.

Martha, meanwhile, was busy preparing the evening meal in the kitchen. It was not going very well and Martha came into the room where they were all sitting, hot and flustered.

"What's going on in here?" she said. "Mary ought to be out in the kitchen helping me, not sitting in here with all you men. Proper rabbis don't teach women anyway. Some of them don't even talk to women!" she said, looking straight at Jesus.

"Martha, Martha," Jesus laughed, "calm down, calm down. There are more important things than dinners. Mary's chosen the better place to be. She'll come and help you, all in good time."

But the spell was broken. Jesus soon finished what he was saying, and Mary got up and went out to help her sister.

"We'll go on another time," Jesus said, as the group dispersed to wash and prepare for the meal.

Another day when Jesus was teaching, some Pharisees brought to him a woman who, they said, had been discovered in the act of adultery.

They pushed her to the ground in front of Jesus. She was dishevelled and dirty where she had been dragged through the streets. She lay with her face to the ground, frightened and ashamed. Some of the men hauled her up on her feet.

"Teacher, this woman was caught in the act of adultery. The Law of Moses says that such a woman should be stoned. What do you say?"

Jesus saw that they were using the woman to test him. What was he to say? He wanted to save the woman, both from the stoning and from the mess that she had made of her life, but he could not contradict the Law of Moses.

TEACHING

He bent down and wrote with his finger in the dust, just like he and the other little boys used to do in the synagogue school, long ago ...

'The man that commiteth adultery with another man's wife, the adulterer and the adulteress shall surely be put to death.'

These angry men, he thought. They blame women for their own lusts.

He stood up and said, gently, "Stone her then, if the Law of Moses says you must. But the law says that both parties to the adultery should be stoned. I don't see the adulterer here with you. Why do you excuse him? But stone her if you must - only let the man who is without sin among you, throw the first stone."

They all stood in a circle round the woman, while Jesus bent down and started writing on the ground again ...

'There is none that doeth good, no not one'.

Sheepishly, one by one they turned, and walked away in silence, hitching their robes up over their shoulders as they went. At last, Jesus was left alone, with the woman standing before him.

He stood up.

"Has nobody condemned you? Then neither do I. Go now, God is merciful. He has forgiven your sin. But better not to do it again, eh?"

Later, when Jesus was teaching, some of the teachers of the Law were listening and asking each other, "Where does this man get all this from? He hasn't studied here in Jerusalem, that's for certain. He hasn't got it from us."

Jesus understood what they were saying and replied, "My teaching isn't my own. It comes from the one who sent me. If anyone chooses to do my Father's will he'll find out whether my teaching comes from God or whether I'm speaking on my own authority."

"We think your teaching comes from the devil. You healed that man by the pool of Bethesda on the Sabbath day," someone said.

"I did one miracle, and you're all astounded. It was a Sabbath. Moses gave you circumcision, or Abraham did, and you circumcise a child on the eighth day, even when the eighth day is a Sabbath. So why are you angry with me for making a man whole on the Sabbath? My Father is working every day of the week, so I'm working too, doing what he does. I do nothing by myself, but what the Son sees the Father doing, the Son does too.

"And I'll tell you another thing. The Father judges no-one. Judgement is all about how you respond to the Son. Whoever hears my words and believes that I am the one sent by God, he has eternal life. He won't be condemned at the judgement. He's already crossed over from death to life.

TEACHING

"God didn't send his Son into the world to condemn the world but that through him the world might be saved. Whoever believes in him is not condemned, but whoever doesn't believe is condemned already, because he doesn't believe in God's one and only Son."

At this the Jewish teachers would listen no more.

"Now we're sure you have a demon, not only because you healed a man on the Sabbath, but because you call God your father and make yourself equal with God. We'll hear no more. Go back where you came from. We don't want to see you here again."

Jesus left them arguing amongst themselves, for they were not all of one mind.

Some were saying, "No, perhaps he is a prophet. Prophets were always strange people and said strange things."

Others were even saying, "Not so fast, what if he's the Messiah. Then it wouldn't be so blasphemous to talk like that after all."

But still others replied, "Ha! We know where the Messiah is to come from - Bethlehem, in Judea, from the city of David. This man's a carpenter from Nazareth."

And Jesus left, to return to Galilee.

thirteen

SAMARIA

As Jesus and his friends made their way back north, they went by the highland route through Samaria. They made good progress and reached the inn at Lubban well before nightfall.

The second day, they stopped as usual at midday outside the town of Sychar, where Jacob's well provided a plentiful supply of water, and the town a plentiful supply of food, for the weary traveller. Jesus was left alone by the well while his friends went into the town to buy food.

There was always a certain tension about these journeys through Samaria. The two races, Jews and Samaritans, were perpetually uneasy with each other. Their attitudes were not so much the hostilities of old wars, but the hostilities of a family quarrel, and the hostilities were all the more long standing and bitter for that.

The Samaritans claimed descent, just as the Jews did, from Abraham, Isaac and Jacob. More specifically, they claimed to be the descendants of Ephraim and Manasseh, the two sons of Joseph, and they did indeed occupy the territory once allotted to those tribes in Israel.

SAMARIA

They claimed to worship the one true God who had revealed himself to the patriarchs, as the Jews did, and they read and kept the Law of Moses, as the Jews did. But they worshipped and offered sacrifice on Mount Gerizim, not in the temple in Jerusalem, from where Jesus and his friends had just come.

The Jews, on the other hand, referred to the Samaritans as Cuthites, descendants of people imported from Persia to colonise the land after the defeat of the northern kingdom of Israel by the Assyrians. The truth was probably that they were both, a mixture of Jews and Cuthites who had assimilated in the intervening years.

Perhaps, like many family quarrels, the dispute was not beyond the possibility of reconciliation. The old Herod had married a Samaritan woman to try to bring the two peoples together, but then other events had aggravated the bad feeling between them.

Jesus himself remembered as a boy the outrage the Jews had felt one year when a group of Samaritans had strewed dead men's bones all over the temple precincts in the middle of the night before the feast of the Passover. The celebration of the Passover and the feast of Unleavened Bread had had to be postponed while the temple was cleansed of this defilement. This incident had left a legacy of bitterness that could break out into open hostility at any time.

THAT MAN JESUS

Jesus was just beginning to doze off under a palm tree, when he was surprised by the sound of someone letting a water jar down into the well. He opened his eyes and saw a woman drawing water.

It was odd that she was coming to draw water in the middle of the day. Most of the women would come at dawn or in the evening when the day was cool, and stop and chat to each other as they waited for their turn at the well.

Jesus spoke to her.

"Gracious lady, would you give me a drink."

The woman stopped drawing and looked up at him. At first she did not speak. Then, hand on hip, she said, "You're a Jew and I'm a Samaritan. You're a man and I'm a woman. That's two reasons why you shouldn't be talking to me."

"Well, I am," Jesus continued, "and if you knew who was talking to you, you'd be asking me for a drink."

"Oh, would I?" she said. "And how are you going to get water out of this well? It's deep, you know, really deep, and you haven't got anything to draw with, have you?"

"No, I haven't. The water I can give you is water for a thirsty soul. You have to go on coming out here to draw water every day, but the water I can give you will last you all your life."

SAMARIA

The woman hauled her jar up from the depths and sat down on the edge of the well to continue this conversation.

"Go on," she said, "I'm all ears."

"Well, of course it isn't really appropriate for me, as you say, a Jewish man, to be out here talking to you, a Samaritan woman, all on our own. What will the neighbours say? You'd better go and fetch your husband."

The woman blushed and was silent.

"Perhaps you haven't got a husband," Jesus said softly. "Perhaps, say, you've had five husbands and the man you're living with now is not your husband at all. Perhaps that's why you come here to draw water in the middle of the day, to avoid the other women, who won't speak to you or let you near the well."

"How do you know all that?" she said. "I've heard of holy men who can see into other people's hearts and lives. Are you a holy man? All the more reason why you shouldn't be talking to me. I'm not a holy woman. But you know that already. And in any case, we don't agree about religion, you Jews and us Samaritans, do we? You go up to Jerusalem to worship and we worship here on Mount Gerizim."

"That's true," Jesus replied, "but does it really matter? The time's coming – in fact it's now come – when people will worship the Father anywhere, on this mountain or that mountain or any other mountain. It's how you worship, not where you worship that counts. All that matters is that you worship God in spirit and in truth. That's the sort of people the Father wants as his worshippers."

"I've heard that there's one who is to come, the Messiah. They say he'll explain everything to us."

"Woman, you are speaking to him right now."

As they were speaking, the disciples returned from the town and were astonished to see Jesus speaking to a woman, sitting together on the side of the well.

"What were you doing, talking to her?" they exclaimed, as the woman jumped up and ran off towards the town in some confusion, leaving her water jar standing beside the well.

"Here's the food we bought."

"I've had food, of a sort," Jesus replied.

"What sort of food? Did that woman bring you food?"

"No. Doing the Father's will's food for me. I've just been having a conversation with that woman. She's led a very complicated life for one reason or another, and now she can't find her way out of the muddle. She's an outcast. No-one wants to talk to her – except me. But this meeting today could be the beginning of a new life for her.

"You see, we have to meet people where they are, not where we want them to be, or where they were before they sinned. It's called forgiveness -

SAMARIA

accepting people and all their baggage, reaching out to them with loving arms, just like the Father does, even before they've repented. They won't all receive our love, but some will. She will."

They looked up, and sure enough a crowd of people, men and women, were coming out of the town towards them.

"See," said Jesus. "You say, 'Four months more until harvest' but I say the fields are already white and ready for harvest. We're going to need plenty of reapers to gather in this harvest."

The woman to whom Jesus had been speaking came up, at the head of a crowd of people.

"Here he is," she announced triumphantly. "Here's the man who told me everything I ever did."

"Man of God," one of the elders said, "if what this woman says is true, we'd like you and your friends to come into the town and stay for a few days as our guests. We'd like to hear what you have to say."

So Jesus and his friends accompanied them into Sychar and stayed with them for several days, while Jesus taught them about the kingdom of God and healed their sick.

Later, as they walked back northwards towards the lake, Jesus was thoughtful and silent. If this was the beginning of something new for the world, a new covenant, a new way of life, a new community, a new Israel, a new kingdom, even a new creation, then sooner or later he was going to have to give it some form or shape.

If it was to spread and grow it could not depend on him alone, on his presence, his preaching, his miracles. Others must be taught and equipped, to be not merely recipients of the kingdom but agents of the kingdom.

From all the people who followed him, he needed to choose a small group whom he could train and teach to do the same things that he was doing. He must choose a team to bring others into the kingdom. He must teach and train them so that they could teach and train others: disciple them, so that they could disciple others.

The new community, those who received their word and believed the good news, would also need to be called out and set apart in some away, to be given a new identity of their own. To continue or to revive the baptism of John would be a fitting way to set people apart for the kingdom. The same repentance and washing away of sin was anyway a prerequisite for entry into the kingdom of God. Those who were sent out to preach and heal in his name could also baptise those who believed their mesage.

Those who believed in him and were baptized in his name would then need to be gathered together into a new community or fellowship. Jesus could foresee the existence of new synagogues of believers. There would come a time when his

SAMARIA

followers would be thrown out of the Jewish synagogues, as he had been thrown out of the synagogue at Nazareth and more or less thrown out of the temple in Jerusalem.

Just as the Jewish people had formed the first synagogues in Babylon when they were deprived of the worship of the temple, so his followers would have to form new synagogues of their own when they were put out of those of the Jews.

Discipleship must also mean discipline. The message of the kingdom and the integrity of the community of believers would need to be protected, against ungodliness in their life together and against distortion in the message that they proclaimed.

It would be an awesome responsibility that he would be giving those men: admitting people or excluding them from this new community. Anyone given responsibility or authority could abuse it. Indeed, in the world, abuse of power and authority seemed to be almost universal. Power always seemed to corrupt people.

In a sinful world such corruption was probably inevitable, even amongst his followers, but this corruption of power was one of the many things in human life that needed to be redeemed, and there was no way to redeem it but to entrust authority to people who were in the process of being redeemed.

In his mind on the journey home, he was already identifying some of those initial disciples whom he would commission and send out. Peter and Andrew, James and John, Matthew, James the sons of Alphaeus, Judas who seemed to be a friend of James, Philip and Nathanael bar Tholomaeus, and who else? How many did he need? Twelve would be a good number. A group that would be neither too big nor too small, and if the old Israel had had twelve patriarchs then these men would be the twelve patriarchs of the new Israel.

fourteen

NOW AND NOT YET

Arriving back in Capernaum Jesus found that he had been invited to preach at the synagogue at Chorazin, an important town just a few miles away. So, accompanied by his usual band of followers, he set out for the town on a Friday afternoon to be ready for the beginning of the Sabbath at sunset.

The ruler of the synagogue took Jesus to stay at his house. Some of his followers had friends and relatives in the town, while the rest found lodgings at the inn.

The synagogue was packed on Sabbath morning, with people standing at the back to hear this controversial preacher from Capernaum. The elders and the ruler of the synagogue liked to see the place full, but today they were experiencing a certain apprehension about who and what they might have invited in. The Jewish grapevine was beginning to buzz with suspicions that this man Jesus was not doctrinally sound, or worse.

After the scriptures appointed for the day had been read, Jesus was invited to speak. Choosing again to read from the prophecy of Isaiah, Jesus unrolled the scroll and found the place.

"'For behold, I create new heavens and a new earth: and the former shall not be remembered, nor come into mind. But be ye glad and rejoice for ever in that which I create: for behold, I create Jerusalem a rejoicing, and her people a joy. And I will rejoice in Jerusalem, and joy in my people: and the voice of weeping shall no more be heard in her, nor the voice of crying.'

"You've heard about the miracles that I've done through the power of God. It's true, the deaf hear and the blind receive their sight, the oppressed are set free and the lame walk. Aye, even the dead are raised. But this is not yet the new heavens and the new earth that God is going to create.

"I have indeed raised a dead man by the power of God, just as Elijah and Elisha did, but that young man will die again. He hasn't been raised to eternal life – not yet – only to an extension of life here on earth. Eternal life belongs to the things to come in the new heavens and the new earth and the new Jerusalem. Death is the last enemy to be destroyed. It will be destroyed one day, but that day is still to come.

"In the same way, I've healed the sick and made the lame walk, but they are not going to be immune from accidents or diseases in the future. That also belongs, not to this world, but to the world to come. Those people will get sick again. They may be healed again, but one day they won't

NOW AND NOT YET

be healed and they'll die. That's the way of all flesh, until the Son of Man comes in glory.

"But these miracles are signs that that day is coming. They are demonstrations of what that kingdom will be like when it comes in all its fullness at the end of time. In the new heavens and the new earth, no-one will be deaf or blind, no-one will be in bondage to the unclean spirits. There will be no more disease, no more infirmity, no mourning, no crying. Death itself will be no more, for the former things will have passed away. The things that you see today are signs of all that, a pledge, a guarantee, a first-fruits of what is to come.

"But even now you can take hold of the kingdom that is to come. You can enter it now; you can have a foretaste of it now. The new heavens and the new earth are breaking in, even into this present world of sin and sorrow. Take hold of it now while you have the chance.

"You don't have to wait until tomorrow, and who knows how many tomorrows there'll be before that day comes. In that day, the sky will be rolled up like a scroll, the earth will be destroyed by fire, and it will be too late. Too late to repent, too late to turn to God. Today is the day to repent and believe. Today is the day of salvation."

As Jesus finished speaking he noticed in the congregation a man with a withered hand.

"Stretch out your hand," he commanded the man.

Full of faith, the man stood up and did so, and as he did his hand was restored, whole like the other. God confirmed the word by the sign that followed.

The ruler of the synagogue concluded the service with the customary prayers and benedictions and the people dispersed - all except for a small group of Pharisees who remained talking to one another outside. As Jesus left the synagogue, they approached him.

"Rabbi," they said, "you have just healed someone on the Sabbath day? If you were in truth a teacher of Israel, you'd know that according to the Law a doctor may only attend a patient on the Sabbath if his life is in danger. That man has had a withered hand all his life. His life was not in danger. So why did you break the Sabbath?"

Jesus replied, "Which is lawful on the Sabbath: to do good or to do evil? Which of you, if you've got an ox or an ass and it falls into a pit on the Sabbath day, won't go and get a rope and pull it out? Go away and learn what this means: 'I desire mercy and not sacrifice', saith the Lord.'"

The Pharisees retired, but watched Jesus and his followers from a distance, hoping to catch him out again.

Jesus started out on the road back to Capernaum. It was no more than couple of miles and they strolled along as the heat of the day increased overhead. They were hungry and some of the disciples pulled the heads off the ears of wheat as they passed. They rubbed the ears in their hands, blew away the husks, and nibbled the grain.

The group of Pharisees, who had been following them at a distance, came hastening up.

"Now, what's this your disciples are doing? This is clearly breaking the Law. Plucking the ears of corn, rubbing them in their hands, blowing the chaff away. That counts as reaping, threshing and winnowing, three of the thirty-nine works forbidden on the Sabbath. Now what do you have to say to that?" they concluded triumphantly.

"And while we're on the subject," another of them pursued breathlessly, "how far do you propose to walk today? Capernaum is more than a Sabbath-day's journey from Chorazin."

"What I have to say is this," replied Jesus, ignoring the last intervention. "Haven't you read what David did when he and his companions were hungry? He entered the house of God, and he and his companions ate the consecrated bread, which it wasn't lawful for them to eat, but only the priests.

"I told you before, go and learn what this means: 'I desire mercy and not sacrifice', saith the Lord. You don't understand that God made the Sabbath for man, not man for the Sabbath. It's supposed to be a blessing to people, not a burden. A chance to rest and to remember the Lord their God, not a day when they have to be even more concerned than usual about whether they're breaking any laws. The Son of Man is lord of the Sabbath."

One or two of the Pharisees spluttered speechlessly, but all turned away abruptly and went back on their way to Chorazin. As they disappeared, Jesus and his disciples could see them gesticulating wildly, angrily shouting at each other, venting their rage and frustration at being contradicted to their faces by this unknown upstart. Jesus could tell that their rage would soon turn to a colder, more calculating opposition, and a more malicious scheming against him.

"They didn't like it," remarked Peter to Jesus, as they walked on together.

"No, I know," replied Jesus. "That's the trouble. They teach rules invented by men as if they were the commandments of God. They pay lip service to honouring God, but in fact they've lost sight of God altogether, of his real nature and purposes. Their god is the Accuser - constantly accusing and finding fault with people. They are slaves. Their forefathers were slaves in Egypt, and now they are slaves to the Law, and to the One who's always lying in wait to catch them out breaking the rules.

"God is a Father who loves his children and wants them to live full and happy lives. He wants them to enjoy life, with him and with one another.

And how are they supposed to do that? They don't know. They're lost. A child grows up under the instruction and discipline of his parents. Then he becomes a young man, and has to make his own decisions. How is he to find his way in life? He's surrounded by bad examples in the world around him. He's easily deceived by the lusts of his flesh. He's a prey to all sorts of harmful and destructive desires. The devil tells him lies over and over again.

"So God, in his mercy, has given us laws, instructions, guidance: a light for our paths and a lamp for our feet. The laws of God are a hedge of protection, not a yolk or a burden for us to bear. They come from God's mercy not from his wrath.

"Think of the Law like a father's guidance. The Law of God isn't meant to be a rod for your back. You're not slaves who have to be beaten into submission to the master's will. God's laws are there to point you towards the sort of life that God wants you to have, the good life."

"But there must be some punishment for sin," Peter continued. "God's just, as well as merciful. How does that work?"

"Aye, there's punishment for sin," Jesus replied. "If you sin, you'll suffer for it. Sin brings its own punishment. Sin is sin precisely because it causes suffering and destruction, to those who sin, as well as to those who're sinned against.

"God's justice is part of the fabric of the world, both physically and spiritually. If you persist in sin to the end, persist in rebellion against God and his will for you, you will die. The wages of sin is death. But God says, 'Have I any pleasure that the wicked should die, and not that he should turn from his ways and live?' There is forgiveness with God. There's always a way back to God from the dark paths of sin. Of course God is angry when people hurt one another and hurt themselves, but 'He will not always be chiding: neither keepeth he his anger forever.' Mercy triumphs over judgement."

For the first time in his life, Peter began to feel free. He had never taken seriously the pettifogging, hair splitting distinctions of the Pharisees but, as a man who, at heart, loved God and wanted to live in accordance with his will, Peter had always been confused about his duty towards God and not sure whether he was fulfilling it or not.

Now he began to experience a new freedom and confidence, that he was serving a God who loved him and approved of him and was not constantly on the watch to find fault with him.

"I think I'm getting the hang of this," he said to Jesus solemnly.

"I think you are too," Jesus replied.

fifteen

CALLING

Some days later news had spread that Jesus was at home again at the house of James and John. People began to appear, bringing the sick and the infirm to be healed. At one point there was such a crowd that there was no longer any room in the house and people were queuing up outside.

Four men arrived carrying a stretcher on which lay a paralyzed man. They had obviously come some distance for they were hot and weary. Seeing the crowd, they looked around and began to heave the stretcher up the outside stairs onto the roof of the house.

To everyone's amazement they then began pulling the roof to pieces. They broke up the clay that formed the surface of the flat roof, then pulled out the withies that lay across the beams.

Having made a hole about six feet long between two beams they then began to lower the stretcher, with the patient still lying on it, into the middle of the room in which Jesus was sitting. Everyone, inside and outside the house, stopped what they were doing and watched, some shocked, some amused.

With the paralyzed man still on his stretcher, now lying on the floor of the house at Jesus feet, the friends on the roof above began to apologise.

"Sorry!" they called down. "We'll make it right before we go, but we couldn't wait. We have to get this chap home before dark, either on the stretcher or on his feet. What do you think?"

Jesus looked at the man on the floor.

"Son, your sins are forgiven. I absolve you from all your offences."

At the back of the room were some Pharisees, standing and watching and listening, looking for some more serious fault with which to accuse Jesus. Now they had found one.

They turned to one another and began muttering, "Yes, this is blasphemy. No-one has the authority to forgive sins except God himself. God has given us all we need to receive forgiveness: the Day of Atonement for the sins of the people, and anyone who knows he's sinned can go up to Jerusalem and offer sacrifice in the temple. This man can't just sit there and say, 'Your sins are forgiven.'"

Jesus knew what they were saying, so he said to them, "Which is easier, to say, 'Your sins are forgiven,' or to say, 'Pick up your bed and walk'?"

There was a stony silence.

"But, so that you know that the Son of Man has authority to forgive sins ..." He turned to the

CALLING

paralyzed man and said, "Pick up your bed and walk."

The man sat up rather uncertainly, rose from his bed, folded up his stretcher, and smiling from ear to ear, walked, somewhat uncertainly, but with increasing confidence, out of the house.

His friends up on the roof, peering down as all this took place, burst into cheers, clapping their hands and shouting, "Hallelujah! Glory to God."

They rushed down the stairs and greeted their friend, now walking easily and freely, hugged him and set off to return to their village in great excitement. The man himself seemed to be speechless, his eyes round with astonishment, unable to take in what had just happened to him. One of the others, remembering the roof, turned round.

"We'll come back and fix the roof tomorrow," he called out, before disappearing as fast as his legs could carry him.

The Pharisees also withdrew, forming a huddle, but Jesus went outside and talked to them.

"You find fault with what I'm doing?" he enquired.

"Aye, we do," one of them replied. "You're leading the people astray with your so-called teaching. You break the Sabbath. You've just uttered blasphemy, and look at the company you keep, tax collectors, prostitutes – oh yes, we've heard about the woman in Magdala – all these riff-raff who don't even know God's Law, let alone keep it."

"It's not the healthy who need the doctor, is it? - but the sick. I didn't come to call the righteous, but sinners to repentance. That's who these people are, you say so yourselves. Sinners. But I don't think you understand the mercy of God. Don't you know the Scripture that says 'He hath not dealt with us after our sins, nor rewarded us according to our wickednesses. For look how high the heaven is in comparison of the earth: so great is his mercy also toward them that fear him. Look how wide also the east is from the west: so far hath he set our sins from us.'

"Think of a shepherd who has a hundred sheep. If he loses one, doesn't he leave the ninety-nine others in the wilderness with the other shepherds, while he goes off to look for the one that's lost? He searches for it until he finds it. Then he puts it on his shoulders and carries it home and gathers together his friends and neighbours, and says, 'Look, I've found my sheep that was lost.' I tell you, there's more joy in heaven over one sinner who repents than over ninety-nine good people who don't need to repent.

"Or think of a woman with ten pieces of silver. If she loses one of them, she sweeps the house and turns everything upside down until she finds it. Then she calls out to her neighbours, 'Look, I've found the piece of silver that I'd lost.' I tell you,

CALLING

there's rejoicing in heaven over one sinner who repents."

The Pharisees had seen and heard enough. They went away, agreeing that something would have to be done to silence this impudent and blasphemous upstart.

That night, while the town was asleep, Jesus rose and went out into the hills to pray. He needed to hear from his Father whom he was to choose to be sent out, to do the things that he had been doing.

He thought over their names and faces. There were quite a number now whom he knew by sight and by name, who were fairly constantly with him. There were also some women who followed him, including the woman from Magdala, Mary, a woman called Susanna, and her friend Joanna the wife of the steward of Herod, no less.

The last two were rich women who often used to provide for them out of their own means. But it would never do to send women out on their own and certainly not with men.

As Jesus reviewed his male followers, he found that some of them, as they came into his mind's eye, seemed to be surrounded by a sort of aura, almost a pool of light. Peter and Andrew, James and John, of course; Philip and Nathanael, James and Judas whom they also sometimes called Thaddaeus; Matthew and who? Thomas whom they called 'the twin'? (though nobody had ever seen the twin).

Then two more, if he was to have twelve. There were two other faces that seemed to appear to Jesus in the same light, but about whom he felt uneasy: another Simon and another Judas.

This Simon was reputed to be a Zealot, maybe part of an underground cell, zealous indeed for the restoration of the kingdom in Israel, but were his ideas of the kingdom and of how it was to be restored the same as Jesus'? And Judas Iscariot? What was it about this Judas that Jesus instinctively distrusted? Nevertheless, he seemed to be chosen by God in the same way as the others, so Jesus swallowed his doubts and went back in the light of dawn to single out these twelve.

One by one, as they turned up at the usual meeting place on the quay, Jesus spoke to them and told them that he wanted them to come away with him, across the lake, because he had special work for them to do. He needed to have them on their own for a while to teach them and prepare them for it.

They got into Peter's boat, and Peter and Andrew, James and John, the fishermen, took the oars. Twelve turned out to be just the right number for the boat as well. It was full but not too full.

CALLING

In the early morning the lake was flat calm, but as the sun strengthened a breeze rose and the men hoisted the square sail. Jesus, having been awake praying for most of the night, fell asleep in the stern. After about half an hour, Peter noticed a big, black cloud building up over the hills of Galilee.

"Look out for that one," he said to the others. "That means trouble."

Only too soon as they sailed on, they could see the sea being whipped up behind them as a fierce squall came down the Gulf of Pigeons and onto the lake.

"Get the sail down, and turn the boat into the wind," shouted Peter. "Oars out and keep her head to wind. We're a bit low in the water for this."

He had done this so many times before; he knew the force of these sudden Galilean storms.

In a very short time the sun had disappeared behind the black cloud, the wind had risen, rain began to beat down, and soon the boat was floundering in a heavy sea. The oarsmen worked hard to keep the boat's head pointing into the oncoming waves so that it rose and breasted them. Only one wave had to break over the side of the boat and it would be swamped.

In spite of their efforts, the water kept lapping over the gunwales and she was beginning to fill with water. There were some old wineskins in the boat, which they used for baling, but they could not keep pace with the water that was coming in.

With the weight of thirteen men in the boat, the situation was beginning to look desperate, but Jesus was still asleep in the stern.

"Wake up, master," Peter cried, shaking him. "We're about to sink! Don't you care?"

In a moment Jesus was awake and looking around, saw immediately the trouble that they were in. He stood up in the lurching boat, held up his hand and shouted at the wind and sea, "Stop! Calm down."

Immediately the wind started to abate, the rain stopped, the sea began to die down, and while they waited, in about five minutes, calm had returned. The black cloud had moved off to the east and the storm was over.

"Phew!" said Peter. "That was close."

But the others were awestruck.

"Did you see that? Did you see that?" Thomas exclaimed. "Even the wind and the waves obeyed him."

Ruefully, they bailed out the remaining water, took up the oars again and rowed over to the other side.

They sat down on the shore under a steep hill and relaxed in the sun, now shining again in full strength. They sat and let their clothes dry out, steaming in the heat, each one thinking about the

CALLING

storm and the calm restored, trying to make sense of what they had just experienced.

A little way down the coast there was a cemetery for the nearby Gentile town of Gerasa. Coming towards them out of the graveyard was a ragged and unkempt figure, almost naked except for pieces of chain that were still attached to his wrists and ankles. His hair and his beard were uncut, and his body was filthy.

As he drew near he began raving at them. "What are you doing here, Jesus, you Son of God? Don't torture me, don't torture me!"

Jesus stepped forward to meet him, and he fell to his knees in front of Jesus.

"What's your name?" Jesus asked.

"My name is Legion," the man replied. "We're too many in here."

Then the voice changed to a sort of gloating, "Too many of us for you to deal with us all!"

"Come out, all of you," Jesus commanded.

Now the voice was a frightened whine, "Send us into the pigs, then. Send us into them."

"Go, anywhere," said Jesus, "but go."

The demons came out of the man and entered the herd of pigs that was feeding up on the hillside behind them. The poor animals immediately started squealing piteously and charged down the slope into the sea and were drowned.

THAT MAN JESUS

They all looked on in horror. The water was full of the carcases of dead pigs, but the man was sitting quietly beside Jesus with his head in his hands, breathing deeply.

"What a day!" remarked Jesus. Then to the man, "We didn't come over for this, but I'm glad you're well."

"Can I stay with you?" said the man.

"No," replied Jesus. "We've got other business over here to attend to. You must go back to your town, and tell your friends and neighbours what the God of Israel has done for you. Bless you, my friend, go in peace."

sixteen

SENDING

"I've chosen you for a special purpose," Jesus began, as he and the twelve men with him settled down in the shade of a clump of trees away from the dead pigs.

The trees were growing on a small promontory projecting out into the lake. With the waters of the lake on three sides of them, and a warm breeze now blowing across from Galilee, the spot was pleasantly cool.

"I'm asking you to make a more permanent commitment, to me and to the kingdom of God. Up until now you've followed me as we've gone about from town to town and village to village. You've seen the things I've done, and you've heard the things I've said. I've chosen you because you've been faithful followers, and because you seem to believe in me.

"But this is just the beginning. You see, God is starting something here that is for the redemption of the whole world. These may seem to you like small beginnings, but as the prophet Zechariah said, 'Who hath despised the day of small things?' This message of the kingdom must be preached to the whole world, but it had to begin somewhere, and it's beginning here.

"God has been preparing for this ever since he first called our father Abraham – not just to receive a blessing for himself and his family, but to be a blessing to the whole earth. Now, I can't do this all on my own. You, as my followers, must become my fellow workers, sowing and reaping a harvest of souls.

"We must spend more time together, apart from the multitude, so that I can teach you and prepare you. Then I'm going to send you out, not alone but in pairs, preaching the message that I've been preaching, about the coming of the kingdom of God, and doing the things that I've been doing, healing the sick, casting out the unclean spirits – just like you saw me doing with that poor man from the tombs just now.

"I know that seems daunting to you, but you're to go in my name, not in your own. You'll preach the kingdom of God in my name, and teach in my name. I know that you have no power yourselves to heal the sick and no power yourselves to drive out the unclean spirits, but you can do it in my name.

"You'll say to the sick, 'Be healed, in the name of Jesus,' and to the demons, 'Come out, in the name of Jesus,' and it will happen, just as you say. The important thing is not to think of yourselves, but

SENDING

of me. If you believe in me, and believe what you say in my name, it will be done.

"One day, as I say, this message of the kingdom must be preached to the whole world, but for now we're sent, both you and me, only to the lost sheep of the house of Israel. I'll be sending you out into the towns and villages of Galilee. You won't even have time to visit them all, before all this comes to a head.

"You're not to take any money with you or take any from those you teach or heal. Freely you've received, freely give. In fact, don't worry about money at all, or what you'll live on or where you'll sleep. Just as you've seen with me, when someone receives you and asks you to stay, go in and stay with him until you move on. God has his people everywhere. Wherever you go, you'll find someone who will welcome you and feed you. If not, shake the dust of that place off your feet and move on somewhere else.

"Concentrate on the work of the kingdom and the rest will take care of itself. God knows your needs, even before you ask, though ask in any case. God likes to be asked, rather than us just taking him for granted. So, ask, and you will receive. Seek, and you will find. Knock, and the door will be opened.

"But a disciple is not above his teacher, nor a servant above his master. As they've treated me, so they will treat you. You've seen that some people have rejected me. They will reject you for the same reasons. They may even drive you out of their synagogues or their villages, just as I was driven out of Nazareth. But don't be afraid. Your heavenly Father is watching over you all the time. Not even a sparrow falls to the ground without your heavenly Father noticing it, and you're much more important than sparrows!

"But don't suppose that I've come to bring peace on the earth – not yet anyway. This message of the kingdom of God is going to divide people. Some people will accept it and believe it, others won't. Even families will be divided, father and son, mother and daughter, brother and sister. Nations will be divided, even Israel will be divided. But anyone who receives you, receives me, and anyone who receives me, receives him who sent me. So, are you ready? Are you willing?"

Jesus looked from one to the other and as they caught his eye each one either nodded in assent, or replied quietly, "Yes, master."

They stayed for some time, talking about the things that Jesus had said, and asking him questions. Finally, they all re-embarked in the boat and, as dark was falling, rowed back to Capernaum.

They were all aware of a new bond between them, with Jesus and with each other. There was excitement, but also trepidation, joy but also solemnity. Each was inwardly surprised to have

SENDING

been singled out and chosen by Jesus. Each was conscious of his own shortcomings and inadequacy.

Looking around, they recognised that none of them was anything special in the world's eyes. They were all ordinary working men. What was it that Jesus saw in them? Yet, whatever it was, that was not what bound them together. It was what that they all saw in him.

* * *

The next day, the twelve were only too aware of their new status amongst the followers of Jesus. They kept closer to him and started to act as his self-appointed guardians, even bodyguards, something which they soon found Jesus did not welcome.

A group of mothers with their children were pressing around Jesus in the market place in Capernaum. Some of the mothers wanted Jesus to touch and bless their babies.

Jesus had stopped and was actually stroking the heads of some of the older children and talking to them as if they were adults. The apostles were immediately offended to see these women and children presuming on Jesus' attention in this way. Surely it was disrespectful to their master. Rabbis never had women amongst their pupils, and these women would never have dared to approach a Jerusalem rabbi in the way that they were now pestering Jesus.

Peter and some of the others began to muscle in and push the women and children away.

"Stand back, there. Our master hasn't got time for you and your children. Let him pass by."

But Jesus intervened.

"No, no, no," he said. "Let them come to me. The kingdom of God belongs to women and children too, not just to you men. In fact, children are much closer to the kingdom of God than you are. They are never in danger of thinking they can manage on their own.

"Look at these babies. They depend on their mothers for everything. You need to become like them, depending on your heavenly Father for everything. You think that children can only know and love God when they're grown up. You're wrong. If you want to know the love of God, you've got to become like them. Full of trust."

Jesus took the babies that the mothers were holding out to him, cuddled them in his arms and prayed for them, asking his Father to protect and provide for each one. The disciples felt chastened and put in their place.

As this was going on, they were approached by Jairus. He was well known in the town because he was the ruler of the synagogue, but he was in great distress. He knelt down in the dust before Jesus.

SENDING

"Master, please come and help. I think my daughter's dying. I left her terribly ill. I don't know what's the matter with her, but she went so still and quiet. We couldn't wake her up. Can you come?"

"Yes, of course, I'll come right away," replied Jesus.

As they went the crowd around them increased. People had heard what Jairus had said, and were curious to see what would happen. But as they were going, Jesus suddenly stopped.

"Who touched me?" he said, looking around.

"Come on, master," said Peter. "We've got to get to Jairus's house. There are masses of people pressing round you. Lots of people are touching you."

"No," Jesus replied calmly, "not just touched me, *touched* me. Someone is in need. I felt it differently from everyone else touching me."

He looked round and there was a woman kneeling behind him in the dust.

"It was me," she said, and hung her head in shame.

"Look up," Jesus said, "and tell me why you touched me."

The woman looked up but covered her face with her veil.

"I don't know how to tell you. I shouldn't be here at all, in this crowd. I've had a flow of blood for the last twelve years. I'm unclean, and I've made you all unclean by coming here like this. I know that everyone I've touched in this crowd is unclean now because of me. I'm so sorry, but I'd heard about you, master, and I thought to myself, if only I could touch the hem of his garment I'd be healed. So I came and I touched you."

She lowered her head again as people began backing away from her where she knelt. But Jesus bent down and took her by the hand. He helped her to her feet and made her look into his eyes.

"Daughter, your faith has healed you. Go where you like now, you're clean."

The woman fell to the ground again and kissed Jesus' feet, before disappearing back into the crowd. Jairus was still at Jesus elbow.

"Please, master," he said.

Jesus turned to him, "Don't worry, my friend, all will be well."

They went on still pursued by the crowd, until they reached Jairus' house. As they drew near to it, they heard the sounds of wailing.

"Oh no, we're too late," Jairus despaired.

"What did I say to you?" said Jesus. "Don't be afraid. All will be well."

Jairus was greeted by his wife, who clung to him, sobbing on his shoulder, while other women kept up the wailing customary when someone had died.

SENDING

"Where is this child then?" asked Jesus.

They led him into the house, followed by the wailing women.

"No," Jesus said to them. "You all wait outside. There's no need for all this wailing. The child isn't dead, she's asleep."

The wailing stopped, but it was clear that the women did not believe what Jesus had just said. They retreated out of the house, somewhat offended, and waited for Jesus to be proved wrong.

It was a small room, so Jesus took only Peter, James, John, Jairus and his wife, and went into where the child's body lay. He bent over the lifeless figure. The girl was about twelve years old, laid out flat on the bed, pale but still warm, her eyes closed in death.

"Little girl, I say to you, wake up."

After a moment, the onlookers saw her chest begin to move as the breath came back into her. As her breaths became deeper, she opened her eyes. She saw the people standing round the bed and smiled.

"I feel better now," she said, and slowly, almost wonderingly, sat up. She rubbed her eyes, as if she was waking up from a deep sleep and stretched.

Her mother gave a cry of joy and embraced her daughter. Her sobbing revived, but now they were tears of joy not sorrow and she went on weeping and kissing the child while Jesus and his disciples quietly left the room.

Outside he met the wailing women.

"See," he said, "I told you so. She wasn't dead, she was asleep!"

seventeen

PLOUGHING ON

The following day, they went their separate ways. The apostles set out in pairs as Jesus had instructed them, taking different roads up into the hills of Galilee and along the lakeshore, while Jesus also went out as usual to preach and teach in the towns and villages.

As Jesus was teaching, a group of men came up to him, announcing themselves as friends of John the Baptizer. Jesus inquired of them how John fared, and thanked them for continuing to support and encourage him.

"Yes," the men replied, "he does sometimes get discouraged. Most of the time he's in solitary confinement in the fortress. We're allowed to visit him once a day and take him food, but otherwise he can only sit and think. He sometimes wonders if he was right, if he really was the forerunner of the Messiah, or whether it was all in his own head. You know, he's afraid sometimes that he was deluded about the whole thing. He sent us to ask you if you really are the one who is to come?"

"Tell John what you see and hear. The blind receive their sight, the lame walk, the lepers are cured, the deaf hear, the dead are raised, and good news is preached to the poor. Aren't these the signs of the coming of the kingdom? Reassure him. Tell him, 'Your labour is not in vain in the Lord.'"

John's friends went away to give Jesus' message to their master. Meanwhile, Jesus turned to the crowd.

"When you went down to the river Jordan, what did you go out into the wilderness to see? Reeds rustling in the wind? If not, what did you go out to see? A man dressed in fine clothes? Not likely! People in fine clothes live in palaces, not in caves by the river Jordan. So what did you go out to see? A prophet? Aye, I tell you, and more than a prophet. John was the one written about in the prophecy of Malachi: 'Behold, I will send my messenger, and he shall prepare the way before me, saith the LORD of hosts.'

"No man, no prophet before him, was ever greater than John the Baptizer. But I tell you, even the least in the kingdom of God is greater than he. And if you can understand this, John is the Elijah figure who was prophesied to come.

"But this is a perverse generation. They're like children sitting around in the market place and complaining to their friends, 'We danced but you didn't want to play at weddings. We wailed, but you didn't want to play at funerals. What *do* you want?' John came fasting and not drinking wine, and they say, 'He's got a demon.' The Son of Man

PLOUGHING ON

comes eating and drinking, and they say he's a glutton and a drunkard, a friend of tax collectors and sinners. Some people are never satisfied, are they?"

Another day, Jesus had cast out a demon. The evil spirit had caused the man to be unable either to see or to speak, but when Jesus had told the spirit to go, the man had recovered both his sight and his speech.

The people had been amazed and had started to say, "Is this the man who's to be the new king of Israel?"

But, as so often, there were Pharisees in the background murmuring, "This is devilish. The man's a sorcerer. It isn't by the power of God that he casts out the demons, it's by the power of Satan."

Jesus overheard what they were muttering, so he said to the crowd as well as to the Pharisees, "If there's civil war in a kingdom, that kingdom is finished. If Satan is driving out his own unclean spirits, then his kingdom is at war with itself and his kingdom is finished. But if it's by the finger of God that I'm driving out the unclean spirits, then you know that the kingdom of God has come upon you.

"You can say all sorts of things about me, and you can be forgiven, but if you see the hand of God in the miracles that I do, and you call it the hand of Satan, then you really are lost. What can open your eyes to the things of God, if you think that opening the eyes of a blind man is the work of the devil?"

Then, turning to the man from whom the demon had just gone out and whose eyes had just been opened, Jesus said, "Take care that you don't let the demons back in. Persistent sin, the worship of idols, the works of darkness, these are things that invite the demons in. Avoid them at all times.

"Your body is like a house. We've cleaned the house up for the time being, but the demons are still out there, looking for a way in. If you give them a chance they'll come back. If that happens, you'll be worse off than you were before."

On yet another occasion, Jesus had been teaching in the courtyard of a house. As he was about to dismiss the crowd, someone told him, "Your family are outside wanting to speak to you."

Jesus replied, "And who *is* my family? The kingdom of God isn't just a kingdom, it's a family. There's one God and Father of us all. We're his sons and daughters, brothers and sisters. But you aren't born into the family of God by nature – you don't belong to this family by human ancestry. You have to choose.

"To be part of this family you have to be born again. Or, if you like, you have to be adopted into it. But, just as adoption replaces the natural bonds, so being born again into the family of God replaces your natural family. You have to put

PLOUGHING ON

your allegiance to me and to this heavenly family before your allegiance to your earthly family or you are not worthy of being my disciples."

The people went away, confused by what Jesus had said. Some were offended, but others saw what he meant, hard as it seemed.

"There are times when you do have to put your obedience to God above the demands of your family. Think of the people in the olden days, when someone said, 'Let's go up and worship the idols of Canaan' - even if it was your mother or your father or your brother who was telling you - you had to say no. Your duty to God came before your duty to your family. I guess it's the same now. If you believe that Jesus is the one God has sent, then you have to put your duty to him before anything else."

As the crowd dispersed, Jesus went out and spoke to his mother and his brothers who were waiting outside.

"Son, we're so worried about you," began his mother. "I know that you've got a calling from God, but look at you – you don't even have time to eat. You'll wear yourself out or make yourself ill, and what use will you be to God then? Come home and rest for a while."

"Mother, anyone who sets his hand to the plough and looks back loses his line. The furrow goes crooked. The ploughman has to keep looking forward, towards the mark on the other side of the field which he's chosen, and plough on towards it. It's the same with me. I must keep my eye on the mark and plough on. I can't look back"

When Jesus returned to Capernaum, he was met again by the friends of John the Baptizer.

"Bad news, master," they began. "We told John what you'd said, and he seemed to find peace again, but a few days later there was a feast at the fortress for Herod's birthday. They all got drunk as usual and then they made that daughter of Herodias dance for them.

"Herod is so besotted with her that he said something stupid. He said, 'Tell me what you want, my dearie. I'll give you anything you want – half my kingdom, if you want it. Come to think of it, you can have the Galilean half, with all those pesky Jews in it.'

"They all laughed in their drunken way, but the girl went and asked her mother what to ask for, and her mother said, 'The head of John the Baptist on a dish.' She's a vicious woman that one, and she's had it in for John ever since he told Herod to put her away, remember? But Herod had to go along with it - I suppose he had no choice after what he'd said - and they went down to the dungeon and cut off John's head.

"They brought it up and presented it to the girl on a plate. Disgusting! But he's dead. We thought we ought to come and let you know."

PLOUGHING ON

"Aye," Jesus replied. "Thank you for coming. I'm really sorry. But that's how they've always treated the prophets, from righteous Abel down to Zechariah who they murdered between the temple and the altar. John's in good company then. He'll have his reward in heaven. Don't worry about him any more. He's at rest, and his deeds will follow him."

Back in Capernaum, some Pharisees invited Jesus to sit down with them for a discussion of some points from their traditions. Some of them seemed to be sympathetic and genuinely interested in what Jesus had to say, others seemed more interested in catching him out and finding reasons to condemn him.

"Master, what do you say about fasting?" they asked. "We believe in fasting twice a week, as you know, because we believe that fasting's a good discipline and it strengthens your prayers. John the Baptizer's disciples fasted as well. What do you say?"

Jesus replied, "Fasting is a good discipline and I'd encourage my disciples to fast, but you won't see my disciples fasting at the moment. Fasting is for days of mourning and lamentation for the sins we've committed, or for the sins others have committed against us. But these are not like days of lamentation. They are days of rejoicing, because the kingdom of God is breaking in, here on earth.

The guests at a wedding are not expected to fast, are they? This is more like a wedding feast."

"Hmm," replied one of the scribes of the Pharisees, "and what about foods? I assume you keep and teach the Law of Moses about foods and cleanness. But you and your disciples don't appear to wash your hands when you come in from the market place before you eat."

"But you scribes and Pharisees go beyond the Law of Moses. You add to the Law rules of your own making. You teach your own traditions as if they were the commandments of God. Sometimes you even set aside the commandments of God in order to observe the traditions of men.

"God said, 'Honour your father and your mother' but you say that if someone says to his father or his mother, 'What you would have got from me is devoted to God,' then he's no longer permitted to do anything for his parents.

"As for foods, God isn't anything like as interested in what goes into a man as in what comes out of him. It isn't what goes into a man that makes him unclean, it's what comes out of him. What you eat goes through your stomach and passes out into the drain, but out of your heart come all sorts of uncleannesses: lust, theft, murder, adultery, greed, malice, deceit, envy, slander, arrogance and folly. Those are what make a man unclean, not food.

PLOUGHING ON

"You Pharisees are too ready to find fault with everyone, including me. But in the same way as you judge others, you will be judged yourselves. If you find fault with others, God will find fault with you. You see the speck in your brother's eye, but you don't see the plank in your own eye. Take the plank out of your own eye, then you'll be able to see properly to take the speck out of your brother's eye."

eighteen

RETURNING

The twelve returned to Capernaum, two by two. When they had all come back, Jesus asked them, "How did you get on then? You must tell me about it. But let's go over to the other side again, away from the crowds, so that we can have some time on our own. I suppose you've heard about John?"

They all got into Peter's boat and pushed off for the other side, the Gentile side of the lake, where they were not so well known. This time there was no storm and they crossed over on a calm sea, talking sombrely about the death of John, then more excitedly about their own experiences.

"It was just as you said. Even the demons were obedient to us. When we told them to leave in your name, they went! They seemed to know the name of Jesus, even when we hadn't spoken about you yet."

"And we saw some amazing healings. There was a man with a lump growing out of his neck. It was so large it was beginning to stop him breathing or swallowing. We commanded the lump to go away, in the name of Jesus, as you taught us, and while we were watching, it slowly came away from his neck and fell off onto the ground!

"Everyone was amazed. We were too. We didn't know what to do with this horrible lump, so we buried it in the ground!"

"That's amazing," cried Nathanael. "Philip and I healed another man with a lump in his stomach. We could feel this thing under the skin of his belly when we laid our hands on it. When we commanded it to go, we could feel it shrinking under our hands. Luckily it didn't come out like yours did. I couldn't have been doing with that."

"You have to let God be God," said Jesus. "One time he'll do it one way and another, another. It's his power at work, not yours. He's in charge."

They landed on the opposite shore and found a shady place to rest and talk together of all the things that they had seen and done. Then Jesus began to teach them again.

"These are wonderful signs. We praise God for them, but they're not the heart of the matter. It's easy to get carried away, and think that that's what the kingdom's all about. But the kingdom of God requires people to respond, you know that. Everyone is glad to be healed, but not everyone will make a response to the invitation to repent and believe.

"God gives good gifts to his creatures, regardless of their response. He makes the sun shine equally on the good and on the evil, he makes the rain fall equally on the just and on the unjust, he heals people because he has compassion on them. But when the end comes, it won't be enough to say, 'I was healed in the name of Jesus,' or 'I was set free in the name of Jesus.' The Father will ask them, 'So what did you do about it?' In some ways, it's worse to have been healed and then to go back to your old ways, than not to have heard the name of Jesus at all. But some respond and some don't.

"Think of a sower. The sower goes out into his field and scatters the seed on the ground. God feeds it and waters it, but not all of it comes to anything. Some of it falls on the path where the earth has been trampled down. The seed lies on the surface of the ground, and as soon as the farmer's passed by the birds come down and gobble it up.

"Some other seed falls on stony ground, where there's no depth of soil. It sprouts, but withers almost at once. It can't get its roots down to the moisture, and so it's burnt up by the heat of the sun. Then again, other seed falls amongst thorns and thistles. It starts to grow, but the weeds choke it and it dies.

"But the farmer doesn't give it all up as a bad job. He knows that some of the seed will have fallen into good soil and it will grow up and yield a good harvest. One seed can produce as much as thirty or sixty or even a hundred times as much as itself. Wonderful isn't it? So we don't give up preaching the good news of the kingdom and healing the sick, even though not everyone responds to it."

"Aye, I see the point," remarked Andrew, "but why do some respond and not others?"

"It's a mystery," Jesus replied, "but again, it's like the farmer and his seed. People are like the soil. Some people's hearts are like the path — hardened. They hear the word but it makes no impression on them. Others are like the stony ground. At first, they're full of enthusiasm. They rush about telling people what they've seen and heard, but the kingdom always causes trouble and there's always opposition to it. When the trouble starts, these people decide to forget it.

"Others are like the seed sown among thorns. They are enthusiastic for a while as well, but they get so weighed down with worries or get so involved with making money or spending it that they forget what God has done for them.

"But then there are others, who hear the word and believe it and give their lives to following the way of the kingdom. They're the ones who make it all worthwhile. They're the ones for whom I've come."

"And in the end, will there be many, or only a few?" asked Andrew.

"There are two roads through life," Jesus replied. "There's a wide and easy one that most people take, but it leads to destruction. And there's a straight and narrow one that leads to life. But not many people find it."

As the day drew on they ate the food that they had brought with them and settled down to sleep under the stars. It was good to be together, enjoying the fellowship of the kingdom.

The following day, they noticed people beginning to arrive along the seashore. Somehow word had spread that Jesus and his disciples were over there.

Some were coming from the Gentile towns on that side of the lake, people who had heard about Jesus from the man who had been delivered from the legion of unclean spirits. Others had set out and made their way on foot round the top of the lake, several hours walk. Others were coming over in boats.

All day they came. Jesus taught them, and he and the twelve apostles prayed for them and healed them. As the day wore on, no-one showed any sign of wanting to go home.

Eventually Philip came to Jesus and said, "What're we going to do with them all? They've come a long way and it's getting dark. They haven't had anything to eat all day. If we send them away now, some of them will faint on the way home."

"Give them something to eat, then," said Jesus.

"We haven't got anything," replied Philip. "There aren't any shops round here, and if there were, goodness knows how much it would cost to feed this lot."

"Well, what have you got?" asked Jesus.

"Nothing," replied Philip.

"There's a lad here with five small loaves and two small fishes," interrupted Andrew, who had been listening to this conversation, "but what's that among so many?"

"Make the people sit down," Jesus said.

"What for?" asked Philip.

"So that when you start distributing the food, there won't be a crush."

"But we haven't got any food," Philip pursued.

"Don't argue, just do it," Jesus insisted.

So the apostles made the people sit down in groups on the grass.

"Sit down and you'll be fed," they said. "But if you don't sit down, you won't be fed."

So the people sat down. The disciples still didn't have any idea of what was going to happen, but they reported back to Jesus when the crowd were all seated. Jesus took the five loaves and the two fish, and gave thanks over them as if it were any other meal.

"Blessed art thou, Lord God of all creation. Thou bringest forth food from the earth, to thee be all honour and glory."

Then he broke the loaves and gave pieces to each of the apostles. As he broke them, the little loaves seemed to swell again in his hands. It was like the feeding of the hundred men in the days of Elisha, or like the widow's jar of flour in the days of Elijah. The more Jesus broke the bread, the more there was to break.

Then Jesus said to the apostles, "Now it's your turn. Take the pieces of bread that I've given you and share them out among the people. As you break them, so they will multiply in your hands."

Wondering, the disciples turned and made their way through the seated people. As they went they broke the bread in their hands and gave a piece to each person. As they did so the bread was indeed multiplied in their hands.

They went through the ranks of seated people handing out the bread until everyone was satisfied. There was a hush over the whole shore and the hillside on which the people were sitting. Everyone could see that something inexplicable was happening, and no-one wanted to break the spell.

As the day was drawing on, Jesus addressed the crowd again.

"I am the bread of life. Our fathers ate the manna in the wilderness. God gave them bread from heaven in those days. You've just eaten God's supernatural provision for you too, but none of this is the true bread from heaven. The true bread from heaven is the one who comes down from heaven and gives life to the world. Our fathers ate the manna in the wilderness, but they died. Those of you who believe in me will live forever.

"I am the bread of life. Anyone who comes to me will never be hungry. Everyone that the Father gives me will come to me, and whoever comes to me I'll never turn away. I've come not to do my own will but to do the will of the one who sent me. And the will of the one who sent me is this: that I shouldn't lose any of those who come to me. This is the Father's will, that anyone who believes in his Son will have eternal life, and the Son will raise him up at the last day."

Dusk was now settling over the shore. The local people set off to walk home, while others settled down to spend the night in the open air. There was a quiet murmuring of voices as people talked over the events of the day, but on one part of the hillside there was a group of men who were standing and talking animatedly together, some of them waving their arms. Some of their words were born over to Jesus on the evening air.

"Now's the time ... While they're all still here ... This is it ... Make him our leader ... Make him our king ..."

Jesus realised that this group – were they Zealots? – might try the next day to inflame the crowd into starting some sort of uprising.

Perhaps they imagined that he would welcome such a move, but Jesus was determined not to be co-opted onto their agenda or to be compromised by their zeal.

Immediately, he told the apostles to get into the boat and to go back to Capernaum across the lake, while he himself went up into the hills to pray. Others who had come across by boat earlier in the day were also beginning to leave. Slightly bemused, and unnoticed by the crowd in the gloaming, the apostles did as Jesus had told them and set off across the water.

As they were rowing slowly across the lake, a strong wind again blew down off the hills of Galilee. As usual, Peter took charge and instructed the oarsmen to keep the boat pointing into the wind. They rode the waves, up and down, but they were being driven back by the wind as fast as they rowed towards the opposite shore.

There was no immediate danger, but it was tiring and tiresome after a long day. It was well into the night when they saw a figure approaching them across the water in the moonlight. It looked like the figure of a man and they were terrified, thinking it was a ghost.

"What on earth's that?" cried James.

They watched in suspense as the figure drew nearer. Then the 'ghost' called out.

"Don't be afraid! It's me."

It was the voice of Jesus.

PRODIGALS

"Jesus? Is it Jesus?" they asked each other.

"Master, if it's you, tell me to come to you, walking on the water," Peter boldly cried.

"Come on then."

While the rowers still kept the boat head to wind, Peter stepped over the gunwale and started to walk towards Jesus on the water. But he had not taken two or three steps when he looked at the water and the waves, his heart failed him and he began to sink.

"Help!" he cried out to Jesus who had by now drawn near to them.

Jesus reached out and took Peter by the hand as he began floundering in the water. He pulled him up and led him back the two or three steps to the boat, where they both got in.

"You began to doubt, didn't you?" Jesus said grinning at Peter. "You can't do it because *you've* decided to do it. You can only do it in obedience to me, but you doubted and you sank. Never mind. Your faith will increase. It grows, faith does. It's like a mustard tree. You start with a tiny seed, so small you can hardly see it, but then it grows, until you can say to this mountain, 'I cast you into the sea,' and it will go. Or until you can walk on the water!"

nineteen

PRODIGALS

Some time later, Jesus gathered the twelve and they crossed the hills of Galilee towards the coast, to the region of Tyre and Sidon.

They all needed rest and rest was now impossible in the Jewish towns and villages where Jesus' fame or notoriety guaranteed a crowd, and many demands were made upon their time.

As they went he was teaching them.

"What do you think it is that offends the Pharisees?" he asked.

"They're offended because you welcome people like me," Matthew replied. "What they call 'tax collectors and sinners.'"

"Exactly, and why do you think I do that?"

"I don't really know,' continued Matthew, "but I'm glad you do. They'd written most of us off long ago, because we didn't keep all their laws and commandments. But you seem to like us, and for some reason you want us to be with you. You seem better than them somehow, nicer, but you still welcome people like us. You'll sit down and eat with us and talk to us. No Pharisee'd dream of doing that. It would make him unclean."

PRODIGALS

Jesus replied, "Once upon a time there was man who had two sons. The younger son came to his father one day and said to his father, 'Look Dad, I can't wait for you to die. I want my share of the family property now.' His father was pretty upset, as you can imagine, but nevertheless he divided his property and gave his younger son the share that would've belonged to him.

"The son went off a long way from home, where no-one knew him, and started to live what he thought was the good life. He had money and he spent it - drinking, parties, gambling, women. He was very popular and he thought it would never end, but one day he found the money had run out.

"All of a sudden he had no friends any more. What a surprise! The only job he could find was looking after pigs for some Gentile farmer. What a job for a Jew! But he wasn't paid much, even for that, and he got hungrier and hungrier, till he was eating the food the pigs ate.

"At last he came to his senses. 'My father's got servants and hired men who're better off than me,' he said. 'What am I doing here? I'll go back. I'm past caring what they'll think of me. When I get home, I'll say, 'Father, I've done wrong to God and to you. I'm no longer worthy to be called your son, but please, take me on as a servant.' Anything's better than this. So he got up and started for home.

"Meanwhile, his father had never stopped watching, and hoping that his son would one day come home. And one day, as he glanced down the road he saw in the distance a forlorn figure that looked like his son. The father's heart leapt for joy. He gathered up his skirts and ran. Some of the villagers saw the old man running down the road with his skirts round his waist and thought, 'What's the old fool up to now?'

"But the father didn't care. It was his son. He reached him, puffing and panting. He threw his arms round the boy, hugging and kissing him. 'Father,' began the boy, pushing his father back enough to talk to him, 'I'm a disgrace. I've disgraced you. I've disgraced the family. I've wasted all your money. I know I'm not entitled ...'

"'Shush, shush, shush, my boy,' his father said, 'no more of that. You're my son and always will be. I'm just so pleased to have you back, safe and sound. Come on, I'll take you home.' And his father escorted him home, past the houses of the neighbours who stood at their doors, surprised and shocked to see the father with his arm round this notorious son.

"When they reached the house, he called his wife and the servants to tell them that the boy was back. 'Bring the best robe for him; a ring for his finger and shoes for his feet. He's in a terrible mess. Let him clean himself up while we kill the fattened calf and roast it. We're going to have a party.'

"What do you think of that then?" enquired Jesus.

"Doesn't sound very likely to me," replied Matthew. "I don't know any father who'd act like that."

"Maybe not," continued Jesus, "but God's like that."

"Meanwhile," Jesus continued, "while all this was going on, the older son was out working in the fields. As he came home at the end of the day, he smelled the calf roasting and heard the sounds of merriment inside. He came to the door and stopped. 'What's all this?' he said. One of the servants told him, 'Your brother's come back and the master's killed the fattened calf.' 'You must be joking,' replied the elder brother. 'Where's my father?'

"His father came over to him and took him outside. 'What's going on?' demanded the older brother. 'That son of yours went off with half the farm. Now I suppose he's spent it all on God-knows-what - whores, I wouldn't be surprised - and you welcome him home! What about me? I've been slaving away here all the time and you've never killed the fattened calf for me. What do I have to do? Go off and disgrace us all as well?'

"'Come on, son,' said his father. 'You can have a party any day of the week. All I've got belongs to you now. Don't resent your brother. He's my son, just as much as you are. You've always been here, but your brother was lost, now he's found. He was dead, now he's alive again. Come on in.'"

Jesus finished speaking. There was a pause.

"And did he?" asked Matthew. "Did he go in?"

"That's the question, isn't it?" replied Jesus. "It's the question for all those Pharisees who don't approve of me mixing with the likes of you. You were lost, now you're found. I can't make them join us, only send you out to call more lost sinners to come home to God, who's always ready to forgive.

"You see, the Pharisees, like the older son, think that they've earned God's favour by being good boys, and that you're all like the younger son, the bad boys. But in the end, they don't love God, they love themselves. They're smug. They want esteem, their own self-esteem, the esteem of other Pharisees, the esteem of God. They're proud of themselves and their own good behaviour. They don't think they owe God anything. In fact, they think God owes them something.

"I'll tell you another story. Two men went up into the temple to pray, one was a Pharisee, the other a tax collector, like you. The Pharisee stood and prayed out loud, 'Lord, I thank thee that I'm not like other men, like this tax collector here, for example – robbers, evil doers, adulterers. I fast twice a week, I give tithes of all I get.' The tax collector, on the other hand, stood a long way off and wouldn't even look up. He knelt down and beat his breast saying, 'God, have mercy on me, a sinner.' I tell you, that man went home justified rather than the other.

"David says in the Psalms, doesn't he, 'The Lord looked down from heaven upon the children of men, to see if there were any that would understand and seek after God. But they are all gone out of the way, they are altogether become abominable; there is none that doeth good, no not one.'

"It isn't that some are sinners and some are not. All have sinned and fallen short of the glory of God, but there are some who know they've sinned and that they need the mercy of God, and there are some who think that they haven't sinned, and don't need the mercy of God.

"God can do business with the first lot, tax collectors like you, my friend, but he can't do anything with the others. To enter God's kingdom, first you have to see your sin for what it is, then be sorry for it, and then repent of it. God is always ready to forgive.

"The worst thing about the Pharisees is that, in fact, they've plenty of sins: pride and hypocrisy, first of all, but then they have all the same old sins as the rest of you - greed, lust, hatred - but they don't want to know about those. It would shatter their good opinion of themselves to acknowledge it. So they take refuge in lies and project their guilt onto others, like you and me."

"It's all about starting again, like the prodigal son. Realising that you're a long way from God and wanting to come home. God's always ready to have you back, to start again with you. The kingdom of God is about starting with the whole world over again, men and women starting again with God, starting again with one another, and starting again eventually in a new world. It's called redemption."

They walked on in silence, each digesting what Jesus had said, not understanding all of it, but glad to be part of it, whatever it was.

twenty

CAESAREA PHILIPPI

They came to a town in the Gentile districts of Tyre and Sidon and sought accommodation at an inn. Judas paid the landlord out of their common purse, and they bought food to cook on a fire in the open courtyard.

There were plenty of other travellers coming and going but no-one took any notice of them. It was a pleasant change to go unnoticed and ignored. Nobody came pleading to be healed. Nobody came to question them or argue with them. They relaxed and talked among themselves, about everyday matters, as much as about the kingdom of God.

They talked about their families and how they were managing at home. They talked about their occupations, or at least about their previous occupations. They talked to one another about Jesus and his teachings. They talked about the future, where all this might be leading.

But after a couple of days, someone must have recognised Jesus, for one morning a woman came over to where they were sitting and asked Jesus to come and heal her daughter.

THAT MAN JESUS

She knelt at Jesus' feet and said, "My daughter's possessed by an evil spirit. Please come and heal her."

Jesus looked at her pensively.

"What do you know about me? I'm a Jew, you're a Gentile. Why do you come to me?"

"I've heard about you in the market place. Some are saying that you're the Son of David, who will restore the kingdom to Israel. They also say that you heal the sick and drive out the unclean spirits. That's why I've come to you."

"They say all sorts of thing, don't they. At this time, I'm only sent to the lost sheep of the house of Israel. One day my kingdom will extend to all nations and peoples, but for now I must preach to Israel. You feed the children first, then the dogs."

"That's true, master, but even the dogs eat the crumbs that fall from the children's table."

Jesus smiled. He could not resist the woman's faith, or her spirit. He had found on several occasions that in spite of his principles and his sense of calling, he could never resist faith, wherever he found it, whether in the centurion in Capernaum or in this Canaanite woman.

"Go on then," he said to her, "I can't resist you. Go home, your daughter is free. The spirit has gone."

CAESAREA PHILIPPI

"Thank you, thank you, thank you," the woman cried, jumping up and running off, sure, it seemed, that what Jesus had said was true.

"That looks like that, then," Jesus said, turning to the twelve. "No more peace here. As soon as that woman starts to tell her story, the whole town, the whole region will be at the gates. It's time to move on."

So, quietly, they slipped out of the town and went back into Galilee. As they passed through the towns and villages of the Galilean hills their progress was slow. Always there were people, sometimes crowds, who would gather about them, bringing their sick to be healed.

At the same time there was an increasing sense of opposition from the Pharisees, and many of the synagogues were no longer open to Jesus as they had once been. At one place, some Pharisees approached Jesus and demanded a sign from heaven.

"If you're from God," they began, "show us some miraculous sign, so that we may believe you."

"What would you like me to do?" asked Jesus, "jump off the pinnacle of the temple and float down to the ground? Nope, you won't get any signs like that. You seem to know how to recognise the signs of the weather. If the sky is red at night, you say, 'It'll be fine tomorrow.' If it's red in the morning, you say, 'Looks like rain today.' But you can't read the signs of the times. They're all around you.

"Well did God say, 'Hear ye indeed, but understand not; and see ye indeed, but perceive not. Make the heart of this people fat, and make their ears heavy, and shut their eyes, lest they see with their eyes, and hear with their ears, and understand with their heart, and convert and be healed.'"

Jesus and his disciples began to realise that a phase of their ministry was coming to an end. They could not go on covering the same old ground again and again, preaching the same message to the same people, encountering the same objections from the same objectors.

They headed north, out of Galilee and the tetrarchy of Herod, into the tetrarchy of his brother Philip. They needed to prepare for what lay ahead.

"Beware of the leaven of the Pharisees and the leaven of Herod," Jesus said to them as they walked together. The twelve looked at one another and shrugged.

"Like what?" asked James.

"Herod is always looking to save his skin, to save his place with the Romans. It's a subtle temptation, compromise. Only say what people want you to say, and do what they want you to do. Don't upset the powers that be. The Sadducees are the same in Jerusalem. 'Don't rock the boat,' that's their motto.

"People like Herod are always trying to calculate the consequences of what they say and do. That's not our calling. We must say what God gives us to say, and do what God gives us to do, and leave him to take care of the consequences.

"The Pharisees, on the other hand, are so afraid of compromise that they dogmatically oppose anything or anyone that threatens their system. It isn't people but rules they put first. Their religion isn't the love of God or of other people, it's regulations, conformity, fear. That's not our calling either.

"Our calling is to love. To love God and to love each other. Love overlooks a multitude of sins for the sake of friendship with one another. Love cares about sin because sin is harmful, to the sinner and to the ones sinned against. But love puts up with sin rather than cutting off the sinner."

As time went on the disciples found that their fellowship with Jesus and with one another was becoming ever more precious. At first, they had been excited by Jesus' teaching and by the miracles of healing and deliverance that they had witnessed, but now they were feeling that their friendship with him and with one another was the most important thing that they had discovered with Jesus.

There was a sense of acceptance and safety in this relationship that none of them had experienced before. They were very different from one another, but their relationship to Jesus was something that they had in common and which now transcended the differences between them.

They reached the new town of Caesarea Philippi. Most of them had never been this far north before, nor visited this pagan area. From a large cave emerged the source of the river Jordan, whose course they had followed all the way up from the lake.

The river's name meant 'the descender', and they had begun to realise in a new way why it was so-called. From here, the Jordan descended steeply to the lake which was their home, then went on descending down to Jericho and eventually to the Dead Sea, which, again, few of them had ever seen.

Up here at the river's source, many Greeks and Romans came to worship at the shrine of the pagan god Pan. Philip the tetrarch, the brother of their Herod in Galilee, a toady like his brother, had recently built a new city around the ancient site and dedicated it to Caesar, binding his own name to Caesar's. Caesarea Philippi.

The Pharisees of Jerusalem would run a mile from such a place as this, or else live in a ghetto, sealed off as far as possible, from pagan contamination. But coming from Galilee with its

CAESAREA PHILIPPI

mixed population of Jews and Gentiles, Jesus and his disciples were less intimidated by the pagan atmosphere.

There was even less chance of their being bothered here than in the region of Tyre and Sidon. Here they could spend time together, and Jesus, in particular, could think and pray about the way forward.

Where did he go from here? All over Galilee and to some extent in Jerusalem and Judea, even in Samaria, there were people who had listened to him, heard the message that the kingdom of God was at hand, and believed.

There were people and families who had experienced healing and deliverance in his name. There were also those, in Galilee and more so in Jerusalem and Judea, who had heard his message and rejected both it and him. So what next? What were the options?

He and his disciples could go back to Galilee, gather together those who believed in him, start a movement, like the Pharisees, though obviously with his values and not theirs. They could be a sort of leaven in the lump of Judaism, a renewal movement in Israel. They would encounter opposition, not least from the Pharisees. They would probably end up with separate synagogues, their own rabbis and teachers. Would they then be able to break out of Judaism and reach out to the Gentiles and the nations of the world? And was that all that God had called and sent him to do? Some or all of this might come to pass in due course, but there was some dimension of his calling that remained unfulfilled.

In a sense, all that was just too cosy. There were principalities and powers that ruled the present world that he had to challenge and to overcome, ultimately they were spiritual principalities and powers, but they were manifested in all-too-real flesh and blood, the power of the Sadducees and the rulers of the Jews, the power of Rome and other earthly rulers.

This was his heavenly Father's world, yet it was ruled by those who neither knew nor acknowledged his Father's authority. Not only the common people, but also the rulers of the world had to be confronted by his Father's will and called to bow the knee to him.

The priests and the teachers in the temple had told him to go away, but he must go back and face them down. It was not their temple but his Father's, and he was his Father's Son. The fight was not finished. And he had not yet encountered Rome. But if he was indeed a king, born to sit on the throne of his father David, he would have to assert his right to rule even against Caesar himself.

The people of Israel had always had to fight. Always the nations around about had regarded the Jews as their enemies. Armies had been sent

CAESAREA PHILIPPI

to conquer and subdue them. There was no escaping the battle. God himself was coming to reclaim his land, and not only the land that he had given to Abraham, Isaac and Jacob but to reclaim the earth that was rightly his. That was what the kingdom of God was all about. This was heaven invading earth, and it would be a fight to the finish, a fight to the death.

But he, and above all his followers, had to be clear that this was a war fought not on the enemy's terms or with the enemy's weapons, but on his terms and with his own weapons, the terms and the weapons that God had given him. The word of truth, the way of righteousness, the weapons of love and compassion.

What use, people might say, were those against swords and spears, horses and chariots? But then, what use were swords and spears and even horses and chariots against the power of Almighty God? If God was on their side, what could man do to them? They should not fear those who could kill the body but who could not destroy the soul. Rather they should fear the one who could destroy both body and soul in hell.

As Jesus resolved these thoughts in his mind, he felt again the love and peace as he was enfolded in his Father's arms. He had known from the beginning in the desert that his mission was to embrace death, even death on a cross, and now the reality of that destiny reasserted itself in his mind and he saw that there was no other way.

It was the very corruption of the world by sin that he had come to redeem, the corruption of the world by hatred and violence, by cruelty and vice, by greed and selfishness. These things could only be redeemed by being borne, by being suffered.

Fighting fire with fire only made more fire. These fires in the human spirit could only be extinguished by love, and for those who failed to respond to that love there was no more that he or his Father could do. They would ultimately be consumed in their own fire.

He would set his face to go to Jerusalem.

twenty-one

THE NEW COMMUNITY

Somehow his twelve friends needed to be warned and strengthened for what Jesus now knew lay ahead of them.

"Who do men say that I am?" he began.

There was a pause while they all looked at each other and wondered who was going to answer.

"Some say John the Baptizer," said Andrew eventually. "They say that you're John the Baptizer raised from the dead. Stupid, I know, but that's what they say."

"Others say Elijah, but then they said that about John the Baptizer too," offered Thomas.

"Others say Jeremiah or one of the prophets," said the younger James.

"And you, who do you say that I am?" Jesus asked.

Peter stood up, as if he were about to make a speech, and looked around at the others seated in a cicle on the ground. They all turned to listen to whatever Peter was going to say.

"When we first met you," he said, "I was doubtful. I wondered if you were some sort of lunatic. I was not sure about John then, either. I liked his message about everyone repenting of their sins, but when he started talking about you as the Lamb of God, I thought it was all getting a bit weird. But I liked you, I have to say - and I still do," Peter added grinning.

"Then, spending time with you, I began to believe that you were someone special. What happened at the wedding in Cana, the way we caught those fish on the lake in Capernaum. And what you said was not crazy at all. It brought the Scriptures alive, and something inside me began to catch fire.

"So, I've been asking myself this question for some time. Who are you? And the answer I've come to is this: you are the Messiah, the one we've waited for, for so long. I can't speak for the others, but I believe you are the Son of God."

There was a general nodding of heads from the others as they all looked at Jesus to see his response.

Jesus smiled.

"Bless you, Simon son of Jonah. You have not come to that conclusion by human reasoning. It has been revealed to you by my heavenly Father.

"When I first met you, I called you Peter. Peter means a rock, and on this rock I will found God's new people. You twelve are the foundation stones of a new temple, a temple built of living stones, and you, Peter, are the first stone to be laid. On this stone a new temple is going to be built.

THE NEW COMMUNITY

"You will be the ancestors of a new people of God, a people called out from among the people of Israel, but also called out from among the peoples of the Gentiles as well. It will be like a new Israel, under a new covenant. There were twelve patriarchs of the old Israel, the twelve sons of Jacob, so there will be twelve patriarchs of the new Israel, you twelve.

"You will be like spiritual fathers who give birth to spiritual sons and daughters, to a spiritual nation, a holy nation, only not living apart from the nations as Israel has done, but mixed in among the nations, like salt or yeast. God said to me, 'It is a light thing that thou shouldest be my servant to raise up the tribes of Jacob, and to restore the preserved of Israel. I will also give thee for a light to the Gentiles, that thou mayest be my salvation unto the end of the earth.'

"A new people under a new covenant. Under the old covenant God required obedience to the Law as the condition of his favour. Under the new covenant, God only requires you to believe in me.

"To you, Peter, because of your faith in me, I am giving the keys of the kingdom of God. You, and the others, will be like stewards of the kingdom. You are to watch over and care for those who enter the kingdom. You are to protect them from false teachers and false prophets. You are to correct and rebuke them. You are to guard both the teaching and the ways that I have given and shown you.

"You will have hard decisions to make, but my Father will guide you. Always remember, it's not your kingdom, but his."

Jesus let this sink in for a few moments, before he went on.

"But first I must go up to Jerusalem. I have to suffer many things at the hands of the chief priests and the teachers of the Law. You have seen how they rejected me the last time we went up to Jerusalem. I deliberately didn't go up to Jerusalem for the Passover this year, because my time hadn't yet come, but next spring I must be in Jerusalem for the feast of Passover.

"You remember, I see, that John the Baptist called me the Lamb of God who takes away the sin of the world. It is at Passover time that the lambs are killed. I shall be killed like a Passover lamb, but I shall rise again."

"Killed!" exclaimed Peter. "Surely not. That doesn't make any sense. Apart from anything else, we won't let it happen. We'll fight, if necessary, won't we?" he said, turning to the others.

"Now, that's the voice of Satan speaking through you, Peter," said Jesus. "Be quiet. You're still looking at things from the wrong side - Satan's side - the world's side, not God's side. I don't want any more talk like that. Listen to me."

THE NEW COMMUNITY

There was a stunned silence. Then Jesus continued.

"If anyone would come after me, he must be ready to deny himself, take up his cross and follow me. Whoever wants to save his life, will lose it. But anyone who loses his life for my sake and for the sake of the kingdom, will save it."

Another silence followed, but the conversation seemed to be at an end and the disciples drifted apart in twos and threes.

"What was all that about?" James said to Judas. "One minute Peter's the voice of God, the next he's the voice of the devil."

"And what's he talking about – going up to Jerusalem to be killed. What's the point of that? Why not stay around in Galilee? Most people seem to like him there. Maybe not the Pharisees, but who cares about them?"

The next day, Jesus called Peter and James and John to come with him. He was going further up Mount Hermon, whose snow-covered peak rose over the city of Caesarea, in order to pray on his own. It was much cooler up here than down by the lake. Caesarea itself was higher than the lake and now they were climbing higher still.

After a few hours they stopped to rest and Jesus went on a little further to pray. The three disciples sat and talked quietly to each other. The year was drawing on and sometimes the sun was obscured by clouds that formed over the mountain.

At one moment, John looked up to see what Jesus was doing. His eyes stayed riveted on what he saw.

"Look," he whispered quietly to Peter and James, pointing upwards.

The other two turned and looked. There, a little way above them stood Jesus, his face turned up towards heaven, shining with an unearthly light.

As they looked the light grew brighter and brighter. Jesus' clothes became dazzling white and his face shone. And then, on either side of him, appeared two wraith-like figures. Jesus turned to them and was talking to them.

The two figures became more defined, almost as solid as flesh and blood, but there was nothing frightening or spooky about the vision. Rather, something awe-inspiring.

"We're here too, master," Peter called out. "What can we do? Make a bit of shade?"

But just then a cloud enveloped them as it passed across the face of the mountain. It was suddenly cold and clammy. Then they heard a voice.

"This is my Son. I love him and I'm pleased with him. Listen to him."

A few moments later, the cloud passed and the sun came out again. Only Jesus was now to be

THE NEW COMMUNITY

seen on the rock above. For a while the three friends simply looked at one another.

"What was that?" James asked. "I heard a voice when the cloud came over us. Did you hear it too?"

The others both agreed that they did, and agreed what the voice had said.

"It was the voice of God," said John, in awe.

Jesus came down to join them.

"Who were those men you were talking to?" asked Peter.

"Moses and Elijah," replied Jesus, just as if he had been speaking to the local butcher and baker. "But do not tell anyone what you've seen. At least, not until everything has been fulfilled."

Still not understanding any of it, the disciples accompanied Jesus back down the mountain towards the city. As they reached the walls they found the rest of their friends surrounded by a crowd, with a man and a boy in the middle of them. It became apparent that their identity as the followers of Jesus had been discovered, and that even up here people had heard of Jesus' reputation.

As Jesus appeared, the man came forward.

"Master, have mercy on my son here. He has fits. He's often fallen into the fire or into the water in one of these fits. We're at our wits end, my wife and I, what to do with him. I brought him to your disciples, but they weren't able to heal him. If you yourself can do anything for him, take pity on us and help us!"

"If you *can* ..." Jesus answered. "Everything is possible for those who believe."

"Well, I do believe," replied the father, "or at least, I think I do. I believe you've helped other people - but then I think, perhaps not me."

"Bring the boy over here," Jesus said. The father took the boy's hand and brought him to Jesus, but as the boy came nearer to Jesus, he started to fit. He fell to the ground, rigid, his back arched and his head went back and he started to foam at the mouth.

"Come out of him," Jesus said firmly, and with a strangled cry something came out of the boy. His body went limp and lay still in the dust.

Some of the onlookers said, "He's dead." But Jesus took the boy by the hand and helped him to stand up on his feet.

"Alright then, lad?" said Jesus, crouching down and looking into the boy's face.

The boy smiled weakly.

"Yes, sir, I think so. Thank you. Is it going to happen again?"

"No. Not now, never again," Jesus replied. "Go and play with your friends."

Later that day, the disciples came to Jesus.

"Why couldn't we cast the spirit out then?" they asked, in a rather chastened tone of voice.

THE NEW COMMUNITY

"There's still too much unbelief in you," said Jesus. "It isn't your fault in a way. You're part of an unbelieving generation. How could you be otherwise? But how long have I got to be with you before you really believe?"

The next day they set off back down the Jordan valley, watching the stream that flowed out of the cave at Caesarea broaden into a river, until it widened out into the familiar shores of the lake of Galilee.

As they went, Jesus again explained to them that they were going up to Jerusalem and that he would die there. This time, no-one dared to contradict him for fear of what he had said to Peter. Even so, no-one understood what he meant, or why he must go up to the great city. Still less did they understand what he could be talking about when he said that he would rise again.

"We're all going to rise again at the last day, aren't we?" they said to one another. "But what's that got to do with it. Does he mean that the last day is coming soon. Perhaps that's what he means."

But they did not like to ask.

twenty-two

JERUSALEM AGAIN

They came back to Capernaum and stayed there for a while. Peter and Andrew, James and John, and the others went back to their families and Jesus lodged again in the small room on the roof of Zebedee's house. People gathered as usual to hear Jesus teach and brought their sick to be healed, but Jesus' messages were now sterner and more pressing.

"There's trouble ahead for you in the towns of Galilee, Chorazin, Bethsaida and the others. If the miracles done in you had been done in Tyre and Sidon they'd have repented long ago in dust and ashes. I tell you, it will be more tolerable on the Day of Judgement for Tyre and Sidon than for you.

"And as for you, Capernaum, if the miracles done in you had been done in Sodom and Gomorrah, they'd still be here to this day. I tell you it will be more tolerable for Sodom and Gomorrah on the Day of Judgement than it will be for you.

"You heard about the Galileans, whose blood Pilate mixed with their sacrifices in Jerusalem. Do you think that they were worse sinners than the rest of you? Not at all. If you don't repent, you

JERUSALEM AGAIN

will all perish. And remember those eighteen people who were killed when the Tower of Siloam fell on them. Do you think that they were worse sinners than everyone else in Jerusalem? Not at all. If you don't repent, you will all perish. But God so loved the world that he sent his only Son into the world, so that all who believe in him shall *not* perish but have everlasting life.

"There is still time to repent and believe, to enter the kingdom of God. But the door of repentance won't stand open forever. At any time your life may be cut off, like the lives of those Galileans or the lives of those people at the Tower of Siloam. And where will you be then?

"You've heard about the Day of Judgement, that great and terrible day, but you think it can be put off forever. It is only delayed because God is patient, not wanting any of you to perish, but wanting everyone to come to repentance. He gives you time, but the Day of Judgement is coming. Take the opportunity, while it's still here. Repent and turn to God and believe in the one he has sent.

"Enter while the door is still open. Once the owner of the house gets up and closes the door, you will stand outside knocking, and pleading, 'Please sir, open the door.' But he will answer, 'I do not know who you are or where you come from.' Then you will say, 'We ate and drank with you, and you taught in our streets.' But he will reply,

'I do not know who you are or where you come from. Go away.'

"Then you will be full of remorse and despair when you see Abraham, Isaac and Jacob and all the prophets in the kingdom, but you yourselves shut out. People will come from east and west and north and south, and take their places at the feast in the kingdom, but you will not be there – unless you repent and believe."

A man in the crowd called out, "Blessed are those who will eat at the feast in the kingdom of God."

Jesus replied, "Aye, but I'll tell you another story. A certain man once gave a great banquet and invited many guests. When everything was ready he sent out his servants to call those who had been invited to come and sit down. But they all alike began to make excuses. One said, 'I've just bought a field and I must go and see it. Please have me excused.'

"Another one said, 'I've just bought five yoke of oxen and I must go and try them out. Please have me excused.'

"Yet another said, 'I've just got married, so I can't come after all.'

"The servant came back and reported all this to his master. The owner of the house was angry and told his servant, 'Everything is ready now. We can't let it all go to waste. Go out into the streets and alleys of the town and bring in the poor and

JERUSALEM AGAIN

the crippled and the lame and the blind. My house will be full, but I tell you, none of those who were invited will taste of my banquet.'"

After Jesus had been back in Capernaum for a few days, some Pharisees came up to him and said, "You'd better leave Galilee. We've heard that Herod wants to kill you."

Jesus wondered what was in the minds of these Pharisees. Were they genuinely concerned for his welfare, or did they simply want to see him leave their towns and villages for good?

Jesus could not tell, but in any case he replied, "Go and tell that fox: I'll drive out demons and heal people today and tomorrow, and on the third day I'll finish what I came to do. I'm on my way up to Jerusalem, Herod or no Herod, for no prophet can die away from Jerusalem.

"Oh, Jerusalem, Jerusalem, you kill the prophets and stone those sent to you. How I've longed to gather your children together, like a hen gathers her chicks under her wings. But you weren't willing before, and I don't suppose you'll be willing this time. One day your house will be desolate. And I tell you, here in Galilee, you will never see me again."

The autumn Feast of Tabernacles was drawing near, and it was time for Jesus and his disciples to set out for Jerusalem. They left their homes and families again and gathered in the market place, as they had often done. They walked out along by the lake, through the towns and villages in which they had preached, and in which he and they had healed the sick and set the captives free.

There was a sense of awe around their party as somehow they all realised that things would never be the same again. Jesus was walking on ahead of them, while the others followed at a distance, at once excited and apprehensive.

Some of them, especially Simon the Zealot and Judas Iscariot, started to whisper that they were going up to Jerusalem to put Jesus on the throne; that this was the king coming into his kingdom, that somehow Jesus would overthrow his enemies and restore the kingdom to Israel.

It seemed possible. Jesus had certainly acquired a considerable following in Galilee. Many of these Galileans would be coming up for the feasts in Jerusalem, now and in the spring. If Jesus could muster a following in the city as well, there might be the chance to form an army out in the hills, as Judas Maccabaeus had done, and begin the liberation of the nation.

It became a subject of speculation among the disciples as the journey went on. They had all seen extraordinary miracles performed by Jesus, and even in their own experience. It was not difficult to believe that God himself would intervene in some supernatural way to support them and to vanquish their enemies once the battles began. Had God not fought for the

JERUSALEM AGAIN

Israelites before - at the crossing of the Red Sea, when the sun stood still for Joshua, when the Lord destroyed the Assyrian army at the gates of Jerusalem?

Some began to be fired up by the prospect of witnessing again some great deliverance of God, whilst others dismissed it all as a foolhardy delusion. Jesus took no part in these discussions. Indeed, the disciples took care that they went on behind Jesus' back. He himself seemed oblivious to whatever was occupying their minds, preoccupied with whatever was filling his own.

But as these suggestions took shape in the minds of some of them, they began to imagine what roles or offices they might occupy in this new kingdom. During a lull in the conversation one day, James and John detached themselves from the rest of the group and walked up beside Jesus.

"Master," began James tentatively, "would you do something for us?"

"Depends what," Jesus replied.

"Well, when you come into your kingdom, can we sit one on either side of you?"

"Hmm," Jesus grunted. "You don't know what you're talking about, do you? Can you drink the cup that I must drink or be baptised with the baptism that I must be baptised with?"

"Aye, we can," John replied boldly, not really knowing what Jesus meant.

"Aye, you will drink the cup that I drink and be baptised with the baptism I'm baptised with, but what you ask isn't mine to give. God will grant those seats to those they've been prepared for."

The other disciples had now caught up with James and John, curious to know what they were asking Jesus. What they heard made them indignant.

"What are you two trying to do? Get one up on us?"

"You've all got it wrong," said Jesus turning to face them.

They all stopped.

"You've seen the rulers of the Gentiles, the Babylonians, the Persians, the Greeks and now the Romans, Herod, and his lackeys. They've lorded it over us, bossing us about, using their power to extract wealth and privileges for themselves. That's *not* how it's going to be amongst you.

"Anyone who wants to be great in the kingdom of God must be like a servant, and anyone who wants to be first must be more like a slave, the least of all. Aye, I've called you to be rulers in the kingdom, but headship in my kingdom means service, not an opportunity to boss people about or seek your own glory. It's service, serving God and serving one another. Even the Son of Man has come, not to be served but to serve – and to give his life as a ransom for many."

JERUSALEM AGAIN

"So what will the coming of the kingdom of God look like then?" Andrew pursued.

"The kingdom of God doesn't come in a way that can be observed," Jesus replied. "You can't say, 'here it is,' or 'there it is.' The kingdom of God is within you and among you.

"The kingdom of God is simply the place where God reigns, where his will is done. Where anyone responds to God's call to trust and obey him, the kingdom comes in that person, and wherever they go, the kingdom goes too. The kingdom of God does not have borders. It isn't a place on a map. It isn't like the kingdoms of the world. It's spiritual, inside you and me."

They walked on in silence.

As they were crossing the border between Galilee and Samaria, they came across a group of ten lepers who were living together in a sort of colony. As usual they were swathed in cloths, but they called out together as Jesus drew near.

"Jesus, master, have pity on us."

When Jesus saw them he went over to them and said, "Go and show yourselves to the priests. They will certify that you are cured."

"But some of us are Jews and some of us are Samaritans," replied one of the men. "If you're a leper, it doesn't matter what you are, no-one wants to know you anyway."

"Then the Jews among you must show yourselves to a Jewish priest and the Samaritans to a Samaritan priest. Then you will be accepted again, by your own people."

The men divided themselves into two bands and went off as they were told, to find priests resident in the nearby towns and villages who would verify their cure. None of them had gone far before, looking back somewhat furtively to where Jesus and his disciples still stood, they began to undo their bandages and inspect each other's skin.

As they did so they saw that indeed they were clean. The leprosy had disappeared. Overjoyed they hastened on, all except one, who came back and knelt at Jesus' feet, and thanked him profusely. He was a Samaritan.

"Weren't all ten of you cleansed?" Jesus enquired. "Then where are the other nine?" he added, looking over to where the other men were rapidly disappearing over the horizon. "The only one to come back and give thanks is this Samaritan! Stand up, my friend, your faith has made you well."

From there, they were taking the highland route to Jerusalem, through the country of the Samaritans. Towards evening they came to a Samaritan village, and James and John were sent on ahead to arrange accommodation for them. But James and John came back too soon, saying

JERUSALEM AGAIN

that because they were Jews and going up to Jerusalem they would not be welcome in the town.

"What a nerve," said James angrily to Jesus, "and just when you'd cured a Samaritan of leprosy too. Can we call down fire on them, like the prophet Elijah did?"

"No, you can't," replied Jesus. "Whenever will you learn? You don't seem to know what spirit you're of. The Son of Man didn't come to destroy lives, but to save them. If needs be, we'll spend the night in the open air – and fast."

twenty-three

BLINDNESS

About halfway through the seven days of the Feast of Tabernacles, Jesus went up to the temple. As he walked through the court of the Gentiles, he saw that once again the market had returned. The traders were exchanging money again, and selling animals for the visitors to sacrifice.

Some of the traders eyed Jesus warily as he passed by, remembering the last time. Some of the money changers began to gather their coins into their money bags in case their tables were turned over again, but Jesus just looked them in the eye and passed on. There would be a time to deal with them again, but not now.

He took his seat in the colonnade of Solomon and began to teach, as the other rabbis were doing. A crowd gathered around him. Many recognised him as the teacher from Galilee, about whom there had been so much controversy when he had last come to Jerusalem eighteen months ago.

What was he going to say or do this time, and what were the temple authorities going to do about him? What did the authorities think about him anyway?

BLINDNESS

Many stories had reached Jerusalem from Galilee. Pilgrims had come to the feasts and told of Jesus healing and teaching and casting out evil spirits. Some of these pilgrims said they thought that Jesus was a prophet like Elijah or one of the prophets of old. Some of them even thought he might be the Messiah. What did the authorities here in Jerusalem think? No-one seemed to know. And here he was, back again, this Jesus of Nazareth, with his north country accent.

"Aye, I've come back to Jerusalem," Jesus began. "You've been hearing about me, no doubt, and about what God's been doing in Galilee. And you think you know where I come from, but you don't. Not really.

"I come from the one who sent me. You don't know him, but I do. You think you know him, but you don't. If you did, you'd recognise that I'm the one he's sent. But I'm only going to be with you for a short time now, and then I'll be going to the one who sent me. You will look for me, but you won't find me. Where I am going, you cannot come.'

One of the hearers said to him, "Where are you planning to go then, that we won't be able to find you? Are you planning to go to the Gentiles and teach the Greeks?"

Jesus ignored their questions.

"I am the light of the world, not just of Israel, but of the world," he continued. "Whoever follows me will never walk in darkness. He'll have the light of life."

Some of the Pharisees who were listening called out, "Who do you think you are? You can't say that sort of thing about yourself."

"Even if I do say it about myself," Jesus replied, "what I say is true, because I know where I come from and I know where I am going. But you've no idea where I come from or where I'm going. You judge by human standards. I don't judge anyone. But if I do judge, my judgement is true, because I listen to my Father who sent me.

"In your Law, it is written that the testimony of two witnesses is valid. I'm one witness who testifies about myself, the other witness is my Father."

"Where is your father then, and who is he, that we should listen to him?"

"You don't know me or my Father. The one who sent me is with me. He has not left me alone, because I always do what pleases him. If you accept my teaching, you will know the truth and the truth will set you free."

"What do you mean, 'set us free'?" the Pharisees replied. "We're not slaves. We don't need to be set free."

Jesus replied, "Anyone who sins is a slave to sin. If you don't believe in me, you will die in your sins. The slave has no permanent place in the household, but a son belongs in the family forever.

BLINDNESS

If the son sets you free, then you are free indeed. I'm telling you what I've heard from my Father, and you are doing what you've heard from your father."

"Abraham is our father," they said.

"If you were Abraham's children, you'd do what Abraham did. He heard the word of God and obeyed it. You're hearing the word of God and you're rejecting it. Abraham didn't do that. You're doing what your father has done from the beginning."

"The only father we have is God himself," they argued.

"If God were your father, you would know me and love me," Jesus continued. "I have come from God. I haven't come on my own account. He sent me. Why isn't that clear to you? It is because you are unable to hear what I'm saying. You belong to your father, the devil, and you want to carry out your father's desires.

"He was a murderer from the beginning and there is no truth in him. When he lies, he's being true to his own nature, because he's a liar and the father of lies. I tell you the truth, and you don't believe me. Can any of you prove me guilty of sin? If I'm telling you the truth, why don't you believe me? The reason that you don't believe me, is that you don't belong to God."

At this they picked up stones and threatened to stone him, but Jesus walked away from them and left the temple. He knew, and they knew, that there was no question of stoning him within the temple precincts, but it was a sign of their hostility towards him. His disciples detached themselves from the crowd and followed him, shaken by this display of their anger.

As they were passing through the streets of Jerusalem they saw a blind man begging by the entrance to the soukh. He had a small notice attached to his cloak: "Blind from birth."

"Jesus, who sinned," asked Philip, "this man or his parents, that he was born blind?"

"Neither," Jesus replied. "Just wait, and you will see the glory of God. While I still can, I must do the works of him who sent me. The time is coming when I shall not be able to do any more of this. But, as I said in the temple, while I'm in the world, I am the light of the world."

This conversation was taking place while Jesus and his friends were standing in front of the blind man. Jesus then bent down, spat on the ground and made a little paste from the dust and his saliva.

"Now, my friend," he said, addressing the blind man, "I'm going to put a smear of this mud on your eyelids. Then you're to go and wash it off in the Pool of Siloam. When you come back, you'll be able to see."

BLINDNESS

The man shut his blind and cloudy eyes while Jesus gently covered the lids with the mud that he had made.

"Go on then," he commanded the blind man, who got up, with a bemused smile and felt his way towards the Pool of Siloam, tapping his way with his stick. Meanwhile, Jesus and his disciples walked on.

It was two days later when Jesus passed the same way again. At the entrance to the soukh one of the stall holders hurried out of the shop where he was selling dishes of brightly coloured and aromatic spices, and urgently laid hold of Jesus' arm.

"Rabbi, you know that man you saw the other day, the one born blind? Several of us were watching what you did and heard what you said. He went, like you said, to the pool, and he came back seeing. Glory to God! But you know what they've done to him now?"

"No," replied Jesus. "What has happened?"

"Well, to start with, people wouldn't believe that he was the same man. Some of the people who knew him here - he's been here for years - said he was the same man, but others wouldn't believe it.

"I *knew* he was the same man of course, but other people disputed it. 'No,' they said, 'he looks like him, but he can't be the same man.' He insisted, of course, that he was. So they said, 'How, then, were your eyes opened?'

"'A man they called Jesus put some mud on my eyes,' he said, 'and when I went and washed it off, I could see.'

"'Where is this man?' they asked him. 'I don't know,' he said. So they fetched some of the Pharisees. There was quite a crowd by now, I can tell you, waiting to see what would happen next.

"So, they came back with the Pharisees who started to give the poor fellow a real hard time. They went over the same old ground again - 'How have you received your sight? Who did this for you?' When the blind man mentioned your name, Jesus, they said, "Oh yes, we know that fellow. He's some sort of sorcerer. We know he's a sinner because he does not keep the Sabbath.'

"There were a few people listening who said, 'But how could a sinner open the eyes of a blind man?' Then they asked the blind man, or the ex-blind man, 'What've you got to say about him? It was your eyes he opened.' 'I think he's a prophet,' he said.

"They still didn't really believe that he was the same man who'd been born blind, so they sent for his parents. It was causing quite a stir by now, I can tell you. More and more people had gathered round and were asking each other what was happening, and people were telling each other what they'd heard. I had to tell some of them they'd got it wrong. I was in on this from the

BLINDNESS

beginning, as I told you, so I knew what'd been said and I could put them right.

"Anyway, this bloke's parents turned up and the Pharisees start to quiz them all over again. 'Is this you son, who you say was born blind?' 'Yes, this is our son, and yes, he was born blind, may God have mercy on him and on us,' his mother said.

"'So how can he now see?' they asked. 'We don't know how he can now see,' his father said. 'He's a grown man. He can speak for himself.' I think the parents were a bit afraid of the Pharisees. Then they said to the man himself, 'Give the glory to God, man. We know this man's a sinner, so don't give the glory to him.'

"'I don't know about any of that,' the chap said. 'All I know is, once I was blind, now I can see.' But they wouldn't let it go. They just kept on and on. 'How did he open your eyes?' Etcetera, etcetera. At this point the chap lost his temper completely. 'I've just told you all that. Why do you want to hear it again? Do you want to become his disciples too?'

"'We're disciples of Moses,' said one of the Pharisees, haughtily. 'We know that God spoke to Moses. As for this fellow, we don't know where he comes from.' 'Here's a fine thing,' said our friend, turning to the crowd. 'They don't know where he comes from, yet he opened my eyes. God doesn't listen to sinners, he listens to men of God. Nobody's ever heard of anyone opening the eyes of someone like me, not since the beginning of the world. If this man wasn't from God, he could do nothing.'

"'You were born in utter sin,' the Pharisees said - because of his being born blind, you see - 'and you're trying to teach us? We'll see to it that you're all put out of the synagogue.' And off they went."

"Bless you, my friend," Jesus said to the shop keeper. "Keep believing and you will see the kingdom come."

Jesus went on his way, but kept a lookout in the streets for the man whom he had healed. He caught sight of him going up to the temple.

Jesus pushed through the crowd to reach the man and took him by the arm.

"Do you know who I am?" he asked him.

"Yes, I know your voice," replied the man born blind. "Are you Jesus? The man who restored my sight?"

"I am," Jesus replied.

"How can I ever thank you?"

"Do you believe in the Son of Man?" Jesus replied.

"Who's that?" said the man.

"You know his voice, and now you've seen his face, and he's talking to you right now."

"Yes, Lord, I believe," he said.

BLINDNESS

"This is what I came into the world for," Jesus said to all about him. "So that the blind see, and those who see, or think they see, become blind."

twenty-four

THE WILDERNESS AGAIN

After the Feast of Tabernacles, Jesus and his disciples went down from Jerusalem to the Jordan valley.

"We're not going back to Galilee," Jesus told them. "We're going to stay out of the way for a bit. You've seen how hostile the priests and the Pharisees are in Jerusalem, but they must be given another chance, and even one more after that. This cannot come to a head before Passover next spring.

"You remember the man I was staying with, when we first met each other by the river, where John were baptising? He said to me, if ever I wanted to stay with him again his door was always open. I'm going to stay there for a few weeks until the Feast of Dedication."

The weather was still warm and the early rains had not yet come. Jesus went up into the hills, into the desert where he had gone after his baptism by John, to spend some time alone again with his heavenly Father. He had much to think and pray about, and he knew that he must prepare himself for what lay ahead.

THE WILDERNESS AGAIN

The silence of the desert enfolded him once again. It was like a warm blanket wrapping itself round him. The silence of eternity, and in the silence, the loving arms of his Father.

How long was it since he had spent those weeks in the wilderness before? How long was it since he had closed the door of the carpenter's shop and walked off down the steep road from Nazareth towards the river Jordan? Was it two years?

It was a life-time. The years at home with his mother and brothers and sisters, the years with the saw and the plane, they all seemed so far away. He supposed that life was going on at home much as before. His return to visit his village and his family had not been a success, for him or for them.

Now he had a new family. His twelve disciples were now closer to him than any of his blood relations. In a short a time they had experienced so much together. These men had stuck with him in spite of their incomprehension, in spite of the rejection from the Pharisees and some of the synagogue rulers, in spite of the hardship of being wanderers, separated from their families and friends. What had he done in calling these twelve men away from their homes and their livelihoods, into a future that was unknown both to them and to him?

"Father, only you could have made these men sacrifice so much for the sake of your kingdom, and kept them with me for so long."

Now, there was only one way forward. The excitement of the days in Galilee, the wonder of the miracles, the joy of seeing men and women healed and set free, the signs of faith in those who had heard him and responded to his message – all those seeds that had been sown by him, and by the twelve when they had gone out on their own, they would all yield a harvest one day – but there was no going back to those early days.

People had had a chance to decide. Were they for him or against him? Some had clearly decided for him, not only the twelve but many others. But equally clearly, others had decided against him, and, strange as it might seem since he had never done anyone any harm, those who had rejected him and his message were not going to let him go on preaching and teaching much longer.

From the beginning, he could sense that the Pharisees were uncomfortable with him, and they had a strong influence on what the common people thought. In everyone's minds, the Pharisees represented pure Judaism, the faith of their fathers and their nation. Jesus had not set out to contradict them, to pick an argument or a fight with them, but he could see that their interpretation of the Law and the way that they were leading the people by their teaching and

THE WILDERNESS AGAIN

example was a blind alley. The blind leading the blind.

His heart ached for the poor, the sick, the despised, the 'sinners' - all those whom the Pharisees regarded as showing in their lives the signs of God's displeasure, knowing in his heart that it was the judgemental and hypocritical Pharisees for whom his Father felt the real displeasure.

It had been the same when he had come to Jerusalem. The priests and the rulers of the people had not been pleased with him. He had upset more than the tables of the money changers. He had upset their sense of being in control.

The temple, and its sacred round of feasts and sacrifices, the observances prescribed by the Law of Moses, were what preserved them and preserved the people from the wrath of God. And who was he, Jesus? Who was he indeed? That was the whole question.

He knew in his own heart who he was. He had suspected it from childhood; he had known it for sure from the day that he was baptised in the river Jordan and the Spirit had come upon him and the voice of God had spoken to him.

"You are my Son, in you I am well pleased."

But how were these priests and Sadducees supposed to know that? To them, he was an upstart from Galilee, and Galilee had produced other dangerous upstarts like him before. He was not one of them, not related to the old ruling families in Jerusalem.

He was not of the clan of Levi that supplied priests and Levites for the worship of the temple. He was not a rabbi who had come up through the schools of Jerusalem and sat at the feet of his elders and betters. He knew that he was descended from David, from the tribe of Judah, but he had grown up in Galilee, not in Bethlehem where David's clan still lived. Again, only his Father could open their eyes to see who he really was.

It was not that people had no way of discerning the truth. John had testified to him: "Behold, the Lamb of God who takes away the sin of the world." The mighty works that he had done, healing the sick, raising the dead: they had heard of these things even if they had not witnessed them for themselves.

Without God, no human being could do the things that he had done. The works themselves were signs of who he was: God his Father testifying to him as his Son.

Above all they had the scriptures; Moses and the prophets and the Psalms. These spoke about him on almost every page. To him, it was almost as if the whole of the scriptures spoke about him, about God's future purpose for his fallen world; a purpose that would be fulfilled in the fullness of time through a man of God's own choice. It was all

THE WILDERNESS AGAIN

there, if only they had eyes to see and ears to hear.

But of course, these very scriptures revealed that it was not going to be like that. The Messiah must suffer before entering into his glory. That was what he must now face.

He could see that the time appointed must be the feast of the Passover. He was to be the Passover Lamb, whose blood would protect his people when the destroying angel passed over. Those who put their trust in him and in his blood would be passed over and spared from destruction. His sacrifice of himself would stand between God and sinners, a propitiation for their sins.

The old regime, the blood of bulls and goats, was only a sign. A shadow of the things to come. A shadow that would fade away when the full light of day dawned.

In truth, these sacrifices offered year after year could never make those who offered them perfect. They were merely a yearly reminder of sin. His oblation of himself, once offered, would be a full, perfect and sufficient sacrifice for the sins of the whole world. The old sacrificial system would be obsolete. Something greater was here.

He had shrunk from the words of the prophet Isaiah when he had heard them in the synagogue school and had learned them as a child:

'He is despised and rejected of men; a man of sorrows and acquainted with grief: and we hid as it were our faces from him; he was despised and we esteemed him not. Surely he hath borne our griefs, and carried our sorrows: yet we did esteem him stricken, smitten of God and afflicted. But he was wounded for our transgressions, he was bruised for our iniquities: the chastisement of our peace was upon him and with his stripes we are healed. All we like sheep have gone astray; we have turned every one to his own way: and the LORD hath laid on him the iniquity of us all.'

Even then he had realised that it was the calling of the servant of God to suffer, and in some way to be a substitute for the sinful world. It was not a shock to realise again that this was his destiny, but now that it drew near he still shrank from the reality of it.

He had never really known pain. He had fallen over as a child; grazes and bruises were a child's lot. He had hit his thumb with the mallet; that was the carpenter's lot. But it was not real agonising pain. No-one would volunteer for that, and he was not volunteering for it now, but he knew that it was the path that he must take. He remembered the words of the psalm:

THE WILDERNESS AGAIN

'Sacrifice and meat offering thou wouldest not; but mine ears hast thou opened. Burnt offerings and sacrifice for sin hast thou not required; then said I, lo, I come, in the scroll of the book it is written of me that I should fulfil thy will, O my God: I am content to do it; yea, thy law is within my heart.'

Yes, he was content to do it. It was written of him in the scroll of the book and he had come to fulfil the perfect will of God.

As he heard the scriptures, read in the synagogue Sabbath by Sabbath, as he recited in his own mind so many of those scriptures engraved on his memory from childhood, so he had always felt that those scriptures were speaking directly about, and even, to him, that he and the prophets of old were somehow contemporaries of each other.

So often, and so clearly, did the ancient scriptures speak of him and of his destiny, that Jesus had had the uncanny feeling that he had always existed, that those who had written and prophesied about him had actually seen him.

And what then? After that sacrificial death? Would God, his heavenly Father, leave his soul in Hades, or his body in the grave? The psalms came to his mind again.

'I have set God always before me, for he is on my right hand, therefore I shall not fall. Wherefore my heart was glad and my glory rejoiced: my flesh also shall rest in hope. For why? Thou shalt not leave my soul in hell; neither shalt thou suffer thy Holy One to see corruption. Thou shalt show me the path of life; in thy presence is the fullness of joy: And at thy right hand there is pleasure for evermore.'

Had not the prophet Hosea also said:

'Come and let us return unto the LORD: for he hath torn and he will heal us; he hath smitten and he will bind us up. After two days will he revive us: in the third day he will raise us up, and we shall live in his sight.'

There were so many scriptures that came flooding into his mind. God's promises of old, promises of everlasting, faithful love, that spoke directly into Jesus' heart as he pondered these things in the desert place, and they gave him peace.

twenty-five

DEDICATION

After all the activity and drama of the last few years, it was a curiously dead time: a time of inactivity. It was like the time after the sowing, when the farmer waits for the grain to ripen before he can put in the sickle, or the time after the kneading when the housewife waits for the bread to rise. The sower and the baker have done all that they can, and then they must wait patiently until the time is right.

Jesus used this time to think and pray, often by himself. With his permission, the apostles took the opportunity to go home, spend some time with their families, and attend to their businesses. Meanwhile, Jesus stayed with his friend from the days of John's baptisms in the Jordan valley.

A few people, hearing where Jesus was staying, sought him out, and as always he healed the sick and taught them wisdom. But gone were the crowded market places and hillsides of Galilee. It was as if, not only Jesus, but the world was waiting to see what the outcome of all this would be.

Back in Galilee, the neighbours were a little surprised to see Peter and Andrew, James and

John and the others apparently taking up the threads of their old lives, living with their families and fishing again in the same old way.

"Not going out with that Jesus any more?" some of them asked. "Come to think of it, we haven't seen him around at all. What's he doing now?"

"He's staying down in Judea for the time being," Peter would reply. "We've come home for a few weeks, but we'll be going up to Jerusalem again for the Passover in the spring. We've arranged to meet up with Jesus again then. You just wait for Passover. That's when things will happen."

They would let the conversation go at that, leaving their neighbours mystified about what they meant. Indeed, the disciples themselves were not sure, but all had the same feeling that their whole adventure with Jesus was going to come to a climax in the spring.

The year drew on and the winter festival of Hanukkah, the dedication of the temple, approached. It was time for Jesus to make another visit to Jerusalem. Moses too had needed to go back to Pharoah many times to call him to obedience, to recognise the sovereignty of God, before the final dénouement of the Passover.

There would not be the crowds in Jerusalem for Hanukkah that there were for the other great festivals. It was not one of the pilgrim feasts commanded in the Law of Moses, merely a

DEDICATION

commemoration of the rededication of the temple after the wars of the Maccabees.

Falling, as it did, in midwinter, it was not a time of year for travelling long distances, even from Galilee, far less from overseas. The climate in the Jordan valley was temperate all the year round, but the highlands of Judea could be cold, even snowy. Hanukkah was celebrated less in the temple and more in the home, where the children enjoyed the lighting of the candles. There would not be the tension in Jerusalem that accompanied the other feasts.

For Passover and the Feast of Unleavened Bread, for Pentecost, for the Day of Atonement and the Feast of Tabernacles, there were always great crowds and always tension in the air. If there were to be riots or uprisings they were sure to happen at such festival times, when religious zeal was running high and the streets and market places were thronged with people.

Zealot cells were infiltrated by Roman spies, paid to report on plots that might be brewing that they might be nipped in the bud. Nevertheless, the smallest provocation could set off a riot and the Romans and the rulers of the Jews were constantly on guard, until the feasts were over.

Everyone understood the politics of Jerusalem; the delicate balancing act that the various powers had to perform in order to preserve the status quo. The Romans were content to stay out of the way, provided there was no threat to public order or to their ultimate authority.

The Jews, they knew, had to be handled with great care, especially in anything to do with their temple or their religion, but if these sensibilities were not offended the Jewish rulers could be left to govern their own people and administer their own peculiar laws. But there were tensions between different parties even amongst the Jews.

The ruling body of the Jews, the Sanhedrin, was presided over by the high priest, who was always chosen from one of the old, aristocratic, families in Jerusalem. They claimed to be descended from Zadok, David and Solomon's high priest, and so were known as the Sadducees. They had ruled Jerusalem, more or less continuously since the return from Exile in Babylon. They were rich, and influential in every aspect of the city's life. But a majority of the Sanhedrin were scribes and Pharisees, experts in the Law of Moses, the spiritual guides and guardians of the faith of Israel.

The interests and concerns of the Pharisees and Sadducees did not always coincide. The Sadducees were primarily interested in power, the Pharisees in purity. Both, of course, believed that they had the best interests of the nation at heart, but their understanding of those best interests often differed.

DEDICATION

Jesus knew that he was unpopular with both groups. He had offended the Sadducees by clearing the temple of the money changers and the traders at the Passover two years ago. If they perceived his preaching of the kingdom of God, or even thought that others perceived his preaching of the kingdom of God, as an incitement to rebellion against themselves or the Romans, then they would certainly try to dispose of him.

He knew also that the Pharisees saw him as a threat to their interpretation or understanding of the Law and of Israel's covenant relationship to God. They saw him as a threat to the integrity and the future of the nation. So, he could not expect any support or sympathy from either party.

There were those in both camps, Jesus had seen, who were in fact stirred by his message and impressed by his miracles. No doubt there were some who were closet believers in him, but not enough to sway the body of the Sanhedrin.

As for the crowds, people would be as divided as they had been in the towns and villages of Galilee, some for him, some against him, and many simply indifferent, wanting to get on with their lives without being bothered. As for the permanent residents of Jerusalem, more than the pilgrims from Galilee, they would be swayed by their rulers.

Jesus could see that the odds were stacked against him in terms of the complicated politics of his nation. In spite of which, he had to go on proclaiming the kingdom of the God who had sent him, and calling men and women of all sorts and of all stations in life to trust and obey his and his Father's words. It was not to worldly success or power that his Father had called him, but to love and faithfulness.

For the Feast of the Dedication, Jesus stayed again with his friends in Bethany, and went up day by day to the temple to preach and to teach.

"You have heard the words of the prophet Isaiah:

'O thou that bringest good tidings to Zion, get thee up into the high mountain; O thou that bringest good tidings to Jerusalem, lift up thy voice with strength, lift it up, be not afraid, say unto the cities of Judah, 'Behold your God!' Behold, the Lord God will come with a strong hand, and his arm shall rule for him: behold his reward is with him, and his work before him. He shall feed his flock like a shepherd, he shall gather the lambs with his arm, and carry them in his bosom, and shall gently lead those that are with young.'

"Now, there are all sorts of shepherds. Good shepherds and bad shepherds, shepherds who feed the flock and shepherds who fleece the flock. The prophet Ezekiel reproached the shepherds of Israel saying,

'Woe to the shepherds of Israel, that do feed themselves! Should not the shepherds feed the

DEDICATION

flocks? Ye eat the fat, and ye clothe you with the wool, ye kill them that are fed: but ye feed not the flock. Behold, I, even I, will both search my sheep and seek them out. As a shepherd seeketh out his flock in the day that he is among his sheep that are scattered, so will I seek out my sheep, and will deliver them out of all the places where they have been scattered in the cloudy and dark day.'

"I am the good shepherd. I know my sheep and my sheep know me. My sheep recognise my voice. I call my sheep by name and they follow me. They won't follow a stranger; they'll run away from a stranger because they don't recognise his voice. But my sheep recognise my voice and follow me.

"I tell you, I am the good shepherd. I'm not like the hired hand. If a hired hand sees the wolf coming, he leaves the flock and runs away. He runs away because he's only a hired hand and doesn't own the sheep. I am the good shepherd. I lay down my life for the sheep, because they are mine.

"While the sheep are in the fold at night, they are safe. When the shepherd comes for them in the morning, the watchman opens the gate and the shepherd calls out the names of his own sheep.

"Anyone who climbs into the sheepfold and tries to get the sheep out any other way is a thief and a robber. The man who enters by the gate is the shepherd. All those who came before me were thieves and robbers. I am the gate as well as the shepherd, whoever enters through me will be safe. He'll come in and go out and find pasture. The thief comes only to steal and kill and destroy. I have come that they might have life, and have it more abundantly.

"I have other sheep as well, who are not in this fold. I must call them too, and they too will listen to my voice. Then there will be one flock with one shepherd.

"The reason that my Father loves me is that I'm prepared to lay down my life for the sheep. No-one will take my life away from me, but I will lay it down of my own accord."

At this point Jesus stopped. His listeners began to talk amongst themselves and disagreed with one another. Some of them were saying, "He's raving mad. Why listen to him any more?" Others were saying, "He doesn't sound like a madman to me – nor like someone possessed by a demon, for that matter."

One of the Pharisees spoke up.

"How long are you going to keep us in suspense? If you're the Messiah, tell us plainly."

Jesus answered, "I've told you, plainly enough. The trouble is you don't believe me. The miracles I've done surely speak for me. But you don't believe me because you are not my sheep. My sheep recognise my voice. They know me and

DEDICATION

follow me. I will give them everlasting life; they will never perish. No-one can snatch them out of my hand. My Father has given them to me, and he's greater than anyone or anything. No-one can snatch them out of my Father's hand. I and my Father are one."

At this, some of the hearers picked up stones again, and threatened to stone him.

"I have done many miracles from my Father. For which of these are you trying to stone me?" Jesus asked.

"We're not going to stone you for any miracle, but because you, a mortal man like us, are making yourself equal with God."

They tried to seize him, but as in Nazareth before, Jesus calmly walked through the midst of them and made his way out of the temple.

His time had not yet come.

twenty-six

JERICHO

The first fingernail of the new moon had appeared, signalling the beginning of the first month of the temple year. The winter was over; the late rains were coming to an end; spring had come. Nature was astir. The fruit trees and the vines were blossoming; the fields were full of the colours of wild flowers; the birds were singing.

Jewish families all over the land were stirring themselves, making preparations for the journey to Jerusalem, for the celebration of the Passover and the Feast of Unleavened Bread. Over the first few days of the new month, Jesus' disciples rejoined him in the Jordan valley with news of their families, many of whom would also be coming up to Jerusalem for the festival.

As they were assembling together, a message arrived from Jesus' friends in Bethany. Someone had been sent to look for him, to tell him that Lazarus was ill, and, knowing that Jesus would be coming to the feast, to ask him to come quickly.

"Thank you for letting me know," Jesus answered, "aye, I'll come."

But when the messenger had gone, he said to his disciples, "It is too soon to go now. We'll go in a

JERICHO

few days. We have to get the time right before we arrive in Jerusalem. This illness of Lazarus' won't end in death – it will end in everyone seeing the glory of God. But we need to stay here another couple of days."

When Jesus sensed that the time was ripe, he told his disciples that they were ready to leave for Jerusalem.

"I suppose you know what you're doing," Thomas said. "The last time we were there they weren't particularly pleased to see us."

"Our friend Lazarus has fallen asleep, and you heard me say that I'd go to Bethany. Now it's time to go. I've got to go and wake Lazarus up."

"Surely, he'll wake up by himself, if he's fallen asleep?" Thomas continued.

"No, I mean Lazarus is dead," Jesus replied. "I'm going to raise him from the dead, like you've seen other people raised from the dead - by the power of God. You'll see. It will help the world believe."

So they set off. The road wound along the floor of the valley beside the Jordan as far as Jericho. There it turned inland, and headed up into the hills of Judea, high amongst which stood Jerusalem.

Towards midday on the first day of their journey they came to the ancient city of Jericho. Some people said that Jericho was the oldest city on earth. Certainly, near the present city stood the ruins of several previous cities, including the one around which Joshua had marched when the Israelites came out of Egypt, the one whose walls had fallen down at the blast of the trumpet. City had been built upon city, each one built on the ruins of the last, the mound getting higher and higher, until Herod the Great had abandoned the old city altogether and started to build a new one two miles further down the valley.

Jesus and his disciples halted in the new city to eat and to rest. Word spread that the prophet Jesus of Nazareth was passing through Jericho. By the time that Jesus was ready to resume his journey, a crowd had gathered outside the inn and, as Jesus left, people were waiting for him. As he made his way slowly through the streets, he caught sight of a man who had climbed a tree and was holding on to a branch, straining to see him above the crowd. Jesus stopped under the tree.

"Who are you?" he asked.

"My name is Zacchaeus," the man replied, somewhat nervously and somewhat sheepishly from up his tree. He obviously felt foolish and undignified. "I wanted to see you."

"Come on down then, and you shall," Jesus answered.

The man climbed down and, on the ground, Jesus could see why he had had to climb the tree. He really was extraordinarily short. Jesus restrained himself from laughing at the little man, but said, "Right, Zacchaeus, I'm coming to

JERICHO

stay at your house tonight - if you will have me, me and my friends."

"By all means, master," Zacchaeus replied. "It will be an honour. We've plenty of room. I've a big house."

At this, there was a murmuring from the crowd around them.

"You bet he does."

"Built out of our money."

"He's the head tax collector here."

"That's fine," said Jesus, looking round him. "Some of my best friends are tax collectors, like Matthew here. So, come on my new friend, lead the way to this big house of yours."

When they arrived, the wife of Zacchaeus and his servants bustled around to make preparations for Jesus and his disciples to stay. Later that evening, while the meal was in progress, Zacchaeus stood up.

"I want to make a speech," he said. "Yes, I am a tax collector, and no, I haven't always been honest. I've used my position to collect more than I should've done. But tonight, I want to say, to you Jesus, and to all my neighbours, that I'm going to give half my possessions to the poor, and if I've cheated anyone I'm willing to pay them back four times over."

There was a burst of spontaneous applause from the disciples and the other guests, while the servants and, not least, Zacchaeus' wife, looked stunned and somewhat alarmed.

Jesus said, "Truly salvation has come to this house today. The Son of Man came to seek and to save what was lost. I promise you, Zacchaeus, you will never regret what you have done today. This is the beginning of a new life for you and all your household. Don't worry about the future. Seek first the kingdom of God and his righteousness and all these things will be yours as well. God is no man's debtor."

The next day, news of Jesus' encounter with the tax collector had spread through the town and an even larger crowd gathered to see Jesus as he went on his way. As they were leaving the town, a blind man was sitting by the roadside begging from the passers by. Hearing a large crowd approaching, he asked what it meant.

"Jesus of Nazareth is passing by," they told him.

So he began to shout out, "Jesus, Son of David, have mercy on me. Jesus, Son of David, have mercy on me."

People told him to be quiet, but he only shouted louder, "Jesus, Son of David, have mercy on me."

Jesus stopped.

"What do you know about me, then?"

"I know you healed a man born blind up in Jerusalem, and I know that you're the one who is to come, the Messiah, the Son of David."

JERICHO

"Bless you, my friend. Flesh and blood did not reveal this to you, but my Father in heaven. So, what do you want me to do for you?" Jesus asked.

"Master, I want to see."

Jesus merely said to him, "Then, see. Your faith has saved you."

The man rubbed at his blind eyes, blinked several times in disbelief, then began to look around him in wonder. The crowd stood still, looking at him as he continued sitting on the ground, turning his head slowly from side to side as if to see as much as he could.

His eyes were not so much open, as out on stalks. No-one could quite take in what it must mean for this man, to see the world and the faces of his neighbours for the first time. Then, an excited cheer broke out from the crowd, and everyone started whooping and shouting for joy as if they had all just received their sight for the first time.

They hauled the beggar to his feet, and as Jesus and his companions continued on their way up to Jerusalem, the crowd escorted the blind man back into the city and began telling the whole town what Jesus had done.

As they climbed the steep hill out of the Jordan valley, Jesus began to tell his disciples again what was to come.

"We are going up to Jerusalem and everything written about me in the prophets is going to be fulfilled. I shall be handed over to the Gentiles, mocked, insulted, spat on, flogged and killed. But on the third day, as the prophet Hosea foretold, I shall rise again."

The disciples were silent. No longer did anyone rebuke or contradict Jesus, least of all Peter. They had realised that Jesus was indeed unpopular with the leaders of the people. They did not understand why they were going up to Jerusalem, if this is what awaited Jesus there, but they were still too afraid to ask. They certainly did not understand what he meant about rising from the dead. But again, they were too afraid to ask.

It was all too mysterious and incomprehensible, so they remained silent, simply knowing that now there was no turning back. Wherever this road was leading they had to follow it to the end.

As they walked on in silence, each one was reflecting on what it was that had brought them to this point. Why had they left home and family, their daily work and all that was familiar, to follow this man Jesus?

They had never known where they were going, but simply followed, trusting that Jesus knew. They could hardly say why they had done it, but he had given them hope. He had opened their eyes to the possibility of something beyond the life that they knew. They had seen amazing things, the blind receiving their sight, the lame walking, the dead being raised, things they scarcely understood

JERICHO

but which were real. Above all, they knew that they were loved by him, and that they loved him.

As they drew near to Bethany, on the slopes of the Mount of Olives, they saw a woman coming towards them. She walked slowly and sadly, her eyes fixed on Jesus. As she drew near, they saw that it was Martha, the sister of Lazarus. She greeted Jesus with a kiss.

"Master," she said, "if you had been here he wouldn't have died." And she burst into tears.

Jesus took her in his arms and comforted her.

"Your brother will rise again," he said.

She choked back her sobs.

"Yes, I know he'll rise again at the resurrection on the last day. I do believe that, but it's hard to bear it now."

"No, I mean, he'll rise again now. I *am* the resurrection you believe in. I give life now to whoever the Father wills, and I will give it to everyone who believes in me at the last day. Whoever believes in me will live, even though he dies now, and whoever lives and believes in me will not die eternally. Do you believe that?"

"Yes, master," Martha replied, "I do believe that you're the Messiah, the Son of God who has come into the world."

"Go back and fetch Mary, while I wait here," Jesus told her.

So, Martha went back to the house and told Mary quietly, "The rabbi is here, and he's asking for you."

Mary got up quickly and went out to where Jesus was waiting. The neighbours and friends from the city, who had come out to comfort the sisters, saw Mary go and followed her, supposing that she had gone to weep at the tomb.

When Jesus met her and saw her tear-stained face, he said to her, "Where have you laid him?"

"Come and see," Mary said.

twenty-seven

ARRIVAL

As they went, Jesus was overwhelmed by the pain and the sorrow of human loss. He remembered the death of his own father a few years before: the death of a man full of years, but nevertheless a death which left a hole in his own heart, a place where all his life his earthly father had been. An emptiness that he had felt in the pit of his stomach which had caused him at the time to howl with grief.

This pain and sorrow was being repeated over and over again, as men and women suffered the death of those they loved, brothers, sisters, husbands, wives, children, friends. Death was the last enemy, but also the most powerful. One that no-one could escape. Death came in many disguises. Sickness, famine, the endless and senseless cycle of war and violence. Poor, suffering, dying humanity!

Jesus' own heart was overwhelmed with grief, not only for Mary and Martha here and now, but for the whole human race in its bondage to sin and death. And Jesus wept again, with them.

By the time that they reached the tomb of Lazarus, everyone was weeping. Mary led the way to the grave, which was on the outskirts of the village. It was a small cave, hollowed out of the rock, with a stone rolled over the mouth. They stopped before the tomb, in silence, except for the sounds of the people quietly sobbing.

"Move the stone away," commanded Jesus.

"But, master, there'll be a frightful smell," Martha replied. "He's been in there for four days now."

"Nevertheless, do as I say."

So a small group of men came forward and rolled the stone back from the entrance to the tomb. Oddly, there was no smell. Jesus knelt, lifted his hands, and prayed aloud.

"Father, I ask you to hear me. I know that you always hear me, but I ask this now so that these people may believe that I'm your only Son. Father, glorify your name."

Then Jesus stood up and called into the tomb with a loud voice, "Lazarus, come out."

Everyone waited in silence.

After a few moments, a figure appeared in the entrance to the cave. A man's figure, but bound in white linen, body, arms and legs, hands and feet, with a cloth over his head.

"Take off the grave clothes," commanded Jesus.

They took the cloth off his head to reveal a smiling and healthy face. Lazarus beamed around at the marvelling crowd and kissed his two sisters

ARRIVAL

awkwardly on the cheek. Then they took the bandages off his hands and his feet, and with his body still covered by the shroud for decency's sake, the dead man walked slowly home, his sisters hanging one on each arm, pressing his flesh to make sure he was real, too full to talk, and the former mourners following behind in an awestruck procession.

Jesus remained by the tomb with his disciples.

"You go too," he said to them. "I'll join you at the house in Bethany as soon as I've attended to a little business in Bethphage."

Jesus went on up into the village of Bethphage and spent a few minutes in conversation with a man who hired out donkeys. Then he also returned to Bethany to the house of Mary and Martha.

Lazarus was now dressed in his own clothes, indeed in his best festal garment, as befitted a man who had just risen from the dead! He came forward, hugged Jesus, and held him in his arms for a long time.

No words could express what he felt or what was in his heart. He might be able to talk of it one day, but not yet, and not at least until he had had days, or weeks, or even years to reflect on what had happened to him.

Martha and some of the neighbours were already busy in the kitchen, while Mary had gone to the market to buy extra food for a banquet that they were preparing as a great celebration for the evening.

During the evening meal, Mary went and fetched a jar of perfume. It was pure nard from India, extremely precious. It had been her mother's before her. She would only use a few drops at a time when she wanted to smell especially nice, a dab here and a dab there, behind the ears and on the wrists. Now she fetched the jar and, coming to Jesus as he reclined at the table, she leaned over him and poured the whole jar of perfume over his head and over his feet.

Everyone stopped eating and smiled at the couple. Jesus looking at Mary as she emptied the jar over his feet, and she looking at him with love and gratitude and worship in her eyes. The fragrance of the perfume filled the whole room and wafted right through the house and out into the street.

After a moment of silence, while everyone was overawed by the extravagance of Mary's gesture, Judas, one of Jesus' disciples protested.

"Master, I know she's done it out of love, but this perfume could have been sold for a lot of money and the money given to the poor. It seems to me that would've been a better use for it."

"Pipe down, Judas," James replied. "This isn't the time for that."

"No, leave her alone," Jesus agreed. "What she's done is something beautiful. You always have the

ARRIVAL

poor with you and you can do good to them whenever you want, but you won't always have me. Mary's done this now, while she can. Wherever stories about me are told in future, this story about what Mary's done will be told as well, in memory of her. And then, you'll see the point of it."

After this gnomic remark, the conversation around the table resumed as before, until late into the night when the guests went home and the household retired to bed, still wondering at the remarkable things that had happened that day.

The following day was the Sabbath, and everyone rested according to the Law. Jerusalem and its surrounding countryside was already filling up with pilgrims from Judea and Galilee, and some from other parts of the Jewish dispersion around the world, people who had made long journeys by land and sea to keep the Passover in the city.

For many there were rites and ceremonies of preparation to be undergone before they could keep the feast, especially for those who were unclean because their lives or their work brought them into contact with the Gentiles. Others had sacrifices to offer for cleansing from sin or illness or contact with the dead.

Already the holiday atmosphere was in the air. Many families were reuniting, meeting up with cousins and relatives only seen at festivals. News was being exchanged, and not least news about the prophet Jesus from Nazareth.

Early on the morning of the first day of the new week, Jesus announced that he would be going up to Jerusalem. Word quickly spread round Bethany and a crowd was gathering in the street outside the house of Lazarus by the time that Jesus and his apostles were ready to set out.

Jesus said to Thomas and Matthew, "I want you to go on ahead to Bethphage. Go into the village and you will find a house with some donkeys tied up outside. There is one there with her colt, a pretty little thing that hasn't been ridden before. Untie them and bring them to me. And if anyone asks you, 'What are you doing untying that donkey?' say to them, 'The master has need of them,' and they will let you go."

The disciples went and found the donkeys as Jesus had said, untied them and brought them back. Meanwhile, Jesus and the crowd from Bethany had set out and were approaching up the road.

Other people, who had overheard the conversation in Bethphage, were also coming out of the village to see what was going to happen. As they met, Thomas and Matthew took off their cloaks and laid them on the colt and Jesus mounted.

As always, when a man rides a donkey, his head was hardly above the heads of the crowd and his

ARRIVAL

feet were nearly touching the ground. But into everyone's mind came the words from the prophet Zechariah – one of the prophecies which they had all known from childhood:

> 'Rejoice greatly, O daughter of Zion; shout, O daughter of Jerusalem: behold, thy king cometh unto thee: he is just and having salvation; lowly and riding upon an ass, and upon a colt the foal of an ass.'

Wild excitement broke out among the crowd. Immediately, they began to pull branches down from the palm trees and wave them, and to raise the liturgical shout.

"Hosanna to the Son of David. Blessed is he who comes in the name of the LORD. Hosanna in the highest!"

As the procession wound up the hill, it grew. People along the way asked, "What's all this about?" and people in the crowd answered, "This is Jesus the Messiah, the man who opened the eyes of blind Bartimaeus in Jericho and raised Lazarus from the dead."

As they came to the crest of the hill, the great panorama of Jerusalem opened up before them. The steep slopes of the Kidron valley descending in front of them, then rising again to the gates and walls of the city, and standing on the mount opposite them, the gleaming buildings of the temple.

At the summit, Jesus stopped and the crowd fell silent. They all regarded the magnificent view laid out in front of them, but tears were filling Jesus' eyes.

"O Jerusalem. Jerusalem," he cried, "if only you knew the things that belong to your peace. But they are hidden from you. Generation after generation, you have killed the prophets and those God has sent to you.

"The days are coming when your enemies will throw up an embankment around you and hem you in on every side. They will dash you to the ground, you and your children within you, because you did not recognise the day of your visitation."

As they began the descent from the Mount of Olives, the crowd broke out again into great shouts of praise and thanksgiving to God. By the time they entered the gates of Jerusalem, the procession stretched right back across the Kidron valley. Men, women and children shouting and cheering.

Some people ran past Jesus to lay their cloaks on the road as they made their way through the streets. The inhabitants of the city came to their doors and windows to see what was happening.

"Who's this?" they asked, and the crowd replied, "This is Jesus the prophet from Nazareth." But some of the Pharisees, who stood by watching,

ARRIVAL

heard the children running along beside Jesus and shouting like their parents, "Hosanna to the Son of David!"

Two of the Pharisees walked up to the colt on which Jesus sat and rebuked him.

"Tell your followers to stop that."

But Jesus only replied, "If they keep quiet, the very stones will cry out."

Stopping at the foot of the steps that led up into the temple precincts, Jesus dismounted and gave the colt back to the two disciples to be returned to Bethphage. He and the other ten, still followed by a great crowd, went up into the outer court.

Sure enough, there were the sellers of cattle and sheep, and the money changers back in the great open space that was reserved for the Gentiles. Once again their eyes met and the traders could see that they were about to be driven out once again. They could also see that, such was the crowd of chanting supporters around Jesus, there was nothing that they, or even the temple guards, could do to prevent it.

So, as hastily as possible they gathered up their animals and their money, as Jesus went from stall to stall and table to table, ordering them to be gone. At last, the precincts were clear, except for the debris left behind by the fleeing traders and their flocks. Jesus was left face-to-face with a group of furious priests and rabbis.

"By what authority are you doing this?" they demanded.

"I'll ask you a question, too," Jesus replied. "If you answer me, I'll tell you by what authority I am doing this. John's baptism: was that from heaven or from men?"

The priests looked at the rabbis and the rabbis looked at each other. You could see what was going on in their minds. If they said from heaven, Jesus would make the same claim. If they said, from men, the crowd would howl them down, for the people all held John in high esteem.

So, after a few moments, they said, "We don't know."

"Neither will I, then, tell you by what I authority I am doing these things."

Jesus turned and made his way through the crowd that parted to let him pass. The apostles followed him. There was a sense of anticlimax after the euphoria of the procession up to the temple, but after a few minutes the crowd dispersed to go about their business.

Jesus, meanwhile, dismissed the apostles, telling them to make their own way back to Bethany while he made arrangements for the Passover meal in a few days time.

twenty-eight

SUNDAY EVENING

On the road back to Bethany the disciples were discussing the events of the morning. Most of them were jubilant and relieved.

"He's much too pessimistic about the support he's got," Andrew asserted. "Look at the crowds. It's only a few miserable Pharisees who don't love him."

But Judas Iscariot was angry.

"You're right, Andrew, but he's blown it. That was it, don't you see? That was the moment to really get things moving, make an impact in the city. With that crowd and us around him we could've taken over the temple courts, even the city, driven out the Saducees, and confronted the Romans. 'Go home and leave us alone! We don't want to fight you, but we don't want you here either!'

"Jesus could've proclaimed himself the new king of Israel, here in the city. Everyone would have rallied round him. It's what they're all waiting for."

"Dream on, Judas," said Philip, "it isn't going to happen."

"So what, then?" Judas persisted. "Where do we go from here? He's let the moment slip. What was all that about, if it wasn't Jesus making his bid for the kingship? And I'm with him all the way, whatever you lot want him to do."

"We all believe he's the new king of Israel," interrupted Peter, "but surely you can see his kingdom isn't going to come like that. When has he ever looked like starting a revolution, or provoking that sort of confrontation with the Romans, or with anyone else?"

"How's his kingdom going to come then?" Judas continued. "I don't know any other way, do you?"

"I've no idea how the kingdom's going to come," added Peter, "but I suppose he does. He confronts people with words and with his miracles and his authority, like he's just done in the temple. Then, people have to make up their own minds about him. That's all he ever does, isn't it. That's all he's ever done."

"And a lot of good that does."

"But it does," persisted John. "You said it yourself, look at the crowds. It's working. More and more people are coming to love him and believe in him. That's how the kingdom will come, not with swords and spears. That's only more of the same. This is different. It's a kingdom of love and peace, and it's working."

"I agree with Andrew," added Nathanael, "Jesus is too pessimistic. All this talk of his about

SUNDAY EVENING

suffering and dying! He takes the opposition too much to heart. They love him. They won't let him die. Neither will we, will we?"

They all agreed that they would all stand by him whatever happened.

"But even still," Judas persisted, "it's got to go further than that. I agree, more and more people are listening to him and believing in him, but if there's never any action, everything'll stay the same as it always was. Mark my words, nothing'll change.

"Maybe I know the world better than you lot do. Whatever happens next, Jesus is not going to last forever, and when he's gone the world'll go on just as it was before, unless we take action. You'll never change the world without action, neither will he. Isn't that right Simon?" Judas appealed to Simon, whose previous Zealot sympathies were well known amongst the twelve.

"Well, I used to think that," Simon replied, "but now I wonder if this isn't a better way. I'm for giving it a go, anyhow. I don't know how this is all going to work out, any more than the rest of you. But we've trusted him so far. I'm for trusting him to the end. I still think he knows what he's doing, even if we don't."

"Hmmph," was Judas' only reply, and he stopped talking and stumped on down the road in front of them, looking defeated and black.

Later in the day, Jesus returned to the house in Bethany and they spent a quiet evening with their friends and neighbours in the village. It was again dark when there was a knock on the door and, as a couple of years before, the late night visitor was the Pharisee Nicodemus.

"Can I come in?" he enquired of Lazarus.

"By all means."

Lazarus opened the door wide and led Nicodemus into the room, where the oil lamps burnt on the low table amongst the remains of the meal. Jesus rose and greeted Nicodemus like a long lost friend.

"What brings you here again tonight?" he asked.

"I've just come from a meeting of the Sanhedrin. You know I'm on the council. There was a hurriedly called meeting this afternoon." Nicodemus paused. "It was called to discuss what to do about you."

"Go on," Jesus replied.

"Your entry into Jerusalem this morning has really got them worried and, I must say, I was wondering what you meant by it myself, when I heard about it at midday. But they think that you mean to make some sort of bid for power, lead an uprising, a rebellion against Rome, or against them, or both. That's what it looked like this morning, didn't it?"

SUNDAY EVENING

"Did it?" asked Jesus. "It's a mystery, isn't it, even in the prophecy: a king riding in on a donkey. It doesn't happen, does it. Kings ride in on chariots or war-horses. Does Pontius Pilate come riding into Jerusalem on a donkey? He'd be laughed out of town, with his feet touching the ground like a peasant.

"The prophecy was supposed to make you think: this is the king you've longed for, but not the sort of king you thought you wanted. And you know how the prophecy goes on: 'And I will cut off the chariot from Ephraim, and the horse from Jerusalem, and the battle bow shall be cut off.'

"I couldn't say it more plainly, could I? Aye, I come as a king, the king of the coming kingdom of God, but no, I'm not the sort of worldly king that some are expecting."

"Maybe *I* get it," Nicodemus replied doubtfully, "and maybe you do. But they don't. I mean the chief priests, and the members of the council. They just see the crowds and the cheering and the excitement. And I'll tell you another thing. A couple of days ago, there *was* an incident over the other side of the city. Nothing serious, but enough to make the Romans nervous.

"Some group of hotheads ambushed a Roman patrol in a narrow street and butchered them all. The assassins escaped, but the Romans will find them. They've got spies everywhere. It just makes everyone even more jumpy than usual. Now they're afraid that your demonstration this morning is the beginning of something more serious. At this time of year, you know, there are always people around who are looking for some excuse to stir up trouble."

"I grant you, there are some who are." Jesus replied. 'Some of them are always looking to make trouble and pick a fight with you and the Romans. I can't help that. One day, mark my words, they will succeed. Succeed in picking a real fight, and they won't win it. But I'm not in the business of picking fights with anyone."

"But they are looking for a fight with you," Nicodemus continued, "especially after today. They're terrified of you. They've been terrified of you ever since they heard about the raising of Lazarus. 'What can we do about him?' they were asking the other day. 'The whole world's gone after him. If we let him carry on like this, everyone will believe in him, and the Romans will come and take away our place and our nation.'

"It was then that Caiaphas said - and this is why I had to come and warn you, Jesus - 'You know nothing, any of you? You don't realise that it's better that one man should die for the people rather than the whole nation perish.' You see, they're determined to kill you."

There was silence round the dinner table. All were looking at Jesus.

SUNDAY EVENING

"I think I knew that," Jesus replied. "I'm not responsible for what other people do or plan to do. I have to follow my own course, the one the Father has prepared for me, and I've got to follow it to the end."

"Why not go home, go back to Galilee? That's where your real support is," Nicodemus urged him.

"No, it's impossible for a prophet to perish outside Jerusalem," Jesus replied.

"Well then," Nicodemus sighed, "the next best thing is for you always to be surrounded by a crowd of friends and supporters while you're in the city. You're very popular with the pilgrims who are in town at the moment. Many of them, like you, come from Galilee, and they've seen or heard a lot about you. Our authorities won't dare to touch you while you're in a crowd, in case it sparks a riot.

"Keep your other movements secret, as far as you can. I'm only trying to give you good advice. I know this city and its ways, and I don't want you to be hurt."

"I truly appreciate your good will, my friend," Jesus told him, "but in the end the only protection I have or need is the protection of God. He will protect me until his purposes for me and his world have been fulfilled. So, go in peace, dear friend, and the blessing of God go with you. Be true to yourself and to me, and all will be well, for you – and for me."

Jesus embraced him and smiled at him as Nicodemus left.

"So what about tomorrow?" Peter asked.

"Tomorrow we go back into the city and we confront the lions in their den."

twenty-nine

MONDAY

Every day the population of the city was increasing: families with their donkeys, some leading lambs ready to be slaughtered at the feast. The inns and guest houses were filling up, and outside the city walls, tent cities were springing up.

Where the slopes of the hills around Jerusalem were not too steep, the authorities allocated fields as camping grounds. The rules required the Passover meal to be eaten inside the city, but for many years the walls of the city had been too narrow to contain all the pilgrims, and the priests had extended the area of Greater Jerusalem to include the suburbs and fields in the immediate vicinity.

Bethany fell just outside this notional extension of the city, although Bethphage was counted within it. The result was that Bethany, over the other side of the hill, remained relatively calm during the festival. The real commotion came into view as Jesus and his friends crossed the ridge of the Mount of Olives once more, on their way into the city the following morning.

Climbing the hill, Jesus passed a fig tree that had just come into leaf.

"Could one of you fetch us some figs from that tree?" Jesus asked.

James the son of Alphaeus went over to it and looked amongst the leaves. "No," he called out, "no figs yet, but no knops either. So there won't be any figs at all this year. Bad luck."

"Then I curse you, fig tree, because you're not bearing fruit," Jesus said to it. "What's the use of a fruit tree that doesn't bear fruit?"

As they went on their way, Nathaniel said to Philip, "What was that all about? He doesn't usually go round cursing things. Hey-ho! I don't think I'll ever understand this man."

"Me neither," Philip replied with a resigned shrug.

Today there was no procession to attract attention but nevertheless, many people, recognising Jesus as he passed on his way, started to fall in behind him, to see what might happen. It was a quiet but numerous crowd that approached the steps and the gates into the temple precinct.

As they emerged into the court of the Gentiles, Jesus could see that the traders and the money changers were back in their places, perhaps not as many as before, but still a brave showing. Much in evidence also were priests and temple guards, prepared, if necessary, for another confrontation

MONDAY

with Jesus, a confrontation that this time they were determined to win.

One of the high priests, with an escort of temple guards, was waiting by the gates as Jesus and his followers entered. The two parties faced one another in silence.

"Peace be with you," Jesus greeted them.

"And also with you," replied the Sadducee, slowly moving aside to allow Jesus to pass. As Jesus moved on towards the Colonnade of Solomon where the teachers sat, the priest and the guards followed at a distance.

Jesus passed through the ranks of stalls at which the traders stood or sat, with a wary eye on him, holding their ground. But Jesus had made his point, twice now, and there was no point in continuing the battle. Without some major reordering of the city's streets and squares, it was difficult in any case to see where else these activities could be carried on.

People had to pay the temple tax, and it had to be paid in the temple coinage, so money had to be exchanged somewhere. Especially at feasts, visitors to the city had to be able to buy animals to sacrifice. Pilgrims from Judea, and even from Galilee, might bring their own animals with them, but those from farther afield had to wait until they arrived in the city to provide themselves with Passover lambs.

There were fields south of the city, between Jerusalem and Bethlehem, where flocks of animals for sacrifice were kept. During the days before the feast, shepherds from the Judean hills drove their flocks up to the city to pen them in the shepherds' fields, to which the traders from the temple would come every day to buy their stock.

The whole operation was on a vast scale, for at Passover, within a few days some ten to fifteen thousand sheep had to be driven in, bought, sold, and then slaughtered in a single day within the temple courts. The logistics of all this had been worked out over generations and Jesus knew that his gesture had been symbolic rather than practical, although none the less powerful for that. But today he passed on, smiling at the stall holders and money changers, who smiled back and even waved in relief.

Jesus sat and waited as a crowd gathered around him eager to hear what he would say. There were his own disciples, pilgrims, including friends from Galilee and Bethany, others who had accompanied him into Jerusalem yesterday, and more than a sprinkling of Pharisees, priests and temple guards. Roman soldiers watched from the walls of the Antonia Fortress, overlooking the temple precincts, ready to come down and take charge if there was any breach of public order.

Before Jesus could begin to teach, one of the priests stepped forward.

MONDAY

"Give us some sign to show that you have authority to disturb the life of the house of God. You came in here yesterday, throwing your weight about as if you owned the place. If you really are someone sent from God, give us some miraculous sign."

Jesus thought for a moment.

"Destroy this temple, and I will raise it up in three days," he replied.

"Just as I thought. You're crazy!" the priest answered. "This temple has taken forty-six years to build, and it's not finished yet. How do you expect anyone to take you seriously?"

So saying, he turned and made his way out of the crowd.

But there was obviously some conspiracy to trap Jesus in his teaching, for immediately another person came forward and asked, "Master, some of us know that you're a man of integrity. You don't take any notice of what people think of you or of who they are. You teach the way of God according to the truth, don't you?"

Already Jesus suspected that the motive behind this flattery was not benign, but he let the man continue.

"Tell us then, should we pay taxes to Caesar, or not?"

Just so, thought Jesus. A trap. If he said yes, they reckoned that he would lose his following among the people. All resented paying the Roman tax, and some actually believed it to be idolatrous. But if he said no, they would report him to the Governor.

"Bring me a Roman coin," he said.

Someone produced a Roman denarius and Jesus looked at it carefully on both sides.

"Whose face and inscription is this then?" he asked.

"Caesar's, of course."

"Then give to Caesar what belongs to Caesar, and give to God what belongs to God."

Jesus gave the coin back, raised his eyebrows in a quizzical way and waited, but no further response was forthcoming.

"What do you say about divorce?" asked another Pharisee, almost immediately. "Is it lawful for a man to divorce his wife for any and every cause?"

Jesus knew that there was a difference of opinion, even amongst the Pharisees, over this question, some being more liberal in their interpretation of the Mosaic law than others. But at least it was a genuine question and not simply a trap.

"In the beginning it wasn't God's plan that people should get divorced at all. You've read in the story of creation how God made them male and female, and for this reason even today a man leaves his father and mother and is joined to his

MONDAY

wife, and they become one flesh. So, what God has joined together let no-one put apart."

"So why did Moses command that a man should write a bill of divorce and put his wife away?" persisted the rabbi.

"Moses wrote that because of the hardness of your hearts," Jesus answered. "God knows that unredeemed human beings cannot always live together in marriage without quarrelling and hatred, and also that sometimes the bond of marriage is broken by adultery and unfaithfulness. So Moses permitted you to divorce. But it wasn't God's intention from the beginning. Any more questions?"

"Yes, rabbi."

This time it was one of the Sadducees.

"Moses wrote for us that if a man's brother dies and leaves a wife but no children, the man must marry the widow and beget children for his brother."

Jesus could see where this one was going, since he had heard the scribes of the Pharisees arguing with the Sadducees about it before.

"Well then, there were seven brothers in a family. The first one married and died without having any children. So the next brother married the widow, but he also died without having any children. And then the third, and so on until all seven brothers had taken the woman as wife. Last of all, the woman died. Now, in the resurrection of the dead, whose wife will she be, since all of them had had her as wife?"

Jesus replied, "When the dead are raised at the last day there will be no more marrying or giving in marriage. We shall be like the angels. There will be no more need to give birth to children, so no more need for a man and woman to be joined together in marriage. There will be love, but not of that sort.

"And as to life after death, I know that you Sadducees deny that there is any such thing, but you're wrong, aren't you? You don't understand either the scriptures or the power of God. Haven't you read in the book of Moses, in the story of the burning bush, how God said to Moses, 'I am the God of Abraham, Isaac and Jacob'? God isn't God of the dead, but of the living. You are mistaken. One day, the trumpet will sound and the dead will be raised incorruptible, and we shall all be changed."

Noticing that Jesus had given a good answer, one of the scribes of the Pharisees stood up and asked Jesus in a much more friendly tone, "Master, of all the commandments in the law, which do you say is the greatest?"

"The first commandment is this: 'Hear, O Israel, the Lord our God, is one LORD, and thou shalt love the LORD thy God with all thine heart and with all thy soul and with all thy might.' And the second is like it, namely this: 'Thou shalt love thy

MONDAY

neighbour as thyself.' There is no other commandment greater than these. On these two commandments hang all the Law and the Prophets."

"Well said, teacher," the man replied. "You have rightly said that God is one, and that to love him with all your heart and all your strength and to love your neighbour as yourself is more than all burnt offerings and sacrifices."

"You are not far from the kingdom of God, my friend," Jesus answered.

"But now, let me ask you all a question," Jesus went on. "It's about the Messiah. Whose son is he?"

"The son of David," various people replied.

"Right, but then how is it that David himself, inspired by the Holy Spirit, said in the psalms, 'The LORD said unto my lord, sit thou on my right hand, until I make thine enemies thy footstool'? You see here, David himself calls the Messiah 'Lord'. How then is he David's son? Nobody calls his own son, Lord."

There was silence. No-one had any answer. Some of the crowd drifted away. Jesus continued to teach those who remained until it was time to return to Bethany for the afternoon.

As Jesus and the twelve were leaving the temple, he stopped by the great chest into which the faithful were putting their offerings. Rich Pharisees would throw in a handful of silver coins

THAT MAN JESUS

that would rattle and jingle so that people would turn round to see who the donor was. But as Jesus watched, a poor widow slipped past and drop in two small copper coins.

Jesus turned to the twelve.

"Did you see that little old lady?" he asked. "I tell you, that poor woman put in more than any of them. The rest are putting in money they can easily afford. They are rich. But that widow has just put in all that she had."

As they turned to leave, Jesus noticed a young man hovering near them.

"I've just heard what you said." He volunteered, "I'm rich. What must I do?"

Jesus replied, "You know the commandments, they are the same for the rich as the poor. 'Thou shalt not kill, thou shalt not steal, thou shalt not commit adultery, thou shalt not bear false witness, honour thy father and they mother, love they neighbour as thyself.'"

"I think I've kept all these from my youth up," answered the young man, "but I still feel there's something I lack. What is it?"

Jesus loved this young man, his simplicity and his obvious desire for more of God.

"One thing you lack. Sell your possessions and give to the poor, and you will have treasure in heaven - spiritual treasure - and become a disciple of mine."

MONDAY

The young man looked hard at Jesus for a few moments, and Jesus could see that he was torn. Eventually the young man's face clouded over and he turned and went away. Jesus watched him sadly as he went.

"He can't let go of his money," Jesus said to the disciples. "Somewhere along the line everyone has to make this same choice: to love God or to love money. To love the things of this world or to love the things of the next. You can only have one god. You have to choose.

"In the end," Jesus continued as they made their way out of the temple, "there's only one distinction that matters. In the world's eyes, there are rich and poor, there are the learnéd and the ignorant, there's the master and the slave. But they are all one to me, and to my Father.

"In the end, the only distinction that matters is between the saved and unsaved. God wills that all should be saved, but he has given everyone the power to choose. Some will accept the invitation to enter the kingdom. Others, like that young man, sadly, will turn away."

thirty

TUESDAY

As the days before Passover went by, everyone felt a rising sense of anticipation. Everyone, from children to old men and women, looked forward to the day when the lambs would be killed and the whole family would sit down to the Passover supper, at which the children would ask the age old questions about why this night was different from all others, and what God had done in it. It would be the highlight of the year for all the Jewish families that had made their way to Jerusalem to celebrate their solidarity as the people uniquely chosen by God.

For the followers of Jesus, there was also another sense of anticipation. That great entry into Jerusalem at the beginning of the week surely could not just fizzle out into anticlimax. Although no-one knew what was to happen next, they all felt sure that Passover would bring some dramatic revelation or intervention by God himself that would set the seal on all that they had come to believe and hope about Jesus.

Jesus and his disciples were up at dawn as usual. The dew was still on the grass by the roadside as they made their way once more across

TUESDAY

the Mount of Olives towards Jerusalem. The air was fresh and clear so early in the day and in the year. As they rounded an outcrop of rock they saw again the barren fig tree they had passed the day before. They all stopped and stared. The fig tree had withered, its leaves hung dry and brown on the branches.

"Did you do that?" James asked Jesus.

"I guess so," Jesus answered. "It's a sign – to you and to them," he added, nodding his head towards the city." As they walked on, he continued, "I'll tell you a story. A landowner had a fig tree in his vineyard, which didn't bear any fruit. So, he called his steward and told him to chop the tree down. 'I've been coming here for three years and I've never found any fruit on it,' he said.

"'Leave it alone one more year,' said the steward. 'I'll dig around it and fertilise it, and if it bears fruit next year, fine! If not, I'll cut it down.'

"Well," Jesus continued, "I've been coming here for three years now and this city has not repented or borne the fruits of repentance. Indeed, the opposite has happened. It is more opposed to me than ever. So God will cut it down."

"But how did you do it?" James persisted.

"Have faith in God. I tell you, if you say to this mountain, 'Go, throw yourself into the sea,' and you don't doubt it, but you know in your heart that what you say will happen, God will do it for you."

They walked on in silence, wondering about what Jesus had just said and done. How was it possible to believe such a thing in your heart and not doubt it? Not only did it seem impossible to believe such a thing, but would it be right to go round cursing fig trees or moving mountains just to prove you could do it? And what did he mean about the city and its inhabitants? How could they be cut down like a fig tree?

They descended the road from the Mount of Olives, passed the olive grove at the bottom of the hill and the olive press where they sometimes met, before climbing the steep slope to the Sheep Gate and into the temple. Jesus took his seat and began to speak. A crowd gathered, prominent among which were many scribes and Pharisees.

"The teachers of the Law and the Pharisees sit in the seat of Moses, so what they teach you about the Law, you must obey. But don't do what they do, and don't try to practice all they preach. They bind up heavy loads and place them on your shoulders. These loads are too heavy for anyone to bear, even themselves, and they won't lift a finger to help you.

"The LORD said to Moses, 'Ye shall not add unto the word I command you, neither shall ye diminish ought from it.' The scribes and the Pharisees do both. They add to the Law all their traditions about the Sabbath, about washing and cleaning, about eating and fasting. They are

TUESDAY

scrupulous about things like tithing – they even tithe the herbs and spices in their gardens – but they neglect the more important things in the Law, like justice and mercy and faithfulness. They strain out a gnat and swallow a camel."

There was general laughter amongst the crowd and many people pressed in closer to hear what Jesus was saying. But amongst the scribes and Pharisees there were some very sour faces.

Jesus continued, "The scribes and Pharisees also take away from the Law. The Law says, 'Ye shall not swear by my name falsely.' But the scribes say, 'If anyone swears by the temple, it means nothing, but if anyone swears by the gold of the temple, he's bound by his oath.' Or, 'if anyone swears by the altar, it means nothing, but if anyone swears by the gift on the altar, he's bound by his oath.' Blind guides!

"Whoever swears by the altar, swears by it and everything on it. Whoever swears by the temple, swears by the temple and by the God who dwells in it. I tell you, it's better not to swear at all, neither by heaven because it's God's throne, nor by the earth because it's his footstool, nor by Jerusalem for it's the city of the great king. Let your 'aye' be aye, and your 'no' be no. Anything else comes from the devil.

"Don't be misled by the Pharisees. They are hypocrites. Everything they do is to be seen by men. They make their phylacteries wide and the tassels on their prayer shawls long, so that you can all see them. They clean the outside of the cup and the plate, but inside they're full of all sorts of greed and self-indulgence.

"They are like whitewashed tombs, beautiful on the outside, but on the inside they're full of dead men's bones and all sorts of uncleanness."

Again there was a ripple of laughter, but by this time many of the Pharisees had heard enough and turned away glowering.

"Before you go," Jesus called after them, "I'll tell you a story."

The groups of Pharisees stopped where they were and listened.

"A man planted a vineyard. He built a wall around it, dug out a pit for the winepress, put up a watchtower and installed a watchman. Then he rented out the vineyard to tenants and went away on a journey.

"At the time of the vintage he sent a servant to collect his share of the profits, but the tenants beat the servant up and sent him away empty-handed. So the owner of the vineyard sent another servant, but the tenants treated him the same way. The owner sent a third servant, but this time the tenants took him outside the vineyard and killed him. Finally, at his wits end, the owner of the vineyard sent his son.

"'At least they'll respect my son,' he thought. But when they saw the son the tenants said to one

TUESDAY

another, 'This is the son. It must mean the old man's dead. The son will be the heir. If we kill him, the vineyard will be ours.' So they set on him and killed him too."

There was a pause, before Jesus asked, "What do you think the owner of the vineyard will do next? I think he'll come and kill those worthless tenants and give the vineyard to others."

Everyone understood exactly what Jesus was talking about, and the crowd waited with baited breath. The Pharisees were furious, and looked around for the temple guards to arrest Jesus. But seeing the crowd around him, they swallowed their anger and hurried away.

"They want you to think that they are more holy than you are," Jesus continued, "so that they can have the places of honour at the feasts and the most important seats in the synagogues. They like to be called 'rabbi' and 'father.' But I tell you, you've only got one Father and he's in heaven. You're all brothers and you've only one rabbi or teacher - the Messiah, sent by God.

"The teachers of the law and the Pharisees are shutting the door of the kingdom of God in men's faces. They themselves aren't going in and they're trying to stop those of you who are. They'll cross land and sea to make a single convert, and then they make him twice as much a child of hell as themselves.

"You see, the scribes and the Pharisees have mistaken the purpose of the law. God gave you the law for your own good. As it says, 'Ye shall walk in all the ways which the LORD your God hath commanded you, that ye may live, and that it may be well with you, and that ye may prolong your days in the land which ye shall possess.'

"If you disobey or disregard the Law, you will suffer for it, as the whole human race has suffered since the days of Adam's first disobedience. It's not because God is a tyrant, who makes laws on a whim, and then loves to punish those who disobey them. He gave you the law for your own good, because he loves you and wants you to prosper, for things to go well with you. He knows much better than you do how you can live a good life.

"But the Pharisees have made the Law into a slave driver and you into its slaves. They picture God like Pharaoh, ever ready to be displeased and to make your lives harder and harder. I have come to set you free from the slavery of the Law, and if the Son of God makes you free then you will be free indeed.

"If you fall short and get into trouble, or if you cause trouble for others, your Father's first desire for you is repentance, not punishment. 'As I live, saith the Lord God, I have no pleasure in the death of the wicked; but that the wicked turn from his way and live: turn ye, turn ye from your evil ways; for why will ye die, O house of Israel?'

TUESDAY

'The LORD is full of compassion and mercy, long suffering and of great goodness. He will not always be chiding: neither keepeth he his anger for ever. He hath not dealt with us after our sins, nor rewarded us according to our wickednesses. For look how high the heaven is in comparison of the earth: so great is his mercy also toward them that fear him. Look how wide also the east is from the west; so far hath he set our sins from us.'"

Jesus rose from his seat and, with outstretched arms, cried aloud, "O Jerusalem, Jerusalem, killing the prophets and stoning those God has sent to you, you will go on doing the same thing until the end. I'll send you more prophets, wise men and teachers, some of them you will kill and crucify, others you will flog in your synagogues and pursue from town to town.

"All the righteous blood that has been shed on earth, from the blood of Abel to the blood of Zechariah, will come upon this generation. Look! Your house lies desolate. I tell you, you will not see me again until you say, 'Blessed is he who comes in the name of the LORD.'"

With that, Jesus walked carefully through the listening people, followed by his apostles, and left the temple, for the last time.

thirty-one

WEDNESDAY

The following day, Jesus set out as usual as if to return to the city. But as they rounded the shoulder of the Mount of Olives and came to the brow of the hill overlooking Jerusalem, Jesus sat down. For a long time he and his followers all sat in silence, regarding the familiar scene.

"The old Herod was a monster by all accounts," Peter began, "but you've got to admit it's a wonderful sight. Look at the size of the stones! And the gold! There isn't a temple like it in the world. Not even in Rome, I'll bet."

"You see those buildings," Jesus replied. "I tell you the truth, not one stone will be left upon another. They will all be thrown down. The temple, the walls of the city, the houses – they will all be destroyed."

"When? Why?"

Peter was surpised, as they all were.

"Will that be the end? Is that what all this is leading up to? We do believe that you're the coming king of Israel, don't we?"

He looked around at the others for confirmation, and they all nodded.

WEDNESDAY

"But we don't know when your kingdom is coming – or how. We have the feeling it's soon, but how soon? And what are the signs of its coming? And is that the end of the age?"

All these questions that the disciples had been turning over in their minds came tumbling out at last, and they all looked expectantly at Jesus for the answers.

"Watch out that no-one deceives you," Jesus answered. "Many will come, claiming to be the Messiah, and many will be deceived into following them. There will be wars and rumours of wars. But don't get excited. This isn't the end. In fact, the world will go on in many ways, as it always has done. Nation will rise up against nation, and kingdom against kingdom. There will be famines and earthquakes in various places. These may be the birth pains of the new age, but it is not the end.

"You yourselves will be arrested and handed over to governors and kings, to be tried. Some of you will be executed. Wherever you go, you are liable to be persecuted for my sake. A pupil isn't above his teacher, nor a servant above his master. If they have persecuted me, they will persecute you. On the other hand, if they've loved me they will love you too.

"But be prepared. When things get tough, many will turn away from the faith, and hate and betray each other, and many false prophets will rise up and try to tell you there's an easier way. But he who stands firm to the end will be saved. Before the end comes, this gospel of the kingdom must be preached to all nations. Then the end will come.

"But as to the destruction of the city and the temple, which we were talking about, I told you before, there will come a day when our enemies will surround the city and throw up an embankment against it on every side. They will dash the people in the city to the ground, men, women and children.

"When you see an army drawing near, then leave the city as fast as you can. Just like the righteous did in the days of the Maccabees, flee to the hills. Don't hang about.

"Don't get trapped in the city. If someone is on the roof of his house, don't let him go down to fetch his belongings. If someone is working out in the fields, don't let him go back into the city to fetch his coat. It will be a terrible time for everyone, but especially for pregnant women and nursing mothers.

"Pray that it doesn't happen in winter. There will be such suffering as has never been since the world began, and, I daresay, never will be again.

"If at that time people say to you, 'Look, here's the Messiah,' or 'there he is', don't take any notice of them. False messiahs and false prophets will appear. Some of them will perform signs and miracles, but do not be deceived.

WEDNESDAY

"If anyone tells you, 'He's out in the wilderness,' do not go out. If anyone tells you, 'He's in the inner room,' do not go in. As a flash of lightening lights up the sky from the east to the west, so will be the coming of the Son of Man. You will not be able to mistake it. People will not be saying, 'Is this it?' or 'Is that it?' Everyone will know."

"But what will be the signs of your coming?" Peter continued, still perplexed.

Jesus answered, "There will be signs in the sun and the moon and the stars. On earth, the nations will be full of fear and anxiety because of the raging of the seas. Men's hearts will faint with terror because of what is coming on the world, because the heavenly bodies will be shaken.

"At that time, the sign of the Son of Man will appear in the sky, and they will see the Son of Man coming on the clouds of heaven in power and great glory. He will send out his angels with a loud blast of the trumpet to gather his chosen ones from the four corners of the earth. See, I have told you ahead of the time.

"But for many people, this will come as a great surprise. It will be like it was in the days of Noah. Before the flood, people were eating and drinking, marrying and giving in marriage, right up to the day when Noah entered the ark and the flood came and took them all away. Or it will be like it was in the days of Lot. People were eating and drinking, buying and selling, planting and building, right up to the day when Lot left Sodom and fire and brimstone rained down from the sky and destroyed them all.

"Keep watch, for no-one knows when that day is coming, not even the angels in heaven, nor the Son. Only the Father knows. If the householder had known when the thief was coming, he would have kept watch and not let the thief break into his house. So you also must be ready, because the Son of Man will come on a day and at a time that you're not expecting him.

"It's like a rich man going on a journey. Before he went, he arranged his affairs with his servants. Some he left in charge of his house and others in charge of his money. To one, he entrusted five talents, to another two, to another one.

"'Go and trade with these,' he told them, 'and tell me how you get on when I come back.' The first servant took his five talents and went off and traded with them and made five talents more. The second also traded with his two talents and made two talents more. But the third servant was too scared to risk his master's money, so he went and buried it in the ground.

"After a long time the master came back. What did he find? The first servant came to report, and proudly produced the five talents that he'd been given and five talents more. 'Well done, my man. I can see you are to be trusted. From now on I will give you even greater responsibilities.'

WEDNESDAY

"The same thing happened with the second man, but when the third one came in he said, 'Master, I know that you are a hard man when it comes to business and you would not have been pleased if I had lost your money. So, I went and buried it in the ground. Here's your talent, safe and sound.'

"But the master replied, 'If you know that I am a hard man when it comes to business, you should have at least deposited my money with the bankers, and when I came back I would have received my money with interest. No, you are a worthless and lazy servant. Take the talent from him and give it to the others.'

"And what about the servants in the house? What will the master find there when he comes home? Will he find the servants he left in charge doing their duty, keeping the house clean and tidy, giving everyone their food at the proper time? Or will he find them getting drunk, beating their fellow servants and bringing disgrace on their master? I tell you, you must watch out, for no-one knows the day or the hour when the master will return."

Jesus stood up.

"Let's go and find our families. Tomorrow is the big day."

Most of the disciples, and Jesus himself, had families who had also come up to Jerusalem for the feast. They were scattered about in various parts of the city, staying with relatives and friends, as was their custom.

The great feasts were the times that brought and kept families together. Not least, they kept alive the sense amongst the Jews that they were the people of God, the family of Abraham, Isaac and Jacob, a people chosen and set apart from the rest of mankind. For them, family was a sacred as well as a natural bond.

During festival time, the family of Zebedee stayed with a cousin of James and John, a man who happened to be a servant in the household of the high priest. It was to this house that the brothers now made their way.

"Do you understand all that?" enquired James, as they walked along together.

"Not really," replied his brother.

"Who are these enemies that are going to destroy Jerusalem?"

"The Romans, I assume," said John.

"It's possible."

"And we are to get out before it happens."

"And what about that stuff about the coming of the Son of Man?" James went on. "Who does he mean by the Son of Man?"

"Well, he usually means himself, doesn't he?"

"But I don't understand it. I know about 'one like the Son of Man coming with the clouds of heaven,'

WEDNESDAY

but is that what he means? That's the end of the world, isn't it?"

"Perhaps that is what he means," replied John. "After the city has been destroyed, the end will come and he will come with the clouds of heaven to rescue us."

"But won't he be here himself?"

"I have no idea. Wait and see," replied John sagely.

Meanwhile, Jesus was making his way back to Bethany, where his own brother James and his family were lodging with his mother in the house of their friends.

thirty-two

PASSOVER

It was the dawn of Passover. The day would be spent in preparing for the meal. From early morning, the women and children would be busy scouring the houses and tents for any signs of yeast, and washing the vessels for cooking and eating the meal. The men would be taking their yearling lambs and inspecting them to make sure they were without spot or blemish, lest they should be rejected by the priest when they arrived at the temple.

Some of the disciples came to Jesus early in the morning and said, "Are we going to keep the Passover together this evening? If so, do you want us to do anything to make ready?"

Jesus told them, "Yes, I have arranged for us all to use the house of a friend in the city. I have also arranged for you to meet him. I want this to be kept secret, if possible - you heard what Nicodemus said the other night - I want us to have this time together, so we are not disturbed.

"Afterwards, we will go to the old olive grove by the press to spend the rest of the night within the boundary of the city.

PASSOVER

"Now, two of you, say, you Philip and Nathanael, are to go into the city. Near the Fountain Gate, you'll find a man carrying a water jar. Follow him, and when you come to the house say to his wife, 'The teacher says, "Where is the guest room for us to eat the Passover?"' She will show you an upper room, furnished and ready.

"Buy us a lamb and slaughter it along with the others. The servants of the house will cook it and prepare it for us, along with the other food."

Philip and Nathanael departed and did as Jesus had directed them. Then they bought a lamb and joined the throng of men carrying lambs on their shoulders as they made their way up to the temple. They took their place in the queue snaking its way half way round the city. Thousands of men and their lambs waited patiently in the sun as the hour for the sacrifice drew near.

They would be allowed into the inner courts in batches of several thousand at a time, where priests and Levites would be lined up in rows ready to perform their sacrificial duties. The priests would inspect each lamb as it was brought in. When the inner courts of the temple were full, the doors would be closed and a trumpet blown so that all could hear.

It was strange how the temple fell silent just before the trumpet was blown. Up until then the air was full of the sounds of men's voices and the bleating of the sheep. But as the hour drew near, both men and animals fell silent, waiting.

At the blast of the trumpet, each man would cut the throat of his lamb. A priest would catch the blood in a bowl and take it to sprinkle it on the altar, while a Levite would skin and eviscerate the animal before giving it back to the men who had brought it in.

The men would wrap the carcases in cloths, and the doors of the temple would be opened. One crowd of men would come out and go their way to their families, while another multitude would be admitted to the courts for the operation to be repeated all over again.

It usually took three shifts to complete the ritual sacrifice, and the womenfolk were not best pleased if their men were the last in. The meal would be late. Roasting a whole lamb was not the work of a few minutes.

The law said that the lambs should be sacrificed in the evening, but for practical purposes this was understood to mean any time from mid-afternoon onwards. The whole business in the temple, now that the crowds were so great, could take at least three hours. It paid to be among the first, not the last.

Philip and Nathanael took their offering to the temple with all the others and then returned to the house in the centre of the city where their hostess was waiting to begin the cooking. They

PASSOVER

checked the upper room in which they were to eat, to make sure that everything was ready, and then returned to Bethany to wait for the sun to set.

When evening came, Jesus and the twelve made their way in the twilight to the house where they were to eat the Passover. It was a blessed evening, calm and clear, with the full moon rising in the east as the sky darkened and the stars began to appear. They came to the stone-built house and went up the stairs to the upper room. The lamps were lit and they took their places, reclining round the low table.

In the corner of the room was a large jug of water, a bowl, and a towel for the washing of their feet. Some of the disciples were looking around, expecting a servant to appear to perform this menial office. But Jesus got up, took off his outer garment, girded himself with the towel, picked up the jug and the bowl and knelt at Peter' feet.

Peter pulled his feet up under his tunic in horror.

"You're not going to wash my feet, master. Here, I'll do it for you. Let me have the towel."

"Unless you let me wash your feet, you have no place here at the table with me."

"What? What does that mean?" Peter asked, hesitantly extending his legs again.

"You don't understand the meaning now, but in time you will understand."

"Then you'd better wash, not just my feet, but my hands and head as well."

Jesus sighed.

"Just do it. If you bathed before you came out then you are already clean. All you need is to have your feet washed. Isn't that so?"

So, one by one, they allowed Jesus to go round the table and wash their feet. It was always a pleasant sensation, having your feet washed, refreshing and comforting in a childlike way, but tonight the ceremony seemed to be filled with some greater significance. When Jesus had finished, he took his clothes again and reclined at the head of the table.

"Do you understand what I've just done?" he asked. "You call me master, and so I am. But if I am your master and I wash your feet, then you must do the same for one another. I have set you an example. You should do as I have just done for you. I tell you, a servant isn't above his master, nor is a messenger above the person who sent him. If you know this, then you should do it."

The ritual of Passover began. Jesus took the first cup of wine, but before he blessed it he said, "It was very important for me to eat this Passover with you before I suffer. I tell, you, I will not eat it again until it is fulfilled in my Father's kingdom."

Then he blessed the cup with the formal blessing and they passed the cup around the table and all drank from it.

PASSOVER

Next they washed their hands, passing the bowl from one to the other. Then they took the parsley, dipped it in the salt water and ate it, reminding themselves of the tears that their ancestors had wept under the oppression of Paraoh.

Jesus took the flat matzo of unleavened bread from the middle of the three loaves on the plate, and broke it. The larger piece he placed under a cloth. There was a discussion as to which of them should play the part of the youngest child, asking the four traditional questions: Why is this night different from all others? They all decided that Thomas was the youngest. They then took it in turns to respond to Thomas's questions, reciting the story of the Exodus, and the deliverance of the people from Egypt. After this, the meal itself began.

They washed their hands again and Jesus blessed the remaining loaves of unleavened bread, the second cup of wine, and they began to eat.

Informal conversation resumed over the bitter herbs and then the roasted lamb itself. Some of them recalled eating the Passover in other circumstances, and they tried to imagine what it had been like to eat the first Passover in Egypt, with the angel of death passing through the houses of the Egyptians and destroying their first-born sons.

At one point, Jesus unexpectedly said, "I tell you, one of you is going to betray me."

There was a stunned silence. They all looked at each other, and looked back at Jesus.

"Who?"

"Me?"

"It is one of you who has been dipping his hand in the dish with me."

In the far corner of the room, there was a movement. There the room was in shadow, but Judas Iscariot had slipped out quietly.

"Where's he going?" someone asked.

"Probably forgotten something," his neighbour replied.

But Jesus was continuing to talk to them.

"Do not be troubled by what is going to happen. Trust in God. Trust also in me. Remember how, when you have been going up to Jerusalem with a caravan of pilgrims, one or two of you would go on ahead to prepare places for everyone at the inn. Then, those who went on ahead would come back and take you all to the place they had prepared.

"This is like that. I am going on ahead to prepare a place for you. There is plenty of room in my Father's house. You don't have to worry about that. Then, when I've gone on ahead and prepared a place for you, I will come back and take you to be with me, so that where I am, you will be too. But you actually know the place where I am going, and you know the way."

PASSOVER

Thomas said, "Jesus, we don't know what you're talking about. We don't know where you're going, so how can we know the way."

And he spoke for them all in their perplexity.

"I am the way and the truth and the life. All you have to do is to follow me. No-one comes to the Father except by following me."

Philip said, "Lord, show us this Father of yours and we shall be satisfied."

"Have I been with you so long, Philip, and you still don't know me? Anyone who has seen me has seen the Father, because the Father and I are one. I am in my Father and my Father is in me. If you can't believe that just because I say so, then believe it because of the miracles you've seen me do. But I tell you, any of you who has faith in me will do the things I've been doing. Indeed, you will do even more of them, because I'm going to my Father. I will do whatever you ask in my name, so that the Son may bring glory to the Father. Ask for anything in my name, and I'll do it.

"If you love me, do what I tell you, and I will ask my Father and he will send you another companion like me, to be with you forever. He is called the Holy Spirit, or the Spirit of Truth. The rest of the world cannot receive him, because it cannot see him and it does not know him. But you know him. He is living among you and he will be in you.

"I have told you I am going to my Father, but I will not leave you alone. I will come to you. Before long, the rest of the world will not see me any longer, but you will see me. Then, you will realise that I am in my Father and you are in me and I am in you.

"I have told you all this while I am still with you, but this other companion, the Holy Spirit, whom the Father will send in my name, he will teach you everything you need to know. He will remind you of everything I have said to you, and then you will understand it.

"Peace I leave with you. My peace I give you. Not peace as the world thinks of it, but a peace that passes all understanding. So do not be troubled about what is going to happen. Do not be afraid."

Jesus then took up the piece of unleavened bread that had been put aside earlier in the meal. He looked upwards, and blessed it, then he broke it, and gave it to the disciples to share.

But as he did so, he paused and said, "This is my body that is broken for you. Do this whenever you meet together, and remember me and what I have done for you."

In silence, they passed the bread around the table, each one taking a piece the size of an olive, as the custom was, and eating it solemnly.

Then Jesus took the third cup of wine and blessed it with the usual words and then said, "Drink this, all of you. This cup is the new

PASSOVER

covenant in my blood. Whenever you do this together, remember me."

There was silence again as the cup was passed from hand to hand and everyone drank from it.

As they finished, Jesus began the Hallel Psalms which were always sung after the supper.

"When Israel came out of Egypt ..."

"... The same stone which the builders refused is become the headstone in the corner. This is the LORD's doing, and it is marvellous in our eyes. This is the day which the LORD hath made; we will rejoice and be glad in it. Help me now, O Lord. O LORD send us now prosperity. Blessed be he that cometh in the name of the LORD: we have wished you good luck, ye that are of the house of the LORD. God is the LORD who hath shewed us light: bind the sacrifice with cords, even unto the horns of the altar. Thou art my God and I will thank thee: thou art my God, I will praise thee. O give thank unto the LORD for he is gracious: and his mercy endureth for ever."

There was a fourth cup of wine on the table, with which to toast the coming of Elijah, but Jesus did not pick it up. Instead he said, "I will not drink again of the fruit of the vine until I drink it new with you in my Father's kingdom."

With that, he rose from the table and said, "It is time to go."

thirty-three

THE OLIVE GROVE

They went down the stairs and left the house. It was nearly midnight and the streets were deserted.

High above, in all its splendour, sailed the Passover moon so that the city was bathed in its pale light. In some of the houses, lamps still burned as families sat round the table together, and from here and there came the sound of psalms. But for the most part the children had been put to bed and the city was asleep.

As they went, Jesus continued to talk, as he had done in the upper room.

"Thou hast brought a vine out of Egypt," he began. "You know the psalm. Well, I tell you, I am the true vine and my Father is the vinedresser. Every branch that does not bear fruit he cuts off, and every branch that does bear fruit he prunes so that it will bear more fruit.

"That is how the vinedresser works, isn't it? No branch can bear fruit by itself, unless it's attached to the vine. Neither can you bear fruit for the kingdom of God unless you remain attached to me. I am the vine, you are the branches. If you remain attached to me, you will bear much fruit,

THE OLIVE GROVE

but apart from me you can do nothing. The branches that are cut off are thrown into the fire and burned.

"As my Father has loved me, so I have loved you. Keep my commandments and you will remain in my love, just as I have kept my Father's commandments and remain in his love. This is my commandment: love each other as I have loved you.

"Greater love has no-one than this, that he lays down his life for his friends. You are my friends. I have never called you servants. I have always called you friends. A servant just does as he's told. He doesn't know his master's business. But I have told you everything that I have heard from my Father, because you are my friends. You did not choose me like most people choose their rabbis, but I chose you and appointed you to go and bear much fruit for the kingdom of God. But this is my commandment: love one another.

"If the rest of the world hates you, remember that it hated me before it hated you. If you belonged to the world, the world would love you. But you do not belong to the world, you belong to the kingdom of God, and so the world hates you.

"I'm telling you all this so that you will not be surprised or led astray. They will put you out of the synagogues; indeed, the time is coming when anyone who kills you will think he is doing God a service. I did not tell you all this at first, because I was with you. But I have told you now so that when the time comes, you will be ready.

"This very night, you will be so frightened that you will all run away. But later, you will stand firm because of what I have told you, and because of that other companion you will have by then."

Peter immediately said, "Not me, master. I'm not going to run away now. I really trust you now. I'll stand firm, whatever happens."

"We'll see. But I'm telling you, Peter, before the cock crows you will deny me three times. But I have prayed for you, Simon, and when you have turned back, I want you to strengthen the others."

Simon Peter shook his head in disbelief, but Jesus walked on, and talked on.

"So, as I was telling you, soon I am going away. But I tell you the truth, it is better for you that I am going away, because unless I go, the Holy Spirit, that other companion I told you about, will not come. But if I go, I will send him to you and he will be with you forever, wherever you go and for all of time, even to the end. And when he comes, he will convict the world of sin and righteousness and judgement. Of sin, because they do not believe in me; of righteousness, because I am going to my Father; and of judgement, because the ruler of this world is judged.

"I have got much more to say to you, but you cannot bear it now. When the Spirit of Truth comes, he will guide you into all truth. He will not

THE OLIVE GROVE

say anything different from what I have been telling you, but he will take the things I have said and explain them to you. And he will tell you about things to come.

"I have told you all these things so that you may have peace. In this world, you will have trouble, but do not be afraid. I have overcome the world."

As he was talking, Jesus was leading the eleven disciples down the hill, beyond the walls of the city, and across the Kidron brook to the olive grove where they had often gathered.

"We will spend the rest of the night here," he said. "You can stay here while I go on a bit further and pray. Peter, James and John, you come with me."

The other eight settled down by the old olive press, and began to doze.

Jesus went on ahead into the walled grove of ancient olive trees, and the three others followed him.

"Sit down here, men," he said, "but stay awake, and pray for the strength to resist temptation when the moment comes."

Going on a little further, Jesus knelt down and began to pray.

His mind was suddenly in turmoil and his body shuddered. The clarity and peace of the evening had left him. He had seen, as a child, the awful suffering of those whom the Romans had crucified. His flesh shrank from the scourge and the nails. He broke out in a cold sweat. Was there not some other way? As he asked himself that question, he heard again the same creepy voice that had spoken to him in the wilderness of Judea.

"You don't have to wait here, you know. You could just walk away. They haven't got you yet. Go home. They'd forget about you quickly enough. Go back to Nazareth. Open the door of the carpenter's shop and take up the old ways again."

But the words that he had spoken to his own mother came back to him.

"The man who puts his hand to the plough and looks back is not worthy of the kingdom of heaven."

No, there was no turning back now.

He glanced back at the three disciples. They were sitting on the ground, leaning back against the gnarled trunk of an old olive tree. They were in shadow. Were they awake or asleep? And what about them? The voice was reproaching him again.

"And what right have you got to involve those poor creatures in all this? It's all very well for you to make yourself a victim, but you're putting their lives at risk as well. They didn't sign up for this, did they? Think of their wives and families. You've no right to put them in danger for your own crazy ideas."

THE OLIVE GROVE

But that wasn't true. He had warned them.

"He who comes after me must take up his own cross and follow me."

They had seen the opposition and the rejection that he had suffered already at the hands of the Pharisees and Sadducees. They had shared the hostility and disgrace with him, and they had not turned back. It was indeed a terrible thing to ask of people, to follow you even to death, but it was not more than his Father was asking of him.

He turned to look at them again. Yes, they were now definitely asleep. They had rolled away from the tree and were lying on the ground. Let them sleep on now while they could.

But if he stayed here to face what he knew awaited him, what precisely was the point of it? A third time he heard the devilish voice.

"What have you achieved so far? You've done your best, but it wasn't enough, was it? They haven't listened to you, have they? You haven't changed the world, and dying here isn't going to change the world, is it? It may be heroic, but it's a useless gesture."

"Abba, Father, is this the right way?"

There was no answer.

Would it not be the end, the end of all that he had done?

But then there came back to him, as so often, words that he had heard and learned so long ago in the synagogue school.

> 'He is despised and rejected of men; a man of sorrows and acquainted with grief. Surely he hath borne our griefs and carried our sorrows. He was wounded for our transgressions, he was bruised for our iniquities: the chastisement of our peace was upon him, and with his stripes we are healed. All we like sheep have gone astray; we have turned every one to his own way; and the LORD hath laid on him the iniquity of us all.'

What, after all, had his father sent him to do? To bring back to himself, to redeem, to reconcile, to heal, a fallen and broken world. A world in which the sort of cruelty that was about to be inflicted on him was inflicted on others daily, a world that had fallen into the power of an evil one who delighted in corrupting and perverting human nature, indeed nature itself, in order to destroy God's creation and his creatures. And how could this work of redemption, of reconciliation and healing be accomplished unless he himself, as his Father's only Son, took upon himself and bore the sins of the world?

THE OLIVE GROVE

Paying back evil with evil simply perpetuated and multiplied evil. The only way to redeem evil was to soak it up: accept it and return it with good. The only way to put a stop to the cycle of bitterness and revenge was to forgive. And only those who have suffered have the right to forgive. That, in the end, was why he had to suffer, because only a God who had suffered had the right to forgive.

"Abba, Father, your will be done."

As Jesus said these words out loud, he heard in the distance the sound of people approaching, and he saw lanterns and torches bobbing along the path through the trees from the direction of the city. He rose and went back to the sleeping disciples.

"Wake up. My betrayer is here."

thirty-four

BEFORE CAIAPHAS

Jesus went out of the olive grove and stood on the path waiting for the people he could see coming towards him. The disciples were now clambering to their feet, rubbing their eyes, and wondering what was going on.

As the crowd drew near, Jesus could see, in the moonlight, Judas leading them. With him were some of the Sadducees, and a contingent of temple guards, with torches and weapons. A short distance behind was a company of Roman soldiers, as if they were expecting trouble.

Jesus took two steps forward. Judas came forward and kissed him on the cheek, then turned guiltily away and made room for the temple guards to seize Jesus.

"Oh Judas! Would you betray me with a kiss?"

"Are you Jesus of Nazareth?" enquired one of the men from the chief priests.

"I am," Jesus replied, "and if it's me you're looking for, let these men go."

For some of the temple guards were already advancing on the disciples, who were standing still, looking confused. As one of the guards

BEFORE CAIAPHAS

approached him, Peter pulled from his belt the fisherman's knife that he always carried with him and lashed out at the man, cutting off his ear, which was left hanging from his head by a piece of skin.

Pulling his own arms free, Jesus rounded on Peter.

"Put that thing away," he commanded him. "That is not the way, and you know it."

Peter dropped the knife in shame and in a moment, panic seized the eleven apostles and they scattered.

Jesus, meanwhile, held the bleeding ear to the head of the high priest's servant and prayed for it to be restored. The shocked and bemused man put his hand to his ear, wiping away the blood that had already flowed down his neck and into his tunic. He shook his head in shock and disbelief. Meanwhile, Jesus had turned back to the officers and the elders.

"Am I leading a rebellion, that you have come out to arrest me with swords and clubs? I was teaching every day in the temple and you could have arrested me then, but you had to wait until the dead of night."

But this time, the guards were tying his hands behind his back and marching him back towards the city. Jesus' wrists were chained to the two guards who escorted him on either side as they made their way back down the Kidron Valley.

The temple mount loomed above them on their right hand side, then the lower hill of the city of David. The band entered the city by the Valley Gate and made their way up the steep western hill, climbing up the great stone steps to the palace of Caiaphas the high priest.

Caiaphas and his father-in-law Annas were waiting anxiously, Caiaphas striding up and down in the hall where the Sanhedrin was accustomed to meet. They had gambled on finding Jesus alone, or with only a few of his disciples, trusting in Judas to show them where his master could be found.

Secrecy and speed were of the essence if Jesus was to be apprehended and disposed of without a riot breaking out amongst the pilgrims and his supporters. They turned with relief as they heard the detachment of temple guards who had been sent to arrest Jesus entering the courtyard of the palace.

"Hold him here now, while we assemble the council and the witnesses," they ordered.

Jesus was shackled to a pillar, while the guards relaxed. After a while, they blindfolded Jesus and took it in turns to come up to him and hit him in the face. Then they called out, "Go on then, prophet, tell us, which one of us hit you."

They all jeered, but Jesus remained silent. But soon tiring of this sport, they settled down to wait.

BEFORE CAIAPHAS

Outside in the yard, servants, who had been told to stay up all night in case they were needed, likewise stood or sat, idly warming themselves by the fire that was burning in the middle of the court. The days might be getting warmer, but the nights were still chilly.

One by one, the members of the council, some raised from their beds, others, more in the know, expecting the summons, arrived at the palace and were admitted by the gate keeper.

A few less respectable fellows also turned up and, saying a few words to the gate keeper, were admitted. From inside the hall Jesus and his guards watched these comings and goings.

Jesus then saw two familiar faces enter the courtyard. John said a few words to the gate keeper, whom he seemed know, and was allowed in, followed by none other than Peter.

Peter looked around apprehensively at the company, glanced through the colonnade to where Jesus was being held, but made no movement to come any closer. He moved towards the fire and sat down, trying to appear at ease, warming his hands.

The man sitting next to him asked him a question, to which Jesus saw Peter shake his head. A few minutes later, one of the guards also spotted Peter and went out into the courtyard to speak to him. Jesus could hear the exchange between them.

"Didn't I see you in the olive grove with him?"

"Who do you mean?" Peter replied.

"Jesus of Nazareth. You know very well who I mean," the guard insisted.

"I don't know what you're talking about. I've never heard of him," Peter answered sullenly, lowering his head, standing up, and moving away from the fire.

A maid was also standing by and she accused Peter again.

"Well, you're certainly a Galilean. We can tell by your accent."

At this Peter swore, and denied again that he knew anything about Jesus. And at that moment a cock crowed.

The voice of the cock struck Peter like a bolt of lightening. He suddenly remembered the words of Jesus.

"Before the cock crows, you will deny me three times."

He blundered out of the courtyard, through the gate, with John following close behind, and Jesus could hear Peter howling in the street in shame and despair.

The first grey light of dawn was visible in the eastern sky before the elders were assembled and the proceedings could begin.

BEFORE CAIAPHAS

Caiaphas took his seat as president of the council and quickly summarised the purpose of this extraordinary meeting.

"Before you, you see Jesus of Nazareth. As you all know, we cannot let this man continue to stir up the people and lead them astray with his teachings. If we do, there will be an uprising and the Romans will come and take our place of worship away, and destroy our nation. It is one man or the nation."

"But of what exactly is he being accused?" enquired Nicodemus, who exchanged a glance of mutual recognition with Jesus.

"We have witnesses. Call the witnesses."

One of the more disreputable fellows was brought forward, obviously primed as to what to say.

"A day or two ago, I heard this man say that he was going to destroy the temple," he said.

"Right, call the next witness. The law says that we need two or three, so two or three we shall have," ordered Caiaphas.

The next man was brought in to the room.

"What did you hear or see?" asked the high priest.

"I heard this man say that he didn't have to pay the temple tax because he was the Son of God," the man offered.

Caiaphas sighed.

"But did you hear him say anything about the temple?"

"Yes, he said that if it was destroyed, he would rebuild it in three days."

The light in the sky was increasing. Precious time was being wasted. Caiaphas lost patience with the phoney proceedings. He turned to Jesus.

"You have heard what these men have said. What have you got to say?"

But Jesus said nothing.

"I adjure you by the living God, tell us on oath: are you the Messiah, the Son of God?"

Jesus slowly raised his head. His face was beginning to show signs of the blows he had received earlier in the night. His eyes met the eyes of the high priest. Everyone held their breath as they waited for Jesus to answer.

"I am," he said. "And you will see the Son of Man coming in the clouds of heaven in power and great glory."

"Blasphemy!" Caiaphas thundered. "You have heard it for yourselves. He is guilty of blasphemy."

"He deserves to die," concurred the old man, Annas.

"I object."

It was a Pharisee named Joseph from Arimathea who had spoken.

"This is a wholly illegal procedure. We have not been properly convened as a court and we cannot

BEFORE CAIAPHAS

condemn anyone without an adjournment. The Pharisees among us, at least, believe in honouring the Law that God has given us. The nation will not be saved by devious means like this, but by honesty and faithfulness to God and the Law."

"You Pharisees live in a world of your own, with all your fine distinctions and exact prescriptions for every situation. Some of us have to live in the real world where such refinements don't apply."

"But what are you proposing to do with this man?" Joseph persisted. "We are not allowed to put people to death in any case."

A crafty smile spread over the lips of Caiaphas.

"My friend, I have no intention of putting this man to death. I know the Romans don't allow us to use the death penalty. I also know that when the Romans are not looking – well, sometimes the mob does get out of hand and, sadly, a stoning may take place. But that is out of the question with Pilate in town and the garrison on alert.

"No. What I propose to you now is that we hand this man over to the Romans. They can do the dirty work for us."

"But what charge can you bring against him before Pilate?"

"He claims to be the king of the Jews. Simple. Quite enough to condemn him in the eyes of the Romans. They will nail him up on a cross for that."

The assembled company considered this for a few moments. It was true that Jesus' entry into Jerusalem at the beginning of the week, about which they had all heard, had identified him in the eyes of all pious Jews as one who was claiming to fulfil the prophecy of Zechariah. But would that persuade the Romans?

Caiaphas called for a vote.

"Those in favour of handing Jesus over to the Governor on this charge, please raise your hands."

Most hands were raised.

Nicodemus, Joseph and a few others abstained, shaking their heads in disagreement.

"Let's go then," Caiaphas said. "We want to get this over and done with before too many people hear about it."

Then, to the captain of the guard, he said, "Send some men out to round up a crowd who will support us. Make it look like a spontaneous demonstration that might get out of hand. Then as soon as the sun comes up we will take the prisoner to the Governor."

thirty-five

BEFORE PILATE

Pontius Pilate had not been prefect over the Jews and Samaritans for very long, but long enough to know that he did not like either of them. This small, hilly, country, sandwiched between the sea and the river Jordan was home to two tribes who, when they were not squabbling between themselves, were plotting against their masters in Rome.

The Jews, in particular, entertained absurd ideas about their own superiority as the result of having been specially chosen by the one true God. This seemed to make them unnecessarily scrupulous about their religion and sensitive about their temple. Nor had they forgotten their military successes in recovering their sovereignty after the desecration of their temple by Antiochus nearly two centuries before.

Judea and Samaria was only a separate prefecture now because of the long history of trouble that this corner of the world had caused to all the people who had ruled over it. Pilate had been given a special induction into the history of the place before he was despatched from Rome.

After the death of the old puppet king Herod, there had been a major revolt, only put down by Varus with the help of three Roman legions. Then Herod's stupid son, Archelaus, had to be deposed and exiled as more trouble than he was worth.

There had been another revolt over new taxation imposed by Sulpicius Quirinius when he was governor of Syria. This new prefecture had then been created to keep a closer eye on the country and since then, things had been relatively quiet. But even in the three years since Pilate had arrived, he had crossed swords with the Jews twice, and had not always come off best.

His first act as prefect had been to set up statues of Tiberius Caesar in Jerusalem, to remind the populace of who was in charge. But a huge delegation of Jewish leaders had arrived in Caesarea to protest, men who only lay down and offered to die when he threatened them with the sword. So, he had been forced to back down and the statues had been removed.

They had also not liked it when he raided their temple treasury to build an aqueduct that the city badly needed. But this time he had bludgeoned them into submission, literally.

Already, this Passover week, some of his troops had been ambushed on patrol, and only the day before had they apprehended the ring leaders. So, Pilate was not best pleased to see a delegation of the chief priests with a shackled prisoner and

BEFORE PILATE

some sort of rabble assembling in the courtyard as he prepared for the day.

"Bring them in," he ordered his servant.

"They won't come, sir. They say they must keep themselves clean for their Feast of Unleavened Bread. They say, will you go out to them."

Pilate sighed. It was not worth the trouble to argue over this.

"So, who is this?" he enquired of Caiaphas

"He is called Jesus, from Nazareth," Caiaphas replied.

"If he's from Galilee, then Herod can deal with it. Herod's in town for the feast. Take him to him. Go away!"

The leaders of the Jewish delegation were reluctant to be turned away, but they could see that Pilate was in no mood to argue, so the procession turned round and left the praetorium.

They made their way through the streets of the city to Herod's town house. The local inhabitants were astir and the sight of a manacled prisoner being led through the streets excited their curiosity. People with nothing better to do tagged along behind to see what there was to see.

When they were announced at the court of Herod, the king, as he liked to be called in his own small circle, welcomed them in. He had wanted to see this man Jesus for some time. He sat down and began to question Jesus about some of the things that he had heard about him, but Jesus would not answer a word.

Finally, despairing of getting anything out of Jesus, he told the high priest's party, "Whatever you've got against this man, he has never been any trouble to me. Take him back to Pilate."

Once more, the procession turned round and made its way back to the former palace of Herod the Great, where Pilate now lived when he was in Jerusalem, in comfort and luxury. By this time, a considerable crowd was following them. Although angry at the delay caused by this abortive visit to Herod, the Jewish leaders could see that in the end it might suit them very well.

"Herod has sent us back to you," they told Pilate. "He says, quite rightly, that it is here in Jerusalem that this man has been stirring up trouble, not in Galilee."

"Is that so? Then what do you accuse him of?" asked Pilate.

"He claims to be the king of the Jews."

"Is he any more than a lunatic?"

"For the last three years, he has been teaching many people, here and in Galilee, about something he calls the kingdom of God, and now he is claiming to be a king. He has attracted a large following, and we believe that if he is allowed to carry on, he will start a revolt that will be difficult to suppress."

BEFORE PILATE

"Have you got witnesses?" Pilate asked.

The Sadducees had lined up a team of witnesses who now came forward one-by-one.

"He put himself at the head of a large demonstration that entered the city in a threatening manner six days ago."

"Yes, I heard about that," Pilate replied, "but my soldiers told me that it looked more like a celebration than a protest. The crowd dispersed peacefully enough afterwards and, as far as I know, there was no violence or disturbance. That isn't evidence."

"We heard him say that we shouldn't pay taxes to Caesar," volunteered a second witness.

The eyebrows of the prefect went up at this and he said, "That's more serious. Is there anyone else who can confirm this witness?"

There was silence. They were all conscious before this Gentile of their status as Jews and could not but remember that one of the prime commandments in the Law of their God was, 'Thou shalt not bear false witness.' For shame no-one was willing to second this blatant lie.

Then another witness stepped forward.

"He threatened to destroy the temple."

Pilate had reached the conclusion that he was being used to settle some sort of score amongst the Jews, a role that he was not prepared to play. He motioned to the prisoner to come into the praetorium so that he could question him in private.

Jesus was unshackled but, with his arms still bound, he followed the governor inside. He stood before the governor's seat. One of his eyes was beginning to close and his lower lip was swollen, but he looked straight at Pilate as he began to question him.

Since his submission to his heavenly Father in the olive grove, Jesus had felt perfectly at peace. He had allowed himself to be taken, and to be marched along without a struggle, knowing in his heart that his Father had everything in hand.

An interpreter stood beside the governor in case he needed help with this Aramaic-speaking, Galilean prisoner. But Pilate spoke the Greek of an educated Roman, and Jesus spoke the low Greek of the common people in Galilee, so they made themselves understood.

"So, are you the king of the Jews?" Pilate asked.

"Yes, but not perhaps as either you or they understand it. My kingdom is not of this world. If it were, my servants would fight."

"Which world is your kingdom of then?"

"A spiritual world, a heavenly world, the world to come, whatever you want to call it. For this reason I was born, and for this reason I have lived: to testify to the truth."

BEFORE PILATE

"Truth!" Pilate mused. "What truth? What is truth? You Jews have got your truth. Other's have got their's. Gods, goddesses, philosophers, stories, myths, lies. What is truth?"

He thought for a few minutes, looking Jesus up and down. Then he rose and took Jesus out into the courtyard again.

"I find no basis for a charge against this man. Take him and judge him according to your own Law if you must."

"We have a Law, and by that Law he ought to die," cried out one of the high priests, "because he calls himself the Son of God."

Pilate paused again, now superstitiously uncertain and afraid. Jesus had impressed him. He certainly was not a common criminal or rabble-rouser. He had a certain dignity, even in bonds, that other men brought before him did not have.

Was he then some sort of god in human form? It was a possibility that Pilate could entertain, and it frightened him. He took Jesus back inside the praetorium.

"Where do you come from?" he asked.

Pilate's wife passed through the room as he sat down to look at Jesus afresh. She caught her breath as she saw her husband's prisoner.

"I have seen this man before," she said. "Last night I had a dream. I saw him in a dream, and a voice said to me, 'Have nothing to do with this just man.' That's what the voice said, 'Have nothing to do with this just man.'"

Pilate began again to question Jesus, but now Jesus stood silent.

"Have you nothing to say?" he asked. "Do you not realise that I have got the power to release you or to crucify you?"

At this Jesus looked up again.

"You would have no power over me at all if it had not been given you from above. The people who handed me over to you have the greater sin."

At this Pilate determined to release him. So he took him out yet again to the waiting crowd of elders and onlookers.

"I find no fault in him," he announced. "I propose to order a beating with rods and to let him go."

But the elders began to shout out, "If you let this man go, you're not Caesar's friend. Anyone who makes himself a king is defying Caesar."

Now Pilate knew very well that he owed his place and appointment to being part of that inner circle in Rome known as 'Caesar's friends.' The Jews had successfully petitioned the emperor before against the rulers and governors sent to them. His word ought to count for more than theirs, but who could tell. You could not trust anyone in the snake pit of Roman politics.

BEFORE PILATE

Then a new thought struck him. These Jews were obviously pursuing some agenda of their own, which probably corresponded to some division in their own ranks. Perhaps he could use that.

"You have a custom at the feast of the Passover that I should release one prisoner for you. As you know, we have in custody the ring-leader of the attack on my troops last week. You choose. Do you want me to release for you that man Barabbas, or this man Jesus?"

The leaders of the Jewish party shouted, "Barabbas!" The crowd took up the cry, "Barabbas, Barabbas!"

Pilate lifted his hand and the noise died down.

"Then what shall I do with Jesus?"

"Crucify him! Crucify him!"

"Shall I crucify your king?" Pilate cried out in despair.

"We have no king but Caesar," they replied.

Pilate could see that he was getting nowhere, but rather that a riot was starting, so he called for a seat and a bowl of water.

Sitting down on the seat with great formality, he waited until the crowd was quiet and watching. He then ordered his servant to pour water over his hands.

"Have it your own way, but you are witnesses that I am innocent of this man's blood."

"His blood be on us and on our children," the Jewish leaders replied.

And Pilate handed Jesus over to the soldiers, to crucify him. They led Jesus away. The chief priests and their followers left the palace.

The crowd dispersed. Pilate was left alone in the middle of the great stone pavement, sitting on the judgement seat, but knowing that it was he who had been judged – and found wanting.

thirty-six

CRUCIFIXION

"Look! The Lamb of God who takes away the sin of the world."

As Jesus was led away, he remembered the words of John the Baptizer by the river Jordan.

As a child he had often wondered what the lambs felt like as they were led away to be slaughtered. Now he knew. In a strange way, he identified with all those lambs that had been sacrificed the day before for the feast of the Passover, whose blood smeared on the lintels and doorposts of the houses in Egypt so long ago had saved the people of Israel from the destroying angel.

He identified with all the lambs offered by the common people as sin offerings in atonement for their sins. At least the poor lambs had only a few minutes of fear and suffering before their ordeal was over, while his own flesh crawled in apprehension of the pain that he was about to endure.

As he was brought into the prison yard, there seemed to be a fight going on. Two prisoners were being separated by their guards from a third man, at whom they were shouting and swearing.

THAT MAN JESUS

"You bastard! You got us into this, and now you're leaving us to take the rap. May you rot in hell, Barabbas."

The man called Barabbas was being escorted out of the cell grinning obscenely, leaving the other two struggling and yelling.

"Shut up, you. It's time to start your treatment!"

Two of the soldiers stripped the first man of his clothes and pushed him face up against a pillar. They tied his arms round the pillar and secured his hands to a hook at head height. The poor fellow began to whimper.

The guards took up the flagella, whips, each with three thongs in which were embedded small pieces of sharp bone. Standing one each side they began to lash the man, the cords making red wheals on his back and the splinters of bone pulling away lumps of flesh. The fellow's initial screams gave way to squeals that became weaker and weaker as the punishment continued.

After exactly forty blows, the soldiers released his hands and arms and he slumped to the floor. Jesus closed his eyes as the second felon was treated in the same way. He prayed for strength and endurance and felt his Father's presence very close to him.

The thought that had formed in his mind in the grove last night came back to him and played itself over and over in his mind as he waited.

CRUCIFIXION

'Only a suffering God can forgive the sins of a suffering world'.

As the first lash of the flagellum struck his back, he gasped with pain. His breath came in short gulps as the pain overwhelmed his senses. There was no room in his mind for thought, no sight, no hearing, except the whip of the cords. He felt blood running down his back and his legs as a sort of numbness began to spread over his lacerated back.

Eventually, he too was released and he slumped to the floor, trembling and sobbing with shock. He was hauled to his feet and sat on a stone seat with his back to the wall. Waves of pain washed over him, interspersed with moments of relief in which he could take in a face or an object in the room.

His eyes met those of one of his fellow prisoners, and their glance united them in shared grief and pain. The eyes of the third prisoner still smouldered with anger and resentment. Against the wall stood three crosses ready to be carried to the place of execution.

There seemed to be a lull in the proceedings. The soldiers stood quietly talking to one another. This was all in a days work for them, their hearts as well as their bodies hardened by both the infliction and the suffering of pain. Occasionally they laughed at some joke. They gave the prisoners back their clothes, to put them on.

A few minutes later, one of the soldiers came in with a sort of wreath woven from a thorn bush that he forced onto Jesus' head.

"Here," he cried to the others, "this one thinks he's the king of the Jews. Better give him a crown and a smart cloak and a stick to rule with."

They draped a soldier's cloak round Jesus' shoulders and gave him a rod to hold. Then they bowed the knee and acclaimed him, "Hail, king of the Jews!"

As they were in the middle of this charade, their centurion came in and the soldiers got quickly to their feet, to await further orders.

"Get them ready to go. Lead the way, sergeant."

One of the wooden crosses was placed on the shoulder of each prisoner and the melancholy procession formed up. The prisoners staggered as they tried to walk under the weight of their burdens, the wood pressing upon their bruised and wounded backs. Jesus felt the well-known texture of the wood in his hands, and remembered the planks that he used to carry into the workshop in Nazareth.

The gates of the compound swung open and the crowd that had gathered outside fell silent as the condemned men appeared. Scenes like this always attracted a ghoulish crowd, some finding a sadistic thrill at the sight of pain, others experiencing a sort of thankfulness that it was not them, at least not this time.

CRUCIFIXION

They began to walk slowly through the streets towards the western wall of the city. The waves of pain increased as Jesus moved forward, step by step. His vision and his consciousness again became restricted to flashes of sight, interrupted by his eyes filling with blood and sweat and times of overwhelming agony.

At one point he fell. A soldier kicked him hard in the stomach, but he could not raise himself under the weight of the cross. He heard the soldier ordering a passer-by to come and pick it up and carry it for him. A couple of women by the roadside came forward and helped him to his feet, wiping his face. They were weeping in pity.

"Don't weep for me," he managed to say. "Weep for yourselves and for your children. If they do this when the wood is green, what will they do when the wood is dry?"

Without the weight of the wooden cross, Jesus could walk more easily and more upright. People whispered as he went by and he guessed that some of them knew who he was. No-one jeered.

Outside the walls, they came to a disused stone quarry. Jesus knew the place. For some reason, it was called Golgotha, the Place of the Skull. The prisoners were dragged up the low hill around the old workings, where holes were already cut in the rock to receive the posts of crosses.

There were a dozen guards accompanying them, who divided themselves into three groups. The crosses were laid down, the prisoners stripped again, and then forced to lie in place, ready to be nailed, each to his cross. The two men who had taken part in the ambush both struggled as they were laid down and had to be restrained and tied, hands and feet to the cross, before the nails could be hammered in.

Jesus lay down without protest, his arms extended. The soldier with the hammer and the nails stepped back in surprise and looked into Jesus' face. Their eyes met.

"Father, forgive them. They don't know what they're doing," he prayed.

The soldier looked reluctant to do what he had to do, but as he bent to the inevitable, Jesus prepared himself for the next shock. He looked the other way, but the pain shot up his arm with each blow of the hammer, and again as the nails was driven into his feet. But this pain was as nothing compared with the agony that raced through every joint and ligament in his body as the cross was raised upright and dropped into its socket with a thump.

The soldiers washed their hands in water from their bottles and gathered up their weapons and tools. They settled down to watch and to prevent anyone from approaching the crosses too closely.

In addition to the waves of pain, the problem was breathing. In order to breathe, Jesus and his two companions had to raise their heads and

CRUCIFIXION

either push up on their feet or pull up on their arms. Every movement brought on fresh waves of agony, but the reflex urge to keep on breathing forced them into this torturing themselves with this exertion.

How long could this go on? Each would keep asking himself this question, but they knew that the whole diabolical punishment was designed to inflict the maximum human anguish for hours, if not days, on end. Somehow the body could not find the oblivion of unconsciousness that it craved. Continual stabs of pain kept it sentient and awake.

The hours dragged by. People from the city came and went. Some priests and elders came to survey the scene, and were apparently satisfied with the result of their night's work. They jeered and pointed the finger at Jesus.

"He saved others, but he can't save himself. If you're the Son of God, come down from the cross and maybe we'll believe in you."

One of the other criminals also jeered at him.

"If you're the Messiah, save yourself and us."

But the other turned his head to reproach him.

"Don't you fear God at all? We're only receiving justice for what we've done. He's done nothing."

He looked again into Jesus' eyes.

"Master, remember me when you come into your kingdom."

Jesus did his best to smile through his own cracked and broken lips.

"My friend, today you will be with me in Paradise."

The heat of the day was increasing. Jesus managed to mouth a few words to a soldier watching him at the foot of the cross.

"... thirsty," he croaked.

The soldier, over whom Jesus had spoken those words of forgiveness, went to fetch a sponge, filled it with sour wine from his bottle and putting it on the end of his spear, held it up to Jesus' lips.

About noon, as the sun was reaching its zenith and the heat was becoming intolerable, heavy clouds began to build up from the west. People began to look up, expecting a storm, but no rain came. It became quite dark and the temperature dropped, but as it did so, an even more intense darkness seemed to come over Jesus.

For the first time since he had been in the wilderness of Judea, after his baptism, the sense of his Father's presence left him. He searched in his spirit for the familiar feeling of his father's love surrounding him, the sense that had sustained him, not only through the years of preaching and teaching, but through these last hours of intense suffering. Where was it now, when he most needed its comfort and strength?

CRUCIFIXION

The words of the psalm involuntarily came to his lips and he cried out, "My God, my God, why hast thou forsaken me?"

There was no answer from heaven. He hung there, as both inner and outer darkness enveloped him.

He did not know how many minutes or hours he passed in this dark pit. Eventually, the clouds moved on and the light returned. Jesus looked down and, near the foot of the cross, saw to his surprise his mother and his disciple John.

"Look after her like your own mother," he said to John, and to his mother, "Treat him like your own son."

Jesus could feel his strength ebbing away with the continual effort of raising himself up to breathe. He knew that he could now die.

Taking one last deep breath, he cried aloud, "It's finished. Father, into your hands I commit my spirit."

He allowed his head to drop forward, and with an effort of will, he relaxed his muscles and prevented himself from breathing again. Unconsciousness came over him, and a few minutes later he was dead.

thirty-seven

BURIAL

The sun was setting. Few people remained on the hill by the crosses. In the distance some women who had come up with Jesus from Galilee sat and watched and wept.

The crowds had long since gone home to prepare for the Sabbath. The noise of the city was dying away. Birds were returning to their nests. The calm and peace of evening was settling over the countryside.

A messenger arrived from the governor and reported to the centurion that, on account of the Jews' rules and regulations, the bodies were not to remain on the crosses over night. The soldiers roused themselves and began the process of taking them down.

"That one's already dead," said one soldier, pointing to Jesus in the middle. "Been dead for some time, I think."

Another soldier took a hammer and with a couple of vicious blows broke the legs of first one, then the other, of the two criminals. Both groaned again and then hung limply as they expired. Unable any longer to press up on their feet, their

BURIAL

chests collapsed, and in a few minutes they died of asphyxiation.

Coming to Jesus, the centurion said, "Yes, I think he's dead, but make sure. Pierce him."

Lucius, the sergeant, came up and thrust his spear into Jesus side. There was a flow of blood and serum down his stomach and thighs. There was no physical response and the centurion said, "Yes, he's dead. You can take him down."

As the soldiers were preparing to take the bodies down, the centurion seemed to be rooted to the spot. He was standing and staring at the figure of Jesus deep in thought. Finally, he said to anyone who happened to be within earshot, "You know, I think he really might have been the Son of God."

As the soldiers were taking the crosses down and unfastening the bodies, two Pharisees, easily identifiable by their prayer shawls and phylacteries, arrived asking to be allowed to take the body of Jesus away for burial. They had with them two servants, who were carrying linen for a shroud, a large water jar and some spices.

The centurion agreed and the two Jewish elders began to wash the body of Jesus with a sponge and anoint it with the spices. The awful sour smell of blood and sweat gave way to a fragrant aroma. They stood again as the servants unrolled the linen and prepared to lay the body on the shroud.

One of the Pharisees said to the other, "Joseph, do you see that?"

He pointed to the board now lying on the ground that had been fastened to the cross above the head of Jesus. It read, JESUS OF NAZARETH, THE KING OF THE JEWS.

Both men put their arms around each other and wept, for grief and shame.

Time was hastening on. They must finish their work before the sun set and the Sabbath began.

With the help of their servants, they lifted the naked body, placed it on the shroud, tied a bandage under the chin, folded the linen back over the body and secured it with strips of cloth around the feet and waist and head.

Together, they carried Jesus down the hill to a small plot of land that Joseph had recently bought and prepared for his own burial, when the time should come. In the rock there was a cave, roughly hewn out, in which a shelf waited to receive a body.

Beside the cave stood a large, round, flat stone, ready to be rolled over the mouth of the cave to secure it. Having settled the body of Jesus in its place, the four men rolled the stone over the entrance and walked slowly back towards the city. Dusk had fallen and the Sabbath had begun.

In the distance on the hill, two other men with a donkey and a cart were loading up the bodies of the other victims. They would take them away

BURIAL

and bury them in a common grave and would be rewarded out of the public funds for their act of piety.

The soldiers picked up their tools and their weapons, fell in, and marched off back to their barracks, their day's work done.

* * *

Once the eleven disciples had realised that they were not being pursued, they had stopped and watched through the trees as Jesus was led away by the temple guards. In ones and twos, they had slunk back to their lodgings in the city, in Bethany and round about.

They all had lain low that next day, the Friday, as pieces of news filtered back to them about the fate of their master. That evening, the women, who had looked on from afar as Jesus was crucified and buried, went round to them one by one, and told them the sorry tale.

* * *

The next day, the village of Bethany was unnaturally quiet, even for a Sabbath. The whole population seemed to be mute with shock. No-one knew what to say, so they said nothing. Everyone in the village had known Jesus, at least by sight.

Many of them had known him from a boy when he used to come to Jerusalem with his parents for the feasts. They all knew Mary, Martha and Lazarus, and to see Lazarus walking down the streets alive was still a source of daily wonder to the inhabitants.

Their guests, for the most part families and friends from Galilee, including Jesus' own family, were even more shocked. They had all shared in the euphoria of the previous week. The triumphal entry into Jerusalem, the waving palm branches and the cries of Hosanna. And now – it had all happened so quickly. So quickly that it had been evening before the full story of what had happened had spread. And then, no-one had been able to think of anything to say.

As the Sabbath wore on, the disciples began to remember some of the words Jesus had spoken.

"The Son of Man will be betrayed into the hands of sinners. He will be crucified and killed."

His words had made no sense to them at the time but now they began to understand that Jesus had foreseen it all. But then other words of Jesus began to come back to them as well.

"If you do not take up your cross and follow me, you are not worthy to be my disciple."

Did that mean that they would be next? Were the chief priests or the Romans even now planning to send out search parties to round them up and do to them as they had done to Jesus?

BURIAL

None of them dared to venture out, but they all realised that they would have to decide what to do soon. How were they to return to Galilee as fast as possible without being arrested or betrayed?

The hours of the day and the night passed uneasily, as they waited for the dawn of the first day of the new week.

thirty-eight

THE FIRST DAY OF THE WEEK

The women who had watched Jesus being buried on Friday evening had agreed to get up early and go to the tomb in which he had been laid.

At first light, Mary of Magdala, Joanna, Mary the mother of the other James, and one or two others, set out to visit the grave. They made their way up the Mount of Olives, down into the Kidron valley below, and up into the city. They crossed the town as it was coming to life on this, the first day of the week.

As they came out on the west side of the city, they glanced up sadly at the place where the crosses had stood two days before, and then looked over towards the garden in which the tomb lay. Just then, the sun rose over the rooves of the city behind them and a brilliant light streamed down into the garden.

The women stopped short. Even from a hundred yards away they could see that the stone had been rolled back. They hurried down, the light increasing all the time, the dew on the grass glistening in the morning sun.

The mouth of the tiny cave gaped open before them, and the low sunlight shone straight into it.

THE FIRST DAY OF THE WEEK

As they stooped to look in, they could see that the body of Jesus was not there. The linen shroud lay crumpled and flat on the stone shelf. The cloth that had been around his head was rolled up in a place by itself.

The women stood up and looked at one another in horror. Who had rolled back the stone, and who had moved the body? It was sacrilege, if nothing else. The only day in between had been the Sabbath. No-one carried burdens on the Sabbath, and contact with the dead would make anyone unclean. Who could have done such a thing? And why?

As they turned to peer into the tomb again, a young man, with dark curly hair, and wearing a long, white robe, had suddenly appeared from nowhere.

"Are you looking for Jesus of Nazareth?" he said. "He isn't here. See the place where he was laid. Go and tell his disciples and Peter."

Joanna was the first to gather her wits.

"You stay here and keep watch," she told Mary of Magdala. "We'll go and fetch help."

The other women began running back towards the city. They lifted their skirts almost to their knees. Going through the city streets, they let their skirts fall again and walked on as quickly as they could. They separated, two of them going to find the disciples who were lodging in the city, and the other two going on to Bethany.

These two were breathing heavily as they ascended the Mount of Olives, for neither of them was young. Down the hill to Bethany, they ran again, and arrived breathless at the house where Peter and Andrew were staying. They burst in. To their surprise John was also there.

"They've taken the master out of the tomb, and we don't know where they've laid him," they cried.

Peter and John were speechless with astonishment, but taking one look at the women they ran out of the house and retraced the women's steps. To Peter's frustration he could not keep up with John, who was the younger man and ran like the wind.

Emerging through the city gate, John recognised the place as the women had described it, and saw Mary of Magdala weeping beside the grave. He ran over to her and, greeting her briefly, peered into the tomb. He, too, saw the linen shroud, and the cloth that had been round his head lying in a place by itself, but he did not go in.

Soon Peter arrived, panting heavily. He pushed past John, bent down, and went into the tomb. He squatted on the floor beneath the low roof and surveyed the scene.

Timidly, John came in too, and they squatted together wondering at what they saw. Suddenly, a wave of hope welled up in John's breast. He could not name the hope, but he knew without any

THE FIRST DAY OF THE WEEK

doubt that all was well, and better than well, unimaginably well.

Peter, however, came out of the tomb pensive and anxious. The words of Jesus had come back to him: "On the third day I will rise again." Was that what had happened? Was this like Lazarus? Did that mean that Jesus might be walking about somewhere, even close by in the garden? If so, did he, Peter, want to see him? Could he face Jesus again, after what had happened in the courtyard of the high priest?

He was at once excited and apprehensive. Forgetting Mary, he walked off slowly in the direction from which they had come. John followed him and cried excitedly, "Let's go back and tell the others. Come on, let's run."

"I don't know," Peter replied. "You run if you want to. I've got to think."

Since Peter seemed disinclined to say any more, John ran off to report back in Bethany what they had seen.

Meanwhile, Mary of Magdala remained, weeping by the tomb, sitting on the ground, leaning her cheek against the great white stone. All she could feel was an immense emptiness, a bottomless pit of grief in her heart, out of which poured an endless flood of silent tears.

Slowly, she became aware of a figure standing quietly in front of her. Through her tear-filled eyes she could see a pair of sandals and the skirt of a robe. Looking up she saw a stranger looking down at her.

"What's the matter, woman? Why are you crying?" he asked kindly.

Supposing him to be the gardener, she said, "Sir, if you've taken him away, please tell me where you've laid him."

The voice said, "Mary."

It was *his* voice. She looked again, wiping the tears roughly from her eyes so that she could see more clearly. It was *his* face.

"Master, my master!" she cried, and threw her arms round his skirts, hugging his knees as tightly as she could, more tears streaming down her face.

"You can't hold on to me," Jesus said, bending over her. "I am going back to my Father. But go and tell my brothers that you have seen me, and tell them that I am returning to my Father and your Father, to my God and your God."

With that, he leaned down, loosened her grip on him and was gone. Mary, her arms empty, did not know quite how or where he went. He did not seem to walk off, he just was not there any more.

Bewildered, but ecstatic, she rose from the gound and started off to tell the others. She did not hurry. She felt as if she was floating through the air, rather than walking on the streets of Jerusalem.

THE FIRST DAY OF THE WEEK

As she was climbing the slope of the Mount of Olives, she saw above her the figure of Peter, sitting on a stone by the roadside, all alone. As she came up to him, she saw that he was staring into space with a beatific smile on his face.

"Hello, Peter," she greeted him. Her words brought Peter back from his reverie and as they looked at each other they both recognised the same glow in their faces.

"You've seen him too!" Mary exclaimed in joy.

"Aye. I can hardly believe it, but I have." Peter paused. "I was walking slowly up this hill and I felt someone beside me. He spoke my name and I recognised his voice. I turned to look and could not focus on his face, but I knew who it was. He was really there. I reached out and touched him to make sure it wasn't a ghost.

"He said to me, 'I want you to gather the others together. Arrange to meet together in the upper room this evening where we ate the Passover supper. I will see you there.' Then he was gone. I don't know where he came from or where he went to, but I saw him. I know he was real."

"I know, I saw him too," Mary said softly. "It was wonderful, wasn't it? I can't get over it."

Peter rose and together they walked slowly back to the village, hardly knowing how to tell the others, or whether they would be believed.

Word of these extraordinary encounters spread among the disciples during the day, but Peter and the men were still afraid that the sight of them in the city might set up a hue and cry. So, at Peter's suggestion, word was taken to the eleven by the women, that they should assemble in the upper room in Jerusalem, after dark.

The moon was rising again as they made their way in ones and twos through the city. When they arrived, Peter fetched the key, unlocked the door to let them in and then relocked it behind them.

When they were all present, Peter told them all from his own mouth of the events of the morning. He told of the empty tomb and of how both he and Mary of Magdala had seen Jesus, alive, but somehow mysteriously changed.

"But where did he come from?" asked James.

"I've no idea," answered Peter. "One minute I was walking along on my own, the next, he was beside me. And he disappeared in the same way."

Just then, there was a loud banging on the door. Not the timid knock that had announced the arrival of the disciples, but an urgent hammering. They looked at one another in horror. Was this the guards or the soldiers coming for them?

"Who's there?" John called out.

"It's us, Mary and Cleopas," a woman's voice called back excitedly. "We've seen the master!"

The door was unlocked and the bar taken down to let the visitors in.

THE FIRST DAY OF THE WEEK

The couple were breathless, and looked hot and tired.

"We've just been home to Emmaus. On the way a stranger fell in with us and we got talking."

The two were telling their story in unison, one taking up the tale from the other as quickly as they could.

"We didn't recognise him at first – I suppose we didn't look too closely at who it was. He started asking us questions, about what had been happening in Jerusalem these last few days. We told him about Jesus, about his arrest and crucifixion, and how we'd hoped that he was the Messiah.

"Then he began to talk to us. He was quoting from the scriptures. He told us that the scriptures had foretold all this – that the Messiah must suffer and die, and then rise again.

"We then told him how Mary of Magdala and some of the women had been to the tomb and found it empty. By this time we were getting near home. He seemed a nice man, so we invited him in to have a meal and stay the night, if he wanted to. So, he came in and sat down.

"Mary went into the kitchen to get some food, while Cleopas and he went on talking. It was getting dark in the room so we couldn't see him clearly. When we came to the table, I lit a lamp and asked our visitor to say the blessing.

THAT MAN JESUS

"It was as he said the blessing and broke the bread," they both said in unison, "that we suddenly realised who it was."

Just then, as they were telling the story, the disciples saw Jesus, standing behind Mary and Clopas.

The room was suddenly filled with a sense of awe. Mary and Cleopas parted and fell silent and no-one spoke.

"Peace be with you," said Jesus, stepping forward and smiling round at them.

Then, he opened his hands and lifted the hem of his robe to show them his feet. They could see the marks where the nails had pierced him. Not bleeding now, but the wounds was still red and ragged.

"Touch me and see, if you want to. I am not a ghost, but flesh and bone. How slow you are to believe what the prophets foretold, and indeed what I told you when I was with you."

They continued to gaze at him in wonder and joy.

"Have you got anything to eat?" he asked.

James picked up a piece of fish from the dishes that their hostess had thoughtfully provided for them. Jesus took it and ate it as they watched. Then they all sat, and Jesus began to explain to them all, as he had done on the road to Emmaus, what was written about himself in Moses and in the prophets and in the Psalms.

THE FIRST DAY OF THE WEEK

"But now," he said, "in the next few days you must go back to Galilee. Let things settle down here in the city. It is too dangerous for you to be seen about here while all this is still fresh. Lie low. You will see me again in Galilee. Then you must come back to Jerusalem again in time for the Feast of Pentecost."

thirty-nine

GALILEE AGAIN

The apostles had been back in Galilee for several days and Peter, for one, was frankly bored. They had stayed on in Jerusalem as unobtrusively as possible until the end of the Feast of Unleavened Bread and then had travelled back north with the caravans of returning pilgrims, including their families and friends.

In the first days after the crucifixion, Thomas had gone to ground altogether. He had not been with them when Jesus appeared in the upper room. Later, Thomas had emerged and rejoined them. But of Judas Iscariot they had seen no sign.

Before they had left Jerusalem rumours had been circulating about a man who had committed suicide in the valley of Hinnom. Some said he had hanged himself, others that he had spilled his guts in the place where the offal from the sacrifices was dumped. Had that been Judas? They might never know. Nor, now, might they ever know why Judas had betrayed Jesus.

But here they were back in Galilee. Eleven of them, at least. Some had gone off to visit and stay with their families again, but six or seven of them were living or lodging in Capernaum.

GALILEE AGAIN

"I think I'm going fishing," announced Peter one evening out of sheer boredom. Zebedee had been keeping his own boat and Simon's boat going with the help of hired men, and he was perfectly happy for his two sons and Peter and their friends to take up their old occupation again. So, after dark, they had all climbed into the boats and pushed out onto the lake.

They fished all night, but caught nothing.

"We must have lost our touch," suggested John.

"But this is weird," replied Peter. "I remember a night just like this before we first heard Jesus preach, from this very boat. Don't you remember? Then he told us to pull out into deep water and we hauled in the biggest catch I've ever seen."

They were rowing back slowly and disconsolately towards Capernaum. The sky was lightening in the east over the hills behind them when they saw a man standing on the shore. He seemed to have a fire going on the beach and he called out to them.

"Caught anything?"

"Nothing at all," they answered.

"Cast the net again, on the right side of the boat and you'll find some fish."

It came back to them all now, and without a word they cast the net where they were told. Sure enough, as soon as they began hauling it in they found the net full of a mass of thrashing silver scales.

"It's the master," John whispered to Peter.

"I know," Peter answered, full of emotion and, unable to restrain himself, he pulled on his tunic, jumped over the side of the boat and waded ashore. The others finished hauling in the fish and followed in the boat.

They pulled the boat up out of the water and counted the fish into baskets.

"One hundred and fifty three," announced James triumphantly.

"Bring some over here. Come and have breakfast," said Jesus, for that was indeed who it was. "I've got a fire going and some bread ready. We can fry the fish!"

It was just like old times, sitting together in the early morning, having breakfast together, as if they were on their travels, visiting the towns and villages up in the hills of Galilee.

Jesus began talking to them.

"The invitation is still open to everyone who will accept it. The kingdom of God is at hand. The only condition for entry is the same as it always was: repentance and faith, faith in you, in the good news you preach, and faith in me.

"There is still healing and power in my name, like there was before. There is still a new life to be had, with God and with one another. Your heavenly Father is still ready to forgive you your sins - yours and the sins of all those who turn to

GALILEE AGAIN

him. But now you understand, as you didn't understand before, that entering the kingdom, while it brings untold blessings, also brings suffering and persecution.

"As I told you before, a servant is not above his master. Nor is a disciple above his teacher. If they have persecuted me, they will persecute you. But if they listened to me, and many did, they will listen to you too.

"But suffering, and even death, are not the end. You have got proof of that now, in me. Here I am with you, alive, and now I can never die again. And that reward will be yours too. He who endures to the end will be saved. You, too, will inherit everlasting life, not in this world but in the world to come.

"I am going to my Father now. There will come a time when you will see me like this no more. But I will still be with you, not far from each one of you, and the Holy Spirit whom the Father will send in my name, he will take my place as your helper and comforter.

"It's better for you that I go away. Here, I can only be with you in one place at one time. When I go and the Holy Spirit comes, he will be with you everywhere, all the time.

"So, 'Be strong and of good courage; be not afraid, neither be dismayed, for the LORD thy God is with thee wheresoever thou goest.'"

When they had finished eating, the disciples put the baskets of fish back in the boat and prepared to row back to Capernaum. But Jesus took Peter aside and together they walked slowly back along the shore.

John followed them at a distance.

"Simon, do you love me more than these others do?" Jesus asked.

"Well, I don't know about the others, but you know that I love you," Peter replied.

"Then feed my sheep," Jesus said.

A little further along, he said again, "Simon, do you love me more than you love these others?"

"Oh yes, master, you know I love you, more than anything."

"Then feed my lambs."

Again a little later Jesus said, "Simon, do you really love me?"

"Why do you keep asking me that?" Peter inquired, but in his heart he knew, and was grateful that Jesus was giving him these three chances to express his love, after he had so shamefully denied him three times.

"Master, you know everything. You know that I love you."

"Take care of my sheep. I tell you, when you were young, you went wherever you wanted, and nobody stopped you. But when you're old, they will take hold of you and make you go where you

GALILEE AGAIN

don't want to go. But, as I told you all, don't be afraid. I will be with you, even then."

Peter noticed that John was still following them.

"And what about him?" he asked, nodding behind them towards John.

"Never mind about him. What does it matter to you if he remains until I come? You just follow me."

* * *

During those days back in Galilee, many people in the towns and villages were asking the disciples about what had happened in Jerusalem. The disciples told the story as best they could in bits and pieces, but, understandably, people were perplexed and curious.

"Let's get them all together and tell them what we know," suggested Philip one day.

So, they began to arrange for everyone who wanted to hear the story to come to the hill where Jesus had first preached to them at the beginning.

On the appointed day, people were coming from all directions, climbing the hill and sitting down, eager to hear the truth. The hills formed a sort of natural amphitheatre here, and the eleven gathered where the crowd could see and hear them. People had clearly travelled from miles around, and the disciples recognised many old friends.

There was Mary, the mother of Jesus, and James, his brother. Nathanael recognised the couple whose wedding they had attended at the beginning, when Jesus had turned the water into wine. There was Jairus and his wife and daughter, who was now engaged to be married.

There was a group from Magdala, and people from Bethsaida and Chorazin as well as from Capernaum itself. Matthew, who was used to counting things, reckoned that there were more than five hundred people there.

Taking it in turns, the disciples told the story of that week in Jerusalem, starting with the great procession into the city with the palm branches and the cries of Hosanna. They told of their last supper with Jesus and their wait in the olive grove before Judas appeared with the temple guards. Peter and John told of what they had witnessed in the courtyard of the high priest, and Peter did not shrink from telling them of his denials.

They told what they knew of the trial before Pilate and of how Jesus had been crucified. They confessed that they had not been witnesses of these things themselves, but had relied on the testimony of friends in the Sanhedrin like Nicodemus and Joseph, in whose tomb Jesus had been buried.

GALILEE AGAIN

They told the story of the empty tomb, and then the stories of Jesus' mysterious appearances, to Mary of Magdala, to Peter, and then to them all, and even of his appearance to them here in Galilee, on the shore of the lake. All appearances that had convinced them that Jesus was not dead, but alive.

When they had finished, people had many questions that they called out from where they sat. The disciples answered them as best they could, but some they could not answer. One man asked the obvious question:

"But how does Jesus come and go, like you say he does?"

"I have no idea," Peter replied. "It's as if there's another world, all around us, a spiritual world, the place where God is, and as if we're only separated from that world by a gossamer veil. It's as if Jesus parts that veil and shows himself to us, and then he goes back behind the veil.

"It's not very good, I know," Peter finished rather lamely, "but it's the best I can do to explain it."

Just then, someone at the back started to step through the crowd of seated people who moved away slightly to let him pass. One by one, their eyes all turned to this figure, and they all knew – it was him.

Jesus came down to where the disciples were standing and greeted them. Then he turned and addressed the crowd of expectant faces.

"You can see for yourselves: it is true. I died, but I am alive for evermore. This gathering is a foretaste of the end. I will go away soon and you will not see me again for a long time. But one day I will come again, this time in the power and the glory of God.

"You will not be able to mistake that day, but how long it will be, I cannot tell you. Even the angels in heaven don't know when it will be. God alone knows. But when the times are fulfilled, I will come again. The trumpet will sound and God will send out the angels to the four corners of the earth, and they will gather in God's chosen ones, just like this. The dead will be raised and those of you who are left alive will be changed, so that you are all like I am now.

"God will create new heavens and a new earth, and a new Jerusalem will come down from heaven. There will be a great feast, like a marriage feast, and there will be dancing on the streets of the city.

"But not yet. Today, you must go back to your towns and villages. Tell your neighbours about me and invite them into the kingdom. Meet together, pray together, study the scriptures together. They will teach you more about me, for they speak about me.

"These apostles I chose at the beginning, I will be sending out into all the world to preach the good news, to baptise people everywhere, and

GALILEE AGAIN

teach them all that I have taught you. So, go in peace, and God be with you, even unto the end."

forty

ASCENSION

A week or two later, the apostles gathered together again and made their way back to Jerusalem, as Jesus had commanded them. They took up lodgings again in Bethany and in the city, and began to wait in expectation. Expectation of what, they hardly knew, but they were filled with the sense of a new beginning, a fulfilment that would at the same time be the beginning of a whole new life for all of them.

One day, about ten days before the Feast of Pentecost, they met together and were praying together and talking about the future, when Jesus appeared among them, as he had done before.

"Come," he said, "we're going out to the Mount of Olives."

Every time that Jesus appeared, it was as if it was the first time. They were all filled with a sense of unutterable love and joy. They walked together in silence. Each had the same premonition, that this was to be the last time that they would see him.

When they reached the summit of the hill, Jesus turned and spoke to them as they gathered in a half-circle, facing him.

ASCENSION

"Stay in the city," he said, "until you are clothed with power from on high. In a few days, you will all be baptised with the Holy Spirit. Remember how John said, 'I baptise with water, but he will baptise you with the Holy Spirit.'"

Peter realised that this was the last chance that he would get to ask Jesus the one question that still puzzled him.

"Master, are you going to restore the kingdom to Israel after all?"

"Aye, after all. At the restoration of all things, as God has promised through the prophets. But not now. I will return, but at a time only the Father knows. There will be new heavens and a new earth; the old heavens and the old earth will pass away. The new Jerusalem will come down from heaven, a city whose builder and maker is God. Then, the kingdoms of the world will become the kingdom of our God and of his Messiah.

"But not now. Now, the kingdom must be built up in people's hearts and minds. People, one by one, will come to believe and trust in me, be born again and enter the kingdom of God. When the Holy Spirit comes upon you, you will be my witnesses, in Jerusalem and in Judea and Samaria, and to the ends of the earth."

With this Jesus lifted up his hands and began to pronounce the priestly blessing over them.

"The LORD bless thee and keep thee. The LORD make his face shine upon thee, and be gracious unto thee. The LORD lift up his countenance upon thee and give thee peace."

As the ancient Hebrew words washed over them, they bowed down to the ground and worshipped him.

A cloud passed over the sun, and when they looked up, he was gone.

TWO THOUSAND YEARS ON

It was a few days before Christmas and the sudden death of the Principal had caused a crisis in the old college.

Term was over and only the choristers were still in residence, apart from the senior members. An emergency meeting of the college council had been called to decide what to do about the Principal's funeral, and about the Christmas celebrations, and in particular the college carol service, due to be held on Christmas Eve, in which the Principal had always played an important part.

"In the circumstances, I suggest that the carol service be cancelled, as a sign of respect for the Principal. We can send the choristers home early and, thank God, our carol service is not due to be broadcast to the nation, like that of another college that we won't mention here."

It was one of the Fellows speaking, a man who made a point of his militant atheism (despite thanking God for the obscurity of his college's carol service).

"It's time that we cancelled the whole absurd ritual in any case. No-one actually believes all that twaddle any more – virgins giving birth, angels, shepherds, wise men. We're a university college not a kindergarten."

"I believe it," the Chaplain affirmed amiably.

"Well, you're in a minority, and a dying minority at that. Let's grow up and move on. Leave the nursery behind."

"That's all very well," the Senior Fellow interrupted, "but we can't cancel a part of traditional college life on a whim. People have lived and died in this place for five hundred years, and we haven't started cancelling things without more serious thought than this.

"Like it or not, the Christian faith is woven into the fabric of this college. Like it or not, we have a Dean and a Chaplain, a chapel and a regular celebration of the Christian liturgy, and although it's a relatively recent innovation - only, I think, about a hundred years old - the carol service is now a traditional event, popular with the friends and relations of the choristers and with the college servants, and even with a few of us Fellows. What do you say, Mr Dean? It's your department after all."

"The idea of cancelling the carol service is preposterous," replied the Dean. "We shall have to make detailed arrangements about the funeral of the Principal after Christmas, but meanwhile, the show must go on, as it has done, in one form or another, for two thousand years.

TWO THOUSAND YEARS ON

"No-one is obliged to come to the college chapel, now or at any other time, but there are many of us who still value its presence in the college and yes, who still believe, as the Chaplain says, in at least the fundamentals of the story of Jesus Christ. I believe that today's secularity is an historical blip.

"We happen to live in a time when we have been blinded by the advancements of science and the profusion of material goods to the spiritual dimension of life. There may not be many of us who keep the torch burning for God, but that does not mean that God does not still exist. The truth is not decided by majority vote. The carol service will go on."

So, on the morning of Christmas Eve, the choir were having a final rehearsal in the chapel, under the direction of their choirmaster.

"This year, as you know, we're going to start the opening carol, Once in Royal David's City, out in the quad. So, let's go out to where we're going to start. I'm going to ask Stephen to listen carefully and tell us what it sounds like from inside the chapel as we approach.

"What I'm aiming at is that the first sounds that the congregation hear are like something mysterious, carried on the air. That's what I imagine it was like for the shepherds, out in the fields watching over their flocks by night. The song of the angels began as something just carried on the wind, getting closer and closer, and clearer and clearer as the angels approached, until the shepherds were surrounded by the glory of God.

"Jeremy, you're singing the first solo verse, aren't you? The congregation probably won't hear the words, 'Once in royal David's city stood a lowly cattle shed' etcetera, but that doesn't matter. It's just a sound borne on the air. After all, that's how the Christian faith begins for most people. The story of Jesus is just a sound borne on the air. Only as they, or the words, come closer, does the story and the meaning become clearer and they start to hear it and believe it. So, that's what I'm aiming at. Let's try it."

At three o'clock that afternoon, Jeremy started to sing the opening solo verse outside the chapel in the quadrangle, as they had practised. The congregation, sitting in expectant silence in the chapel, at first heard nothing. Then, a few thin treble notes, coming closer. Then, as the second verse began, the harmonies of all the voices, swelling into the well-known tune as the choir entered the chapel door.

The sound resolved itself into words, "He came down to earth from heaven, who is God and Lord of all."

As the procession passed through the nave and entered the chancel the congregation stood and sang with the choir of the childhood and humanity of Jesus. As the carol approached its climax,

TWO THOUSAND YEARS ON

Stephen pulled out all the stops on the organ for the last two verses:

> And our eyes at last shall see him
> Through his own redeeming love,
> For that child so dear and gentle
> Is our Lord in heaven above;
> And he leads his children on
> To the place where he is gone.
>
> Not in that poor lowly stable,
> With the oxen standing by,
> We shall see him; but in heaven
> Set at God's right hand on high;
> Where like stars his children crowned
> All in white shall wait around.

Lightning Source UK Ltd.
Milton Keynes UK
UKOW05f0019190714

235409UK00002B/17/P